THE ORION MASK

Reviewers Love Greg Herren's Mysteries

"Herren, a loyal New Orleans resident, paints a brilliant portrait of the recovering city, including insights into its tight-knit gay community. This latest installment in a powerful series is sure to delight old fans and attract new ones."—*Publishers Weekly*

"Fast-moving and entertaining, evoking the Quarter and its gay scene in a sweet, funny, action-packed way."—*New Orleans Times-Picayune*

"Herren does a fine job of moving the story along, deftly juggling the murder investigation and the intricate relationships while maintaining several running subjects."—*Echo* Magazine

"An entertaining read."—*OutSmart* Magazine

"A pleasant addition to your beach bag."—*Bay Windows*

"Greg Herren gives readers a tantalizing glimpse of New Orleans."—*Midwest Book Review*

"Herren's characters, dialogue and setting make the book seem absolutely real."—*The Houston Voice*

"So much fun it should be thrown from Mardi Gras floats!" —*New Orleans Times-Picayune*

By The Author

The Scotty Bradley Adventures

Bourbon Street Blues

Jackson Square Jazz

Mardi Gras Mambo

Vieux Carré Voodoo

Who Dat Whodunnit

Baton Rouge Bingo

The Chanse MacLeod Mysteries

Murder in the Rue Dauphine

Murder in the Rue St. Ann

Murder in the Rue Chartres

Murder in the Rue Ursulines

Murder in the Garden District

Murder in the Irish Channel

Murder in the Arts District

Sleeping Angel

Sara

Timothy

Lake Thirteen

Dark Tide

The Orion Mask

Women of the Mean Streets: Lesbian Noir

Men of the Mean Streets: Gay Noir

Night Shadows: Queer Horror
(edited with J. M. Redmann)

Love, Bourbon Street: Reflections on New Orleans
(edited with Paul J. Willis)

Visit us at www.boldstrokesbooks.com

THE ORION MASK

by

Greg Herren

A Division of Bold Strokes Books

2015

THE ORION MASK

ISBN 13: 978-1-62639-355-4

This Trade Paperback Original Is Published By
Bold Strokes Books, Inc.
P.O. Box 249
Valley Falls, NY 12185

First Edition: July 2015

Credits
Editor: Ruth Sternglantz
Production Design: Stacia Seaman
Cover Design by Sheri (graphicartist2020@hotmail.com)

Acknowledgments

When I was a teenager, I discovered the genre of romantic suspense, and I spent most of the next twenty years reading every book ever written by exceptional women like Dorothy Eden, Anya Seton, Phyllis A. Whitney, Norah Lofts, Mary Stewart, and Victoria Holt. I always wanted to write one, and I owe an enormous debt of gratitude to Radclyffe and Bold Strokes Books for giving me the opportunity to finally write in the subgenre of mystery/romance that I've always loved. I truly miss those great women writers and love to revisit their works from time to time.

Bold Strokes Books has been an exceptional home for me and my work. The support from everyone behind the scenes—from Radclyffe to Sandy Lowe to Stacia Seaman to the marketing people—has been the kind of publishing experience I've always dreamed of having. Thanks, ladies, it's an absolute joy working with all of you.

My editor, the incomparable Ruth Sternglantz, always manages to spot the mistakes and come up with ways to make the story better, the writing stronger, and the characters more believable. Working with her has been an education in novel writing, and I am still learning. Thank you, Ruthie, for always saving me from myself, helping me better my work, not minding my blown deadlines (or at least not letting me know), and for being such a phenomenal friend.

I am also incredibly lucky that in my day job I get to work with some amazing people who are changing the world. Thanks to Allison Vertovec, Nick Parr, Mark Smith, Alex Leigh, Lena Williams, Joey Olson, Drew Davenport, Louis Monnig, Christal Leon, Vanessa Alford, Augustin Correro, and all the volunteers who make the Community Awareness Network and the Gay Men's Wellness Center a great place to work. Josh Fegley, Tiffany Medlock, Martin

Strickland, Robin Pearce, Ryan McNeeley—I still miss you guys every day when I come to work, but I'm proud of the things you've done since you moved on.

Beth Hettinger Tindall is the most amazing web goddess ever. Thank you, my darling.

I'm also incredibly blessed with an amazing network of friends who support me and love me and can always make me laugh. Thank you to Konstantin Smorodnikov, Jean Redmann, Gillian Rodger, Stan and Janet Daley Duval, Priscilla Lawrence, Pat Brady, Michael Ledet, Jesse and Laura Ledet, Butch and Bev Marshall, Dan and 'Nathan Smith, Jeffrey Ricker, Michael Wallenstein (SB), Michael Thomas Ford, Annamaria Alfieri, Heather Graham, Connie Perry, Lisa Morton, Vince Liaguno, Wendy Corsi Staub, Rob Byrnes, Felice Picano, Dan Hale ("phrasing!"), Josh Aterovis, Erin Mitchell, Bryon Quertermous, Carolyn Haines, Dean James, McKenna Jordan, John Kwiatkowski, Carson Taite, Trinity Tam, Nell Stark, Lynda Sandoval, Rachel Spangler, Lee Lynch, Elaine Mulligan, Anne Laughlin, Timothy J. Lambert, Becky Cochrane, and so many, many others. Thank you all for being you.

I've spent the last few years sitting on the National Board of Directors for Mystery Writers of America, which has also been an amazing experience. Thanks to everyone I've served with; you are all not only great writers but great people.

Every one of my Facebook friends makes me smile on a daily basis, but no one as consistently as Paul Emery. Some day we will meet, kind sir.

The FL's are the best ever, despite their penchant for kicking ass rather than kissing it, being tossed to the wolves only to come back leading the pack, and playing bitches on television. Remember—it's only true when it comes from MY lips.

And of course, Paul, who has made every day of the last twenty years more amazing than I could have ever dreamed.

This is for Lauren, who also loves Victoria Holt

CHAPTER ONE

Taking this trip was probably a mistake I would regret. I finished my cup of coffee and glanced over at my shiny black suitcases. They were new, bought specifically for this trip. My old bags were ratty and worn and wouldn't have made the kind of impression I wanted to make. My cat was asleep on top of the bigger bag, his body stretched and contorted in a way that couldn't possibly be comfortable. I'd put the bags down just inside my front door. I'd closed and locked them securely. I'd made out name tags and attached them to the handles. I'd taken pictures of them with my phone in case they were lost or misdirected by the airline. My flight wasn't for another three and a half hours, and even in heavy traffic it wouldn't take more than fifteen minutes to get to the airport. I had plenty of time; as always I'd gotten up earlier than I needed to, and finished getting ready with far too much time left to kill before leaving for the airport. I checked once again to make sure I had my airline employee ID badge, my driver's license, my laptop, and the appropriate power cords in my carry-on bag. I was flying standby, of course, but I'd checked the flight before leaving work the previous night and there were at least thirty seats open with a no-show factor of fifteen. The only way I wouldn't get on Transco flight 1537 nonstop from Bay City to

New Orleans was if another flight to New Orleans canceled, or this one was canceled for mechanical problems. But should that happen, I had my cousin's cell phone number already loaded into my phone so I could give her a call and let her know what was going on.

I got up and poured what was left in the pot into my mug, making sure I turned the coffeemaker off.

The occupational hazard of flying standby was that your plans were never carved in stone and were subject to change at any moment.

They'd offered to buy me an actual ticket, of course, but I'd said no.

I wasn't really ready to take any money from the family I didn't know just yet.

I sipped my coffee. *Has it really only been two months?* I thought again.

I'd known they'd existed, of course, since that day when I accidentally found my birth certificate when rooting around in my father's desk drawer. I wasn't supposed to be in there—his office was off-limits to both me and the woman I'd always thought was my mother, a place of solitude for him where he could get away from us, from the pressures of his day job, and just have quiet alone time. The office door was always kept locked. It was what was originally called the maid's apartment when our house had been built back in the 1920s, in the heyday of Bay City's Hyde Park neighborhood. It was just a back bedroom, really, off the kitchen with a small private bathroom. I had no memories of living anywhere other than the house, and as long as I could remember that room had been my father's office.

I was home alone that day—they'd gone to some function or another, promising they'd be home around two that Saturday afternoon, and to bring me lunch home from McDonald's.

McDonald's was a rare treat around our house; both of my parents thought fast food was garbage and a waste of money. I'd finished my homework already and was bored. There was nothing on television to watch, and I'd read the books I'd taken out from the library the previous week. I wasn't allowed on the Internet if they weren't home—they made sure of that by not allowing me to know the password for the Wi-Fi. Whenever I wanted to use it one of them had to sign me in, and they never allowed my laptop to store the password, either. I'd gone into the kitchen for a glass of orange juice when I noticed the door to the office wasn't completely closed. That was unusual: Dad's privacy was paramount. He must have been in a hurry and didn't notice the door hadn't shut. I knew I shouldn't go in there, that if he ever found out I'd be in serious trouble, but I couldn't resist. I'd *seen* inside before, even though I wasn't allowed to go inside, catching glimpses when my dad would go in or out. The room was done in a dark faux-wood panel, with hideous green shag carpeting that had been popular in the 1970s.

I took a deep breath and walked across the kitchen. I pushed the door softly with my right hand, my heart beating faster as the door swung farther open. Feeling brave, I swallowed and stepped through the doorway. Going inside almost felt like entering Narnia through a wardrobe. I was sweating from nerves in spite of the air-conditioning. I glanced around the room. It was bigger than I'd always imagined. There was a large desk nestled into a corner, with work space branching out in an L shape. There was a computer on one arm of the L, some files, envelopes, and papers scattered over the other side. A reclining chair faced a television stand, complete with a big television set, the cable box, and a VCR blinking 12:00. There was an open white door to my left leading into the bathroom. The sliding doors to the closet were closed.

It was a little disappointing, to be honest. I don't know what I was expecting, but I thought there would be *something* more than this.

Of course, with an imagination weaned on the Hardy Boys and the Three Investigators, I'd always liked to believe there was some dark secret hidden inside the room, some reason why Dad didn't want either Mom or me to ever go inside. But now I realized, standing in the center of the room and looking around, that it was nothing more than just private space he wanted, some place that was solely his.

I was a mere couple of minutes from making the big discovery that would change my life forever.

I walked over to look at the papers scattered on the top of the desk. We were going on vacation to Cancun later that summer, and on top of a stack of papers was my passport application. I'd had to go down to Walgreens with my mother a few days earlier to get the pictures taken. We hadn't done a family vacation in a couple of years, and when Dad told us he'd decided we were going to the beach in Cancun this year, I'd started making plans. Dad promised we could visit Chichen Itza and other Mayan ruins I'd read about in some of the mysteries I was forever checking out of the library.

I exhaled and decided to get out of there before they got home when I noticed something strange on my birth certificate, just to the side of the passport application.

I didn't read that right, I thought, picking up the certificate and staring at it in disbelief.

There had to be some mistake.

Mother: Genevieve Melissa Legendre Brandon

Only *my* mother's name was Sandra—or so I had thought.

My heart started beating really hard and fast. According to my birth certificate, I'd also been born at a place called Touro

Infirmary in New Orleans, Louisiana—not Bay City, Florida, which was where we'd always lived.

They'd lied to me.

My mother wasn't really my mother.

I finished my coffee and rinsed the mug out in the sink. Skittle, my enormous orange-and-white Maine Coon cat, hopped up on the counter and rubbed his head against my forearm. He always knew when I was going away—he knew from experience what suitcases next to the front door meant. He was purring, wanting attention, afraid he was being abandoned. Absently I scratched behind his tufted ears. My stepmother would come by later to take him back to the house where I'd grown up. She was going to keep him while I was gone—for the whole two weeks, for a couple of days, who knew how long I was going to be gone?

It depended on how things went once I got there.

It was hard to believe it had been a little less than two months since I'd first noticed the bald man sitting in the airport lobby.

Mondays were always busy days at the ticket counter, and this particular Monday had been one of the worst I could remember. My feet and calves were aching from being on my feet all day, my lower back throbbing from lifting and carrying luggage back to the TSA agents. The line of passengers checking their bags and getting boarding passes hadn't let up from the moment I'd signed in to the computer at my assigned station at noon. I somehow managed to keep a smile plastered on my face and my voice friendly. I tried not to look at the clock on my computer screen too often. I'd learned early in my airline career that watching the clock just made it seem to move slower. It was a hot June day in Florida. The airport was kept at what sometimes seemed like subzero temperatures inside, but every time the electric doors opened to let in yet another group of passengers dragging their luggage to the stanchions marking the start of the lines, a wave of hot air blew in behind them, making my scalp sweat and my skin sticky.

I only had about an hour left to go in my shift that night. I knew I looked awful. My white dress shirt was sticking to my back, and I knew there were damp half-moons at my underarms. I didn't have to look in a mirror to know my hair was a mess—the combination of thinning bangs and sweating forehead just wasn't an attractive look on anyone.

I smiled at the harried-looking woman in front of me who was keeping a wary eye on the three children under ten she was traveling with, handed her a ticket jacket with her boarding passes and baggage-claim tickets, and directed her to the gate. I picked up her heavy suitcases from the scale and walked them back to where the TSA agents were working, so they could be put through the X-ray machine, and returned to my station. My feet were aching and my calves were sore, but I plastered the required smile back on my face that gave passengers the illusion I was actually glad to be helping them. I took a deep breath and was just about to call the next passenger in line to come down to the touchscreen check-in station when I saw him.

He was sitting in one of the lobby chairs facing the Transco Airlines ticket counter, his legs stretched out in front of him and crossed at the ankles. He was bald, and his scalp gleamed in the lights of the Bay City airport central terminal. He was wearing a very tight black cotton T-shirt with a V-neck that emphasized the thick muscles of his shoulders, chest, and arms. His knee-length khaki shorts were looser, but his hairy calves were also strongly developed. I figured him to be somewhere in his mid to late forties. He was handsome, with a round, full face and enormous brown eyes beneath thick black brows. His nose was wide and almost a bit flat, but his lips were full and his chin strong. There were creases beneath his cheekbones that probably signaled deep dimples when he smiled. He was looking right at me, his right eyebrow raised a bit, and I could feel my face starting to color slightly.

Yeah, right, Heath—a hot-looking guy like that is definitely checking you *out. That's why you have a boyfriend, right?*

When you work at an airport, part of the job is watching people, paying attention, and noticing things out of the ordinary. I kept watching, not calling the next passenger down, and began to wonder if I should call airport security.

And tell them what? A hot guy in a tight T-shirt is watching you? Or the ticket counter? He might just be waiting for someone to arrive, or someone to get off work—you don't know anything about him, and it's not like he fits the profile of possibly dangerous passengers. Although I suppose he could be a drug runner or something.

When he realized I'd noticed him watching, he looked down quickly and started fiddling with the phone he was holding. *Maybe he* was *checking me out—and if he is, that would make it even more embarrassing if I called security*, I thought, finally motioning for the next passenger. I glanced over at him again but he was still playing with his phone. I smiled at the elderly couple now standing in front of me and said, "Where are y'all traveling today?" When I finished helping my passengers—they had trouble using the automated system and I had to come out from behind the counter to help—I looked back over again. He was gone. I hadn't seen him go or where he went.

Oh, well, probably just as well. He's a little too good-looking for me. And that would just mean heartbreak in the long run. Just hope he's not a criminal or something.

I waved at the next people in line and went back to work, forgetting all about him.

Then he showed up during my shift on Tuesday.

While Mondays were always busy until later in the day, Tuesdays and Wednesdays were the slowest travel days of the week. The vast majority of leisure travelers booked their travel around the weekends, so most weekday passengers were traveling on business with carry-on luggage only so they could bypass the ticket counter and head directly to the gates while yakking away nonstop on their cell phones. Those were the days when airport employees could catch our breaths a bit, in anticipation of the onslaught of weekend travelers that would start kicking in on Thursday. Low seniority had stuck me with Tuesdays and Wednesdays as my days off ever since I was hired, almost right out of high school. But that Tuesday I'd picked up a shift from a coworker who'd gone to the West Coast for a few days to visit her sister. I didn't mind having what everyone else considered crappy days off, frankly. Tuesdays and Wednesdays—unless there was a holiday—were painfully slow, and an eight-hour shift on those days seemed to last longer than the Middle Ages. This particular Tuesday was no exception. I started at eleven and by three o'clock I was climbing the walls with boredom. There's nothing worse than standing on your feet all day with nothing to do, and there's only so many times you can check your Facebook feed on your phone.

I was coming back from my lunch break when I saw him. He was sitting in the same place he had been on Monday. He was fiddling with his phone and hadn't yet seen me. He was wearing another black T-shirt, only this one had a crewneck, and he was wearing blue and red madras shorts. "That's odd," I said as I signed back in to my computer.

"What's odd?" the woman working at the next station

asked without looking up from her computer screen. Brenda Steen was a thirty-year veteran of what we jokingly called the ticket-counter wars, a grandmother with gray streaks in her short red hair. Some of the other agents didn't like her, but I thought she was funny. You always knew where you stood with Brenda, and she did not suffer fools gladly. She spoke her mind, even if it made her sound like a bitch. She always wore the knee-length uniform dress with low heels—you'd never catch Brenda in the slacks—and navy-blue hose. She was never late, never called in sick, and never took an extra minute on her breaks than was allowed by the corporate handbook. She was a stickler for the rules. I always imagined that her house was regimented—everything had a place and everything in its place—and she'd trained her husband and children accordingly. She never broke the speed limit, never ignored a stop sign, and never rolled through a red light while turning right. She never asked anyone to cover a shift for her, only taking her allotted vacations. She came to work, did her job, and went home. She never gossiped about coworkers and was always politely friendly but distant with the passengers. However, she did enforce the rules on tickets. I'd seen her make passengers repack their suitcases to avoid overweight charges any number of times. If there was a fee to change your ticket, Brenda collected it. She had no problem arguing a point with a passenger, and she never, ever backed down.

Another agent called her Brenda Steen the Queen of Mean.

She thought it was funny, which made me like her all the more.

"You see that bald guy sitting there in the black T-shirt?" I said in a low voice, pointing with my hand below the counter so he couldn't see me if he was looking.

She looked up and pushed her glasses up her nose. She

glanced out into the middle of the lobby and looked back down again. "The good-looking bald one? What about him?" she asked, keeping her voice low, as though she was afraid he might hear her.

"Nothing, I guess. He was there last night. It's just weird, is all."

Brenda frowned, her eyes narrowing to slits. "That is odd. Do you want me to call security? Is he acting suspiciously?" She picked up the phone at her station.

Sorry I'd said anything, I was opening my mouth to tell her not to when he stood up and walked over to the up escalator, heading to the level where the trams to the gates were located.

"If he comes back or you see him again," Brenda said, putting the phone down with a frown, "you need to let security know. We probably should anyway. You know we're supposed to report suspicious behavior. *Any* suspicious behavior. Just because he doesn't look like a terrorist doesn't mean he's not a drug smuggler or something."

"I know," I replied, "but I don't think he's up to anything bad."

"You never know," she replied darkly, turning back to her computer screen. "You can't trust anyone these days." Without looking back at me, she added, "Even the hot bald ones in tight T-shirts." The corners of her mouth twitched as she struggled not to smile.

I grinned to myself. Underneath that tough exterior she really did have a soft caramel center.

By the time my shift finally ended, I was exhausted. The evening had been even slower than the afternoon, and I didn't think it was ever going to be time to log off and clock out. I closed out my drawer—I'd only run a few charges—and dropped the report into the safe before grabbing my lunch box and punching out on the time clock. Some of my coworkers were going out for drinks the way they always did, unwinding from the day by telling horror stories of stupid passengers and even stupider management decisions. Sometimes I went, but I usually said no. Forty hours per week was enough for me— the last thing I wanted to do when I was finally off the clock was sit around and talk about work some more. I said no this time because I only had about forty dollars left in my checking account before payday on Friday, and the last thing I needed was to blow what little was left of my money on alcohol.

Besides, if I wanted to drink there was a six-pack of beer, already paid for, in my apartment refrigerator.

I took the elevator down to the baggage claim level, where shuttle buses to the employee parking lot departed every ten to fifteen minutes. As I headed for the electric doors I saw one pull away from the curb. I swore softly under my breath and dug out the paperback Alison Gaylin mystery novel I was reading from my backpack as I passed through the door into the swampy Florida night. There was at least a thirty-degree difference between the inside and the outside. I started sweating as I walked over to one of the cement benches to wait for the next shuttle. My feet ached from standing for eight hours, and I just wanted to get home, crack open a beer, and go to bed early. I sat down and opened the book to where I'd left off reading during my lunch break. No one else was around.

I was lost in the book but was vaguely aware the electric doors had opened again with that weird hissing sound. I didn't bother to look, figuring it was either one of my coworkers or someone who worked for one of the other airlines. I turned another page when a deep masculine voice said from behind me, "Your name is Heath Brandon, isn't it?"

Startled, I spun around.

The bald man was standing just a few feet or so behind me. He had looked good from a distance, but he looked even better up close. His skin was tanned a dark reddish-golden brown, and I could see the bulging veins tracking his forearms and large biceps. There was a slight smile on his face—I'd been right about the dimples. There was a slight bit of dark stubble on his shiny head. His enormous and expressive brown eyes were crowned by thick black eyebrows and framed with long lashes. There were creases in his forehead, and his nose was broad and looked like it might have been broken once. His lips were thick and red. A slight five-o'clock shadow on his lower face actually made him look sexier than he would have clean-shaven.

Up close, he looked familiar. I could swear I'd seen him before, but I couldn't place him. That happens a lot when you work at the airport, though.

"Yes, it is. I'm Heath Brandon. Who wants to know?" I asked, unsettled and feeling a lot more nervous than I should have. I gave him a quick once-over. He didn't appear to be armed, though I slipped my hand into my backpack and put it on my phone, just in case.

You can never be too sure—especially at the airport.

He held up both of his hands with the palms out toward me, the muscles in his arms flexing and the veins bulging even more. "Sorry to startle you, but there's no reason for you to be concerned," he said, his smile getting wider and the dimples deepening. "I'm not crazy and I don't want to rob or hurt you. I just want to talk, if you have a few minutes."

"You've been watching me now for at least two days," I replied, not bothering to keep the coldness out of my voice as I pulled my phone out and touched the button to wake it up. "What am I supposed to think? I'm not supposed to think that's creepy and weird?"

"I don't blame you—I just needed to be sure you were

who I thought you were." He took another step forward, his hands still up in the air.

"Don't come any closer or I'll call airport security—and believe me, you don't want to mess with them." I held up my phone. "They're speed dial 1."

"Okay, okay, okay," he replied. He slipped his right hand into his shorts pocket and produced a card, holding it out to me. "I just want to talk to you. My name is Jerry Channing. I'm a writer."

The name sounded familiar. He added, "I wrote a book called *Garden District Gothic*?"

"I loved that book," I replied, staring at him and trying not to get too excited. I got up from the bench and took the card. Now that I knew who he was, I recognized him from the author photo on the back cover of the book. The book had been an account of a murder case that still, twenty or so years later, occasionally made headlines in the tabloids and got coverage on the cable news networks.

A wealthy New Orleans blue blood had married a beauty queen of much humbler origin, and the wife had been the primary suspect when their youngest child, a beautiful seven-year-old girl, was mysteriously murdered and her body found in the carriage house on their property. Channing was a personal trainer at the time, with most of his clients drawn from New Orleans society, and as he wrote in the introduction, "personal trainers are told as much gossip as hairdressers." He had written the book as a casual observer, managing to make the book more than just a true-crime story, using the murder mystery and the way it was covered in the news as a framework to give the reader an inside look into New Orleans society, and how the class betrayal of the marriage impacted the lives of the family and may have even led to the daughter's murder.

It was extremely well written, and I'd read it numerous times. It had never gone out of print since its first publication and had been made into a really bad movie I'd streamed on my computer and given up on halfway through.

"I've always wanted to be a writer," I said as I examined the card. It was thick cream vellum, with his name, phone number, and email address written on it in raised, cursive black letters. I fingered it for a moment before slipping it into my shirt pocket. "It's nice to meet you, Mr. Channing. But what do you want with me? I'm just a part-time college student who works at the airport," I said, very conscious that my socks were soaked through, my shirt was clinging to my back, and I smelled…well, interesting was a polite way to say it.

He was very good-looking, and his body was amazing.

His right eyebrow arched as I spoke, and the corners of his mouth went up. "You want to be a writer?" His voice was smooth, warm, and friendly. "What I want from you is to talk to you about your mother. Is there somewhere more private we could go? Maybe have a drink or two?" He gestured toward the short-term parking garage, just across the street from where we were standing. "I have a car in the short-term lot."

"My mother," I replied, confused. Why would a writer want to talk to me about my mother? Much as I loved her, my mother was hardly interesting enough to merit interest from a writer. She'd been a librarian, retired during my father's final illness, and was now just back from a trip to the Bahamas with her sister. "Why?"

He sat down on the bench next to me. "I meant your *real* mother." He lowered his voice, even though there wasn't anyone else out there who could hear. "Genevieve? You do know about Genevieve, don't you?"

Unable to speak, I just nodded.

"I'll make it worth your while," he continued smoothly,

his silky voice almost purring. "If you'd like, I'd be happy to read some of your writing, maybe give you some pointers?" He held out his hands again, palms up. "I like helping aspiring writers."

I didn't answer him because I couldn't. I just stood there, staring at him in shock. My heart was pounding in my ears, my head spinning.

How does he know about my real mother?

After I'd found the birth certificate, I debated whether I should mention it to my parents. I went back to my room and tried to read a Hardy Boys mystery I'd bought with my allowance, but the words had just swum on the page in front of my eyes. I couldn't focus on Frank and Joe's adventures in Alaska.

I couldn't forget, or get past, the fact that they'd never told me.

But I didn't know how to bring it up without admitting I'd gone into my father's office.

"You're awfully quiet today," the woman I'd always thought was my mother said as we sat at the kitchen table eating our McDonald's lunch later that afternoon. I just shrugged and didn't reply. I didn't know what to say to them, or how to even talk to them anymore. We'd always been close—they were good parents, never missing one of my school functions, always supportive and helpful—but now I felt a distance opening up between us.

If they'd lied about this, what else had they lied to me about?

I looked for information on my real mother—this Genevieve Legendre—online, but there was practically nothing to find. A death notice, listing my father and me as survivors, in a small newspaper called the *Avignon News* and another in the *New Orleans Times-Picayune,* both of which listed her occupation as painter. There were other family members listed in the obituaries: her parents, Geoffrey and Nina; a sister named Olivia; a brother Henri and his wife Denise and their daughter Virginia—all of them relatives of mine, relatives I didn't know existed. More searches turned up the information that my uncle Henri and aunt Denise were dead, drowned in a yachting accident.

But the most important information of all was that the Legendres owned a famous plantation in Louisiana, about seventy miles north of New Orleans along the Mississippi River, a place named Chambord.

Images of Chambord were everywhere online, and as soon as I saw it, I recognized it. One of my favorite movies, a grim black-and-white film starring two actresses in the twilight of their careers, had been filmed there. I would often sit at my computer, staring at the pictures of the magnificent brick house, with its rows of gleaming columns, wondering what my mother had been like, wondering what those relatives I didn't know were like, and how different my life would be had my mother not died when I was so very young. I looked up information on Chambord at the library, discovering that the Legendres had built the place before the Louisiana Purchase made them American citizens, and not only did the Legendres make their fortune growing cotton and indigo and sugar, but they were premier glassmakers as well. Chambord glass, similar to the famous Venetian glass, was prized throughout the South, and after the war the glassworks on the estate kept the Legendres going.

An old book, long out of print, called *Plantation Parade* by Harnett Kane thrilled me with its stories and legends about the Legendres of Chambord and their glittering history.

Whenever I was angry at a punishment from my parents or any time something bad happened to me at school, I would imagine what my life would be like if I were living at Chambord, if whatever my father's reason for cutting that part of my life away had never happened.

And I began to resent him more and more with each passing day.

My junior year in high school, I took my first creative writing class. I had always wanted to be a writer. I had learned how to read very young and had always found solace in books. The public library and bookstores were my favorite places to be, and I wanted to write books of my own, to give other people the pleasure I found myself in reading. My first story for my creative writing class was set at Chambord, and I gave free rein to my imagination. The story got an A; my teacher read it aloud in class and wanted to publish it in the school's annual literary magazine. My ego overruled my worry about my parents' reaction.

"How long have you known?" my father said quietly after he read the story.

I looked at my mother, who had tears in her eyes, and back at him. "Since I was about thirteen, I guess."

"Why didn't you say something?" my mother asked, her voice trembling.

I couldn't look at her. I thought they would be angry, but it never occurred to me that she would be hurt. I couldn't bear to see her cry. "I figured you both had a reason to lie to me, I guess."

And that was when my father lost it completely.

"Your mother was an evil woman!" my father snapped, his face turning red. He stood up. "She killed herself, Heath! She didn't love either one of us! She didn't think we were worth living for!" His face twisted in anger. "You want to know what kind of people they are?" He was screaming now, and I recoiled from him. "Not once have they ever tried to see you. Not once! I did you a favor getting you away from them. Monsters—they're *monsters*!" He stormed out of the room, angrier than I'd ever seen him.

I turned to my mother—my *stepmother*—and said, "Mom—"

She took my hand and squeezed it, the tears now flowing from her eyes. "Your mother hurt your father really badly," she said softly, "and he still can't talk about her without getting angry. Please try to understand." She didn't say it, but I could see it on her face. He'd never gotten over my mother's suicide. She walked into the kitchen and came back, pressing my birth certificate into my hand. "He needs time, Heath. I'm sure someday he'll be able to talk to you about her."

I stared down at the name written on the line marked *Mother.*

"Don't ever ask him about her," she whispered, wiping at her tears. "Promise me. Let him be the one to bring it up. Will you promise me that, please?"

I'd promised. And I'd never mentioned my real mother to either of them ever again.

And my father never brought up the subject again, even when he was dying.

But I wasn't able to forget his words.

They'd abandoned me like I'd never been born in the first place.

And that was just fine. I had parents who loved me, a relatively happy life in Bay City, Florida, and I didn't need them.

I didn't need the Legendres any more than they needed me.

Best to leave that door shut tightly.

My fantasies about Chambord and that side of my family were over.

When my father died, I thought about them again. I wondered if maybe they'd get in touch with me, that maybe they were respecting his wishes or something, and now that he was gone it would be different.

But I didn't hear from them, so I decided to put them out of my mind completely.

Sure, every once in a while, when money was tight or when I was too exhausted from working to study, I thought about them. I thought about asking them for some help, so I didn't have to work full-time while trying to get my degree. Maybe if I didn't have to work so much, I could study more and get better grades, find time to work on my writing. It was easy to get lost in fantasies about being welcomed into the Legendre family with open arms, offers to pay for my schooling, and an allowance granted so I wouldn't have to work. About giving up my little apartment and moving into the graceful mansion on the river, where the warm breezes would be scented by jasmine and magnolia, with servants waiting on me hand and foot.

And then I'd remember that not once had they ever reached out to me.

Not once.

"All right," I replied slowly. "There's a little dive bar just outside the airport, called the Runway, on Bayshore Boulevard. You can't miss it, you just turn right when you exit the airport and it's right there on the other side of the road. You can buy me a beer and I'll listen to what you have to say." The parking lot shuttle drove up. I picked up my backpack and my lunch box and climbed on board. The driver closed the doors behind me and pulled away from the curb.

All the way to the employee parking lot at the edge of the airport I wondered what he wanted to talk to me about. Was there some question about my mother's suicide? The obituaries hadn't said anything other than her death had been sudden—if my father hadn't told me about the suicide I wouldn't have known. I pulled out my smartphone and did another Internet search, typing her name into the search engine as the shuttle van drove through the night.

Was he writing a book about my mother?

The Web search didn't turn up any new facts about my mother, just that she'd been a painter and died nineteen years ago. There were some articles I hadn't seen before, about her paintings—their value had gone up in the years since she'd died, and she was now considered an important and sadly overlooked painter of the second half of the twentieth century. But there was nothing about her death other than a date, and some references to tragic circumstances. I didn't see how her suicide—which apparently had been kept out of published reports—could be the basis for a *Garden District Gothic*–type book.

Why on earth would he be interested in my mother?

I clicked on a link for the website for Chambord. I stared at the pictures of the majestic old plantation mansion in Redemption Parish, Louisiana. There were now cottages for rent on the property, as well as a five-star restaurant and a glass museum—Chambord glass was now rare, expensive and collectible. I didn't bother clicking on any of the interior pages. There was nothing I'd be interested in on the website.

But just looking at the picture of the columned mansion on the home page was making me get angry. *They've known where to find me all these years*...I closed the browser and put my phone away. Fuck the Legendres.

The Runway Bar was weathered and old and had gone through many different iterations and name changes over the years. Someone had told me it had been built during Prohibition, when Bay City was a popular destination for rum runners smuggling contraband liquor into Florida from Cuba. Located a block or so away from the airport entrance, it was a popular after-work watering hole for airport employees. The icy air-conditioning blasted me in the face when I opened the door and walked inside. Some of my coworkers were there, sharing a couple of pitchers of beer in their uniforms. An old Garth Brooks tune was blaring from the jukebox. I saw Jerry Channing sitting at a small table back in a corner, nursing a Corona with a wedge of lemon floating inside the bottle. I walked back to where he was sitting and sat down across from him. "All right," I said. "I'm here. What is this about?"

"I'm interested in your mother." He tilted his head to one side and narrowed his eyes. "What did your father tell you about Genevieve?" He said it familiarly, like he'd known her, as he picked up the bottle and took a drink.

"He refused to talk about her, so he didn't tell me anything," I replied, ordering a bottle of beer from the waitress who'd materialized while I was speaking. Once she moved away, I shrugged slightly. "So I don't really know much about her, other than what I could find online. She was a painter. She killed herself. That's pretty much it." *And the one time my father talked about her, he said she was an evil woman. But you don't need to know that.* "Did you know her?"

"She lived and died before the Internet exploded," Jerry said with a shake of his head, ignoring my question. "Believe me, if the Internet had been what it is today when she died, there would be plenty about her for you to find. Although your grandfather did a really good job keeping it all quiet, and out of the papers. That must have cost him a pretty penny, but I imagine he thought—still thinks—it was worth it. The Legendre name is damned important to him."

The waitress set my beer down on the table, and he paid for it. Once she left, I asked, "Why was it such a big deal to keep it out of the papers? Was it because she was a Catholic? And suicide is a sin?"

He raised his eyebrows. "Are you telling me you don't even know how she died?"

"She committed suicide when I was three years old." I sipped my beer. "Big deal."

"She committed suicide?" He took a deep breath and stared at me, a puzzled look on his face. "I—you know, maybe I was wrong, and this isn't such a great idea. I mean, I thought you at least knew some of this. I don't know if I should be the one to tell you the truth."

"The truth? There's more?" I heard my father's voice, shouting in my head again, *Your mother was an evil woman!* "I told you my father refused to talk about her. He got angry if she was ever mentioned, so how would I know anything other than what I can find online?"

He watched me as the jukebox switched from Garth Brooks to Toby Keith's "I Love This Bar." He took another drink, almost draining the bottle empty. "Your mother was…It was more than just a suicide, Heath. Your mother was having an affair. She was cheating on your father. She killed her lover and took her own life."

No wonder Dad didn't want to talk about her. I saw the pain on his reddened face again as he shouted those words at me. *Your mother was an evil woman!*

I shook my head, hoping my shock didn't register on my face. "All he told me was she killed herself, that she didn't love either him or me enough to go on living. He didn't say anything about an affair," I said, picking the label off my beer. The amber bottle was covered with condensation. I felt oddly numb, and even more sympathetic for Dad. How awful that must have been for him.

"And you've never met any of your mother's family?" His

face was unreadable, and he was speaking in a professional monotone.

I stared at him. "I—" I stopped myself from finishing the sentence. "No. All I know about the Legendres is what I've read on the website for their estate, Chambord." I raised my chin. "They've never once tried to reach out to me. Not once, in all the years since she…since she died. They don't care about me, so why should I care about them? The Legendres can go to hell."

My words were strong, were what I'd always believed, yet I could feel doubt forming, creeping in. *Are you sure? Dad didn't tell me everything. Maybe there's more to the story.*

"Are you sure?" His facial expression didn't change. "Family is everything to your grandfather, and your mother was your grandparents' favorite child. I can't believe your grandmother Nina died without ever trying to see you, to see Genevieve's only child." He leaned toward me. "Are you sure they never reached out to you? From everything I've been told, your father was really angry when he left Louisiana—not that I can blame him, given what happened. Maybe they tried and he wouldn't let them."

I stared at him, remembering how angry my father had been when he told me the truth. He'd been angrier than I'd ever seen him. He wasn't a man with a temper, he rarely got angry, and he had a lot of patience.

Your mother was an evil woman!

My father had been an accountant and worked for a firm in Bay City. We'd never been poor—I always had a roof over my head, food on the table, clothes on my back, we took family vacations—but my parents spent what they earned and never really saved. When Dad died right before my high school graduation, there really wasn't money for me to go to college, but I'd gotten lucky and landed the job with Transco Airlines.

I was taking classes part-time at Bay State University, and my mother—my *stepmother*—was trying to help when she could, but I felt guilty about taking money from her. One of the great things about working for Transco was the flight benefits— Mom got to fly free, too.

My childhood had been a happy one; my friends had always envied how great and loving my parents were, and how supportive.

Could he really have been so vindictive, so angry about my mother's betrayal, that he would have deliberately kept me away from her family?

"You're one of Geoffrey Legendre's only grandchildren," Jerry was saying. "You have a first cousin who's a few years older than you, Ginny. Her parents are also dead, they were killed in a yachting accident twenty years or so ago—so Geoffrey's only surviving child is your aunt, Olivia. She lives at Chambord—well, they all live at Chambord. Geoffrey is really big on family." He was staring at me. "You're certain they never tried to get in touch with you? That doesn't sound like Geoffrey at all, and I can't believe Nina wouldn't have tried, especially when she was dying."

I felt like I'd been punched in the stomach. I could feel tears rising in my eyes, but I wasn't sure if they were from anger or upset or hurt… Could Dad have kept me from my *family*?

"You're certain they've never tried to reach you?" he asked again.

I looked across the table at him. He looked incredulous, and there was sympathy in his eyes. I shook my head. "I don't know. As far as I know, no. I mean, it's possible that Dad… But he's been dead for several years now, so if he was the one keeping them from me…" I shrugged. "Well, they haven't tried in the last four years now, have they?" I finished my beer. "And why do you care about any of this? Are you writing another book?"

He didn't answer at first and licked his lower lip. "Yes," he said finally. "I'm writing about your mother's death. I know the public story isn't true, and I know there was already a cover-up—your grandfather made sure the public never knew the real story." He leaned across the table and lowered her voice. "It wasn't easy for me to find out what really happened the day your mother died, and how, and I do think there's a hell of a lot more to the story than what little I've been able to find out." He coughed. "Most people don't know your mother's lover was even there—it was certainly left out of the police report. But I'm not so certain..."

"Do you think she was murdered?" I stared at him.

He nodded. "I think someone killed both her and her lover."

"But why?" I started shredding the beer label into bits. "Why would someone kill her?" A horrible thought, something I couldn't believe or wrap my head around, popped into my head. "Do you think my father killed them?"

"I don't really have a theory," he replied. "It's just that there are so many inconsistencies in the story, and the more I look into it, the more it doesn't make sense." He gave me a slight smile. "Your father couldn't have done it, though, Heath. He was in New Orleans that day, when it happened. So don't worry about that."

"I don't understand why you want to talk to me about her. I don't even remember her. I don't even know what she looked like."

"You don't remember her at all? Nothing?" He was peering at me, watching my face. He fiddled with his phone and held it out to me. There was a picture on the screen of a beautiful woman with a heart-shaped face and long blond hair. She was laughing, and her eyes sparkled.

I knew immediately she was my mother.

I looked a lot like her.

"I didn't even know my stepmother wasn't my mother until I was thirteen," I replied bitterly. I pushed my chair back and stood up. "Well, this has all been really interesting, but I'm really tired and I want to get to bed—I have a busy day tomorrow." It was a lie; all I had to do was laundry and clean my apartment. But I wanted to get out of there, get away from him, think about the things he'd said.

He stood and held out his hand to me. "Thank you for talking to me, Heath. I know this wasn't easy for you." Again, he gave me that searching look. "You should think about calling your grandfather—I mean, what have you got to lose? And if you remember anything about your mother—"

"I'll call you." I got out of there as fast as I could. Once I was safely in my car, I turned the ignition key but sat there for a long time in the darkening parking lot, thinking.

Maybe—just maybe I should reach out to them. Maybe they could help me with money for college. Maybe it was Dad keeping them away from me all this time. I am blood, after all, and if there's just me and my cousin—well, it couldn't hurt to ask for some help, would it?

I slammed the car into drive and headed home.

Chapter Two

If one of the great things about working for an airline was flying for free, the best thing about working at the airport was getting seated in first class. The gate agents always tried, whenever possible, to bump their coworkers up from coach, and even on a flight as short as the one from Bay City to New Orleans—about an hour and a half—it was so worth it to collapse into one of those plush leather seats and get free drinks. I was nervous when I boarded, and when the flight attendant—a hot blond with broad shoulders and a ridiculously tiny waist—offered me a preflight drink, I asked for a cup of coffee with Baileys. He gave me a surreptitious wink when he placed it on my tray, and I took a sip as I allowed my body to relax into the comfortable seat. I watched the rest of the passengers boarding as I finished the coffee. It was good, and the Baileys gave it the right amount of kick. The seat next to me on the aisle was vacant and, unless some frequent flier turned up at the last minute, would stay that way. I accepted a second cup when the handsome blond came by again but decided it would be the last one. The Baileys was helping to mellow me out, but I wanted to be lucid when I arrived.

I switched to water when we were in the air, and read the latest Alex Marwood suspense thriller while ignoring the flight attendant's attempts to flirt with me. But I couldn't focus on the book, no matter how hard I tried. I had to keep rereading the pages I'd just finished, unable to keep track of the complicated plot. I finally gave up as we started the initial descent, looking out the window as the plane banked northward in from the Gulf and down over Lake Pontchartrain. *Here we go,* I told myself as the plane landed smoothly on the runway and slowed down, heading for the gate. I slipped my book into my shoulder bag and pulled out my cell phone, switching it back on and waiting impatiently for a signal as the plane taxied. The signal finally kicked in just as the Jetway was attached to the plane and everyone stood up. I fiddled with my phone so I didn't have to make eye contact with the flight attendant as I walked off the plane, getting slapped in the face by the heavy, hot, thick swampy air that let me know I was in Louisiana.

"Enjoy your stay," he called after me as I hurried up the Jetway.

You really shouldn't judge all flight attendants because you had a bad experience with one, I scolded myself as I headed through the terminal to baggage claim. I walked past a four-piece jazz ensemble playing near the down escalator. *They're not all the same—still, the nickname "air mattress" wasn't invented in a vacuum.*

I grabbed my bags off the carousel and looked around, trying to spot my cousin Ginny. According to my grandfather's last email, she had volunteered to meet me at baggage claim. My palms were sweating, and I dried them on the black jeans I was wearing. I was moments away from meeting a member of my mother's family for the very first time. I'd never had a cousin before. My father had been an only child and his parents had died when I was really young. My stepmother had a sister who'd never married. I'd grown up envying the other kids I knew for their big sprawling families, but I'd never realized how badly I wanted more family of my own until the last few weeks.

Honestly, the last two months had gone by so quickly I'd barely had time to process everything that happened. It had taken me a few days after that first meeting with Jerry to drum up the nerve to talk to my stepmother. "You don't need my permission, Heath," she'd said to me with a sad smile. "If you want to get in touch with your mother's family, you should. Better to do that than spend the rest of your life wondering, right? I don't know why your father was so against it. I know she hurt him, but her family is your blood." She'd taken my hand. "Sometimes letters would come from Louisiana, and he would send them back unopened. I thought it was wrong—we argued about it a few times—because even if he was angry, no matter how badly they'd hurt him, no matter what your mother did, she was still your mother and they were—*are*—your people. I should have said something to you before... but when your father died"—she swallowed and her eyes filled with tears, the way they always did whenever we talked about my father—"I was hurting too bad, and I didn't want to lose you, too. I was being selfish. I hope you'll forgive me for that. And then, then it was just easier to leave things as they were. There weren't any more letters, there hadn't been for a long time, and we were happy. Don't hate me, Heath." Her voice shook when she said the last few words. Her inability to conceive had always been hard for her to accept, so she had embraced me as her one chance at motherhood. She'd been a great mother.

"There's nothing to forgive, Mom. I could never hate you. They may be my blood, but you're my mother." I put my arms around her and squeezed her tightly. "But I think I am going to talk to them."

"Maybe they'll help you with school," she whispered. "Maybe you won't have to work so hard."

Your mouth to God's ears, I thought, even if it did make me feel a little mercenary.

I'd called Jerry, and he put me in touch with the Legendres for the first time. I'd gone to their website again, gone through the many pictures of the estate, the rooms in the mansion and the guest rooms, the restaurant menus. I'd gotten the reservations number and called, hanging up with a mumbled *Sorry, wrong number* when the bright, cheerful female voice chirped, "Chambord Plantation Bed and Breakfast!" The website listed my grandfather as the owner/proprietor of Chambord, and Jerry had filled me in on the rest of the family over dinner one night before he went back to New Orleans. "Your grandfather is the one who came up with the idea to turn the old place into a boarding house and restaurant," Jerry had said over steak and lobster at a fine restaurant overlooking Gaspard Bay. "Geoffrey inherited the place when the house was practically a wreck and all the money was pretty much gone. Nina, your grandmother, was an heiress, but don't think for a second Geoffrey married Nina for her money! They loved each other very much—your grandfather has really never gotten over Nina's death."

"How did she die?" I asked, sipping the expensive white wine he'd ordered that I could have never afforded on my own.

"It was rather sudden. A real tragedy. She had breast cancer, and it looked like she'd beaten it, but she tripped and fell down the main staircase at Chambord. She broke her neck." He poured some more wine into my glass when I set it back down on the table. He gave me an odd look. "She never tried to get in touch with you?"

"She may have." I shrugged. "My mom—my *stepmother*—told me that letters used to come from Louisiana, and my dad would send them back unopened. They eventually stopped coming." I felt a spark of anger against my father. No matter what my birth mother might have done, it wasn't right for him to keep me from my grandparents. "Who else is there in the family again?"

Jerry looked at me for a long moment before continuing. "Well, Geoffrey and Nina had three children. There were two girls—your mother, Genevieve, and your aunt, Olivia—and one son, Henri, who was the middle child. Olivia never married— she's the only surviving child." I must have involuntarily flinched or something, because he stopped talking again and gave me a long, careful look. "Are you okay?"

I took another, bigger sip from my wineglass. "Yes," I replied, even though it wasn't true. It was a lot to take in. I was trying very hard not to get angry at my father for keeping it all from me, but it was getting harder and harder the more I thought about it.

He kept me from my family. No matter what my mother may have done, there's no excuse for keeping me from my grandmother. And now she's gone…I'll never get the chance to know her. Or my uncle. Wasn't it bad enough I lost my mother when I was a little boy? Did he have to steal my family from me?

"You're sure?" He kept looking at me, and when I finally nodded, he went on. "Olivia has always lived at Chambord, and she runs everything having to do with the house itself—she oversees the running of the house, the gift shop, the museum, the servants, the tours, anything involving Chambord itself, including the guest business." He laughed. "Your grandfather hates letting people in to look at the place, but of course the tours don't include the part of the house where the family lives."

"He must really hate the B and B, then."

"Well, none of the paying guests stay in the main house—all the paying guest rooms are in the outbuildings. The restaurant, though, is the real moneymaker. More wine?"

"No, thank you." I put my hand over the top of my glass as he picked up the bottle.

"Between all the individual businesses, the Legendres do pretty well for themselves." Jerry refilled his own glass and shrugged. "And of course, there's the money from your grandmother. She inherited a considerable fortune."

My grandmother inherited a considerable fortune. Did she leave anything to me? I toyed with the remains of the lobster on my plate. "The website said something about a glass museum?"

"Your grandfather's pride and joy." Jerry gave me an appraising look. "Your grandfather takes a great deal of pride in the family history. In the old days, before the war—"

"When there were slaves at Chambord?" I was feeling a bit tipsy and the wine was making me reckless. My tone was a lot sharper than I'd intended, and he flinched a bit.

He sipped his wine. "Yes, of course there were slaves at Chambord. But the Legendres weren't just farmers, you know. The Legendres were glassmakers, and Chambord sustained itself for years from the glass industry."

The story was that the original Legendre, Remy, had apprenticed on the island of Murano as a young man and learned the glassmaking techniques of the Venetian masters. He had left Murano and come to the New World, bought the land and slaves, and set himself up as a glassmaker. For generations, Chambord glass was just as desirable as Murano glass—and Chambord supplied all the Carnival krewes of Louisiana with glass beads and masks for their balls and parades. It was when the krewes moved away from using glass beads and started using plastic ones that Chambord revenue began to dry up—which was why, I supposed, my grandfather had to marry my grandmother for her money. Glass was no longer manufactured at Chambord, but the old foundry where the glass had been made for almost two centuries had been converted into a museum, with prime examples of Legendre glass beads and masks. Some were shown on the website—they were quite beautiful.

"Your uncle Henri married very young, a local girl of no great family—your grandfather didn't approve, of course, but made the best of it." Jerry was saying, after telling the waiter we didn't want dessert. "They had a daughter, Ginny, and when Ginny was about five years old Henri and his wife were killed when their yacht sank out in the Gulf. Your grandparents both never really got over that, and then your mother died not long after that, you know."

"So Ginny's a little older than I am?"

He nodded. "Your grandparents and your aunt raised Ginny—she's a bit of a troublemaker. She flunked out of Tulane, but eventually got her business degree from LSU. There was a lot of trouble there, apparently, but she finally married someone your grandfather approved of—Constantine Poulos—Costa. He's Greek—his parents were from Greece and ran a Greek restaurant in New Orleans for many years. Costa is a Cordon Bleu–trained chef, and naturally after he married Ginny, the two of them took over the running of the restaurant from Geoffrey."

My head was spinning a bit, but that might have been from the really good wine. Jerry had kept refilling my glass whenever it was less than half-full, and I was worried about getting drunk. He was a very attractive man—handsome, and that amazing body, and smart on top of it all. I worried that I might make a fool of myself if I drank too much and got too bold. After all, what would a man like that—rich, handsome, sexy, smart, talented—see in someone like me? I'd never had much luck in the boyfriend department, unrequited crushes and a lot of first dates that never went anywhere. "And my grandmother died when exactly?"

"About six years ago."

"So she did die before my father." My voice sounded thick, like my tongue was too big for my mouth, and I felt light-headed. I took a sip from my water glass and decided it was smarter to avoid the wine from there on out. My stepmother couldn't remember exactly when the letters from Louisiana had stopped coming, but she thought it was a year or two before Dad died. It made sense, in a sad way.

The letters stopped coming when my grandmother died.

No one else had cared enough to reach out to me, apparently.

"You said that my mother…that my mother killed her lover?" My words were slightly slurring—definitely, I told myself, lay off the wine. "Who was her lover?"

I'd tried to find out more information about all of this online but hadn't had any luck. If Jerry was telling me the truth, my grandfather had been very successful in keeping everything out of the papers and completely under wraps.

But Jerry didn't answer my question. He deflected it with some nonsense about finding out about my mother from her family. I somehow managed not to make a fool of myself the rest of the evening—but didn't have more wine, either. And when Jerry dropped me off at my apartment, I didn't have the nerve to ask him in.

He did, however, urge me to contact my grandfather. "And if you do decide to come to Chambord for a visit, you have my number." He smiled. "I hope you'll use it, seriously."

Maybe it was the wine, but I emailed Geoffrey Legendre when I got back home to my apartment. He responded far more warmly than I expected—I wasn't certain he'd answer at all, since the letters had stopped coming after his wife died—and we started a correspondence, careful and halting, neither side revealing very much. After the first few days, the emails from Chambord became warmer, and we started chatting on the phone every few days. He was curious, wanted to know my major at Bay State and pretty much everything there was to know about me, but it seemed every time I hung up I knew no more about the Legendre family—and my mother—than I had before. It was like my mother was hidden behind some thick veil of secrecy. He would talk about the restaurant, the museum and the estate, the history of Chambord, but he was reticent when it came to the family itself.

"You need to come visit"—he would brush aside any questions I dared ask—"and learn for yourself by meeting us. When will you come?"

Initially I was reluctant to visit Chambord, to even think about it. But as the calls became warmer and friendlier, I started looking into changing my vacation plans. I had two weeks off in late June and early July, and had planned on going to Europe. I'd always wanted to go to Italy and had been scraping and saving every cent I could to put toward two weeks there.

Italy will still be there, I finally decided, *and I can save even more money by next summer. Who knows—maybe Geoffrey will help me with my school expenses and I'll have even more money for the trip!*

He was delighted when I told him I could come for a visit earlier than I expected, and I canceled my Italy plans.

And that was how I found myself at the baggage claim area at the New Orleans airport, looking around for my cousin Ginny. Grandfather had said she was looking forward to meeting me, and she had insisted on picking me up at the airport. He'd sent me a picture of her attached to an email so I'd know who to look for.

Ginny was a beautiful young woman, and the picture was obviously taken by a professional. She was sitting on the ground in a pair of khaki shorts, wearing a purple LSU T-shirt that hugged her upper torso like another layer of skin. She had large breasts, a small waist, and her legs were trim and nicely formed. Her long blond hair was blowing in the wind, and her blue eyes—so like my own I caught my breath when I noticed them—were filled with joy, and she was clearly laughing. My guess was she was seated on top of a levee, because behind her the wide and brown Mississippi River contrasted against the vibrant blue of the cloudless sky. She and her husband had no children.

I'd practically memorized my grandfather's email, and I fiddled with my phone to pull up Ginny's picture. I dragged my two bags—a large square hard-sided one on wheels, the other a duffel bag with a handle and wheels—away from the belts Transco Airlines used. I frowned as I looked around again. There wasn't anyone who even slightly looked like Ginny, even assuming she looked prettier in the picture than she did in real life. I was about to give up and call Chambord when I heard a female voice call my name.

"Heath?"

I turned. The woman addressing me appeared to be in her late forties. She was short, maybe a few inches over five feet tall. Her dark brown hair was cut short and there were streaks of iron gray in it. She was tanned, and her figure was slight but sturdy. She was wearing a white tennis skirt and a navy-blue collared pullover with short sleeves. She was tentatively smiling as she took a few steps toward me.

"Ginny?" I asked, confused.

She laughed. "Hardly. I'm Charlotte Draper. I'd have

recognized you anywhere—you have your mother's eyes." She tilted her head to one side as she scrutinized me. "It's amazing how much you look like her." She stuck out her small hand for me to shake. "Geoffrey may or may not have mentioned me." She shrugged her shoulders slightly. "My father and Geoffrey were roommates in college. He took in my brother and me when our parents were killed, raised us like we were his own children." A slight shadow crossed her face, but it was gone so quickly I might have just imagined it. "Anyway, it's nice to meet you. Is that all you have with you?"

"Yes." I was fumbling. My grandfather hadn't told me anything about her, and I racked my memory trying to remember if Jerry had mentioned her. I'd done as much online research as I could on my newfound relatives, but I hadn't seen anything about Charlotte Draper.

"Well, all right then, follow me." She started walking away quickly and I hurried to catch up to her. I had a lot of questions—ones I'd hoped to have Ginny answer for me.

"I thought Ginny was going to meet me," I said as I followed her out the electric doors and down the sidewalk to the crosswalk.

"Yeah, well, Ginny had other plans, apparently." She blew out her breath in a raspberry as we crossed the street to the concrete island separating the taxis and buses from the cars circling. "She just disappeared this morning and wasn't answering her phone, so your grandfather asked me to come." She smiled at me. "I was happy to. I was…I loved your mother very much. I've been so excited—ever since Geoffrey told us you'd contacted him, I'd been hoping you'd come."

"That's very kind of you." I said, making sure to smile at her. "About Ginny—does she…does she disappear a lot? Should I be worried?"

She gave me an odd look before barking out a laugh. Her

face twisted. "Well, you'll learn soon enough what she's like. Spoiled, spoiled, spoiled. Geoffrey has spoiled her rotten, and she has the most dreadful manners. I could wring her neck myself. Ginny only cares about Ginny—you'll find that out soon enough for yourself, I suppose." She shook her head as we reached the tall parking garage opposite the terminal. She stabbed at the elevator button and turned back to me. "You might as well know—Ginny didn't want you to come, and she won't be happy you're here. Geoffrey ordered her to pick you up today, she said she wouldn't, and so of course she went missing last night. No one knows where she is." The elevator doors opened, and we stepped inside. "So of course everyone's looking for the spoiled brat, and I was drafted to come pick you up. She's been coddled and spoiled so much she thinks all she has to do is hold her breath until she gets her way." She pulled a key ring out of her shoulder bag as the elevator doors opened on the top level. "And she always does. That's something else you'll have to get used to." She pressed a button on the fob and a corresponding chirp sounded from a nearby row of cars. She gave me a sly smile as we stepped back out into the sunshine and the wet heat. "Ginny's been getting her way since she was a little girl. She thinks now that you're here that might change, and she doesn't like it. She has to be the center of attention."

"Well, I don't want to cause any trouble," I said carefully. I didn't know how to respond to her comments about my cousin, so I chose not to say anything. I didn't know this woman and wasn't entirely sure I could trust her. *No need to worry about me, Cousin Ginny,* I thought as the wheels on my two suitcases clacked over the paved parking lot, *I'm not here to take your place. I just want to know my family and maybe get some help with college. You can have the rest for all I care.*

I followed her down the row. The sun was incredibly bright, and I was sweating. Bay City was hot and humid, like all of Florida, but I wasn't used to this kind of intensity. At least in Florida there was always a breeze blowing in from the Gulf. The air here felt stagnant, like it was just hanging there. I could feel sinus pressure building in my temples, and I coughed. She clicked on the fob again and a silver BMW's trunk popped open. I put my suitcases in the trunk, taking the time to retrieve a Claritin from my shoulder bag before slamming the trunk closed. I dry swallowed the tablet before getting into the passenger seat and buckling the seat belt. She started the engine and instantly cold air began blasting out of the vents in the dashboard.

"It's about an hour's drive to Chambord," she said as she backed the car out of the space. She gave me a weird smile as she put the car into drive and headed for the exit. "It's really nice that you're here, Heath. I know I'm glad you're here. The place—hell, the family—could stand some shaking up."

Shaking up? What the hell is she talking about? "You think I look like my mother?" I asked after she'd paid the lot attendant and headed out for the highway. "You said I have her eyes."

It took her a moment to answer. "Yes, I knew your mother—we grew up together," she finally said, her voice soft. "Everyone loved Genevieve, you know." She smiled at the memory. "She was so alive...people thought she was wild, but that was just Genevieve, you know? She loved life, wanted to squeeze all the juice out of it. I've never known anyone like her...She was amazing, so loving and kind and generous. She loved to laugh. I always wished I could be more like her. Geoffrey said your father never told you anything about her—is that true?"

I nodded. "Did you know my father, too?"

She barked out a laugh as she merged into the traffic heading west on I-10. "Oh, I knew him, all right. Your

father...he was a nice guy, smart and kind and gentle, totally
the opposite of every man Genevieve had ever been involved
with before—she really liked wild boys, you know? The kind
who'd always find a way to get some booze and pot and a
private place to go party. All through high school Genevieve
was wild...Oh, the fights she used to have with Uncle Geoffrey
and Aunt Nina! They'd ground her and she'd just sneak out
at night. And then all through college, the same thing. She
was always getting into some kind of trouble. You could
have knocked us all down with a feather when she turned up
married to him. They weren't suited to each other, not suited
at all...it was just a matter of time, we all figured, before they
realized they'd made a mistake and she'd leave him. They
didn't live at Chambord, you know, and Geoffrey didn't like
that one bit." She laughed grimly. "Geoffrey and Nina gave
them a house in New Orleans as a wedding gift—your father
refused to live at Chambord, but they always came out for the
weekends and holidays and things, and of course, after you
were born Geoffrey stepped up the big campaign to get you
and your mother back to Chambord full-time." She took her
eyes off the road long enough to look at me. "You were such a
sweet little boy. It was a dark day when David took you away.
He shouldn't have done that, no matter what he thought about
Genevieve, no matter what he thought about the family."

"The only thing he ever told me about her was that she
was an evil woman and that she committed suicide when I
was a little boy." I turned and looked out the window. I tried
imagining what it must have been like for him, married to
someone so different from him, whose father opposed her
marriage and wanted her to move back to her childhood home.
My stepmother was a better match for him, I thought sadly,
feeling some of the anger for him I'd been holding on to
slipping away. We were driving on a bridge, over a marsh. I

assumed the broad expanse of water just beyond the reeds and the drowned trees was Lake Pontchartrain.

"He would say that," she replied dourly. "Evil." She shook her head. "No, Heath, your mother wasn't evil. She was foolish and high-spirited and, yes, she made mistakes, but she wasn't evil. She owned up to her mistakes, tried to make them right. She was a remarkable woman. Everyone loved her." She clicked her tongue. "No, *Genevieve* was not evil."

The obvious response to that was *Well then, who was?* but I decided to change the subject. "So, what's my grandfather like?"

She clicked her tongue against her teeth and reached down to turn on the car stereo. Jazz music I didn't recognize began playing softly through the speakers. I watched the lake shimmer in the sun as we drove along at a steady clip. "Geoffrey has slowed down some since the stroke," she finally said, gripping the steering wheel tightly. "He gets frustrated now—he used to be so vital, and now, well, now he can't do all the things he used to do. Sometimes he has to use a wheelchair—there are days when he just doesn't have the strength to stand or walk, you know, and that frustrates him." She smiled faintly. "He was so...I don't know how to describe it. Vital? Alive? He was never a very big man—he's not as tall as you are—but he took up a lot of space. After Nina died, he seemed to shrink a little bit. And the stroke..." She shook her head.

He hadn't mentioned anything about a stroke or a wheelchair to me. "Is he in good health?"

She shrugged. "He has good days and bad days." She patted my knee. "That's why he wanted you to come visit sooner rather than later. Every once in a while he goes to a dark place and thinks he doesn't have much time left. Olivia pretty much runs everything now other than the restaurant." Her face darkened. "Ginny and Costa supposedly run that together, but

Ginny rarely sets foot in there anymore. She's too busy with her, um, other pursuits."

What other pursuits? hung there in the air between us, but I wasn't going to ask. Whatever was going on between my cousin Ginny and her husband was none of my business, and definitely nothing I wanted to get involved in. I looked out the window. We were out of the swamp and driving now through the lush Louisiana countryside. Everything was green, with the occasional splash of color from a flowering vine. The car's air-conditioning, which had seemed like a godsend at first, was now so cold I was getting goose bumps. Charlotte kept talking in the same tone of voice, rising and falling, as she told me stories about my family and her own past. I thought it best not to comment on anything she said. I didn't know her well enough to trust her, so I just made appropriate noises when it seemed necessary.

Apparently my grandfather and her father had met as pledge brothers at Beta Kappa fraternity at LSU and had been roommates all through their college years. They married best friends—my grandmother Nina and her mother Amanda had been sorority sisters—and the two couples remained close, and their children were close as well. "So when our parents died, Geoffrey and Nina took us in—my brother Dylan and me," she said, glancing over at me for a moment before returning her attention to the road, where it belonged. "They treated us like family, of course, but more like poor relations." The last bit came out with a bit of malice, her lips tightening and her knuckles turning white on the steering wheel. "They made Dylan go into the military—he died in the Gulf War, right around the same time your mother died." Again, the malice dripped from her words, and I wondered why she clearly had issues with my mother. She was the first person I'd met besides my father who'd known her.

"Your mother's suicide was a difficult time for everyone," she went on, unaware of my discomfort. "And then of course David just grabbed you and took off for Florida." She glanced over at me again, giving me a gentle smile. "I haven't seen you since you were three years old, and now look at you—you're a grown man." She looked sad. "I loved your mother a lot, Heath. She was the only Legendre who never treated me like a poor cousin." She bit her lower lip.

Then why did you sound so bitchy when you talked about her dying? I thought, wondering if maybe I had misread her tone.

"You might as well hear this from me," she went on as she turned on her blinker, veering off onto an exit with a sign reading *Avignon*, "before someone else says it to you. My husband Cole—" She sighed. "When we were all younger, Cole...people thought Cole was in love with Genevieve. He wasn't—he married me—but there was always some gossip about them. Mean-spirited stuff. Genevieve would have never cheated on her husband, never. Just small-minded small-town people, trying to cause trouble. I never believed it, and you shouldn't either, if anyone says anything to you about it." She sniffed as she turned left at the stop sign at the foot of the exit. "You're young—you don't know how people are yet."

I didn't say anything, but she kept talking. She and her husband still lived at Chambord, but not in the main house— they had an old bachelor house on the grounds. Cole Draper was the owner of the local paper, and she was a housewife. "We never had any children—we thought about adopting but we never got around to it, and now, well, now we're of course too old." She sighed. "After Henri and his wife died, I helped raise your cousin Ginny." Again, her face twisted when she said my cousin's name.

Apparently, there was no love lost there.

We reached another crossroad. A directional sign pointing right said *Avignon 5 miles* and another pointing left read *Chambord Plantation 3 miles*. She turned left, and before long we were driving alongside an enormous levee, covered in grass. After a little while a tall brick fence appeared on the left side of the road. "That fence marks the property line," she said as she accelerated a bit, so she could pass a slow moving pickup truck loaded down with furniture bound by string. "Chambord is enormous, it runs all the way back, almost to the swamp line."

She turned to the right and drove through a gate with *Chambord* inscribed in wrought iron over the entryway. I gasped, in spite of myself.

I was prepared for my first glimpse of Chambord. I'd seen the house before, in any number of movies and TV shows, pictures on the website, and from searching through Web images. The house looked impressive in the pictures, but they didn't truly capture the stunning grandeur of the reality. Chambord was enormous and gleaming white, so white it almost glowed in the bright sunshine. Enormous live oaks spread their branches out to shade the house on every side, and a row of willows stretched out behind the house along the paved road leading back to other buildings, which I knew from my research to be the guesthouses, the gift shop, the museum, and the five-star restaurant.

But the main house itself was remarkably beautiful. It rose from the ground, three stories with enormous white marble columns supporting the gallery roofs. Two graceful wings branched off from the central main portion of the house, their galleries also graced by columns. The expanse of vibrant green lawn was broken by the occasional fountain, or a beautifully carved classical-style sculpture. Flower beds exploded in a riot of colors. Enormous rosebushes and bougainvillea vines, magnolia blossoms, and mimosa trees were scattered at various intervals throughout the grounds. There was a swimming pool in a pavilion just behind the house, as well as tennis courts. Charlotte drove the BMW into the parking area just in front of the main portion of the house. Several other expensive cars were also parked there. She shut the car off and popped the trunk open while she examined her phone with a frown. She dumped it into her shoulder bag. "Still no sign of Ginny— sorry, but she'll turn up eventually. She always does," she said as she opened her door and got out. "It's probably for the best, anyway. No need for you to meet her when she's in this kind of mood."

I got my bags out of the trunk and followed her up the wide steps to the first-floor gallery. She opened the front door with a key and stepped aside. "Welcome to Chambord," she said. "Ignore the smell. There's always another room rotting somewhere inside the house."

I walked into the incredibly cool interior of the house, my mouth slightly open. The hardwood floors were polished to a glowing shine. Doorways were made of dark wood, the walls of the long hallway painted a pale yellow. Lighting fixtures on the walls were made of cut glass that sparkled in the light from the bulbs within. Antique tables were placed at strategic intervals along the hallway. At the far end, I could see big wooden double doors with frosted glass windows. An enormous chandelier hung from the ceiling, with teardrop-shaped crystals flashing red and blue and yellow fire when a facet caught the light. At the far end of the hallway, just before the double doors to the back gallery, was a beautiful hanging staircase that I remembered from the website. It was famous, I recalled from my reading, and was a rare example of the work of the architect who'd designed Chambord; most of the other homes he'd designed and built were long gone.

At the top stood a tall, slender woman, her hands clasped in front of her, a severe look on her face as she slowly began to descend the staircase.

Her long gray hair was pulled back into a braid, and she was wearing a long denim skirt that reached her knees over sensible flat patent-leather shoes. Her blouse was bright yellow and open at the throat, where she had a blue scarf tied around her neck that matched the blue of the denim skirt. Her face was unlined, and she wasn't a pretty woman. She had a large hawk-like nose, thin lips, and no makeup on her face. But her eyes—her eyes looked like mine, that icy bright blue Charlotte had mentioned at the airport.

Her eyes flicked up and down, judging me and apparently finding me wanting. She didn't say anything.

"Heath, this is your aunt, Olivia," Charlotte said. "If you'll excuse me, I think I'm going to go hunt down my husband. See you at dinner." She disappeared down the hallway, and I heard a door shut as I stood there, my gaze locked on my aunt's.

"I trust you had a pleasant flight?" she finally said, her voice low and husky and not completely unfriendly. No offer of a hug or even a handshake.

She doesn't want me here, I thought, saying aloud, "It was uneventful," in a tone matching hers.

"Is that everything?" She gestured to my bags. Her hands were probably her best feature, the fingers long and tapering and elegant, the nails perfectly shaped and manicured, painted a dark red. An enormous ruby set in a plain gold band was the only jewelry she wore, and the ruby was so big it emphasized how slender her fingers were. "I will show you to your room." She turned and started back up the stairs. She was about halfway up when she stopped and turned. "Come, come," she snapped at me.

I picked up my suitcases by their handles and followed

her up the stairs. On the second floor another staircase led up again, but she walked down the hallway. I followed her, and when the hallway branched off to the left she turned.

"I'm putting you in the west wing," she said over her shoulder as I walked hurriedly, trying to keep up with her. "I assumed you would want privacy. No one else is staying in the west wing. My father's rooms are on the third floor in the main part of the house, and my rooms are in the east wing, which is where your cousin and her husband also have their rooms. You have a house phone, of course, so if you're hungry or need anything you can call down to the kitchen. Maya has been instructed to give you anything you need." She paused in front of a door, turned the knob, and stepped aside. "Make yourself at home. Dinner will be served at seven. The dining room is on the first floor, down the hallway from the staircase. You can't miss it." She walked over to the dressing table. "A map of the house with every room clearly marked has been left for you here." She tapped it as I placed my suitcases on the bed.

"And when can I meet my grandfather?"

Her facial expression didn't change as she walked back over to the doorway. "He's resting now. You will meet him at dinner. He's not well." She paused in the doorway and turned back to face me. "I believe in honesty, so I will be honest with you. I told my father, and now I am telling you. Inviting you here was a mistake, a terrible mistake, and you shouldn't have come. I didn't want you here."

I felt my cheeks getting warm. "I can understand why my father wanted to keep me away from this family."

"Your father was a wise man. You should have listened to him." She stepped closer to me and raised her right hand to my face, placing her palm against my cheek. "You look like her. I can see her in your face." For a moment, the mask dropped and I saw pain, but then the mask dropped back into place and she blinked her hooded eyes. "Are you like her?" she asked softly. "Are you going to cause trouble the way she always did?" When I didn't answer, she turned and closed the door behind her.

I exhaled with a sigh and wondered yet again if coming here was a mistake. I walked over to the French doors, unlocked them, and opened them wide. My room faced out over the lawn, and I could see the outbuildings. The big one, which used to be the stables, was now the restaurant. The parking area in front of it was empty; they closed it down at two and it didn't reopen for dinner until six. There were no cars in front of any of the guesthouses, other than Charlotte's BMW. I assumed that was where she and her husband lived. I stepped out onto the gallery. It continued to the back corner of the house, where it turned and followed the line of the house again. It also went around to the front and connected to the main house's gallery. I heard a rumble of thunder in the distance. Otherwise, it was very quiet. I closed and locked the doors behind me and lay down on the bed. It was comfortable, and there was time for a bit of a nap. I yawned—air travel always made me sleepy—and set the alarm on my phone for six, which would give me time to wake up and shower before going down to dinner.

I closed my eyes, thinking, *Well, that wasn't exactly a warm welcome.*

Of course, I could always catch the next flight back to Bay City.

And on that cheery note, I drifted off to sleep.

CHAPTER THREE

I sat up in a strange bed, wide awake, my heart pounding. Disoriented, I looked around in the gloom, not sure where I was or what had woken me up from my already restless sleep. I shivered. A storm was raging outside as my mind began the process of clearing out the fog. Wind was whipping around the house, rattling the windows and the French doors. The rain was coming down in a steady stream. As I sat up farther in my bed, lightning lit up the room, and I recoiled in horror. The brief flash of illumination had exposed the shadow of someone outside against the curtains over the French doors. I bit back a scream as I wondered if there was anything within reach in this strange room that I could use as a weapon. My eyes were still seeing spots as thunder shook the house, and I remembered there was a table lamp on the nightstand next to the bed. As my vision cleared, I could see that the doorknob on the French doors was turning. I reached out to the table and fumbled for the switch on the lamp. I found it and clicked it on, filling the room with bright yellow light.

I thought I heard footsteps running away along the gallery. I threw the covers aside and climbed out of the massive bed. I dashed over to the fireplace on the other side of the bed, grabbed one of the brass pokers, and carried it over to the

French doors. I flipped the lock off, turned the knob, and the wind immediately grabbed the doors out of my hands. They slammed against the walls and swung back. The wind pushed me back a few steps. Curtains moved away from the walls, and the canopy over the bed rippled as I struggled to latch the doors against the walls. Once this was accomplished, I tried to step out. Lightning flashed again as I stepped onto the wide gallery. I wrapped my arms around me and wished I'd put on at least a T-shirt. The wind was blowing the rain onto the gallery, and the heavy drops were splashing my legs as I looked through the gloom in each direction.

I didn't see anyone.

My heart still pounding, I closed and locked the doors again before heading back to the bed, still holding the poker in my hand. I put the poker into the bed next to me and slid underneath the covers. Maybe it had been a dream, maybe there really hadn't been someone out there on the gallery trying to get into my room, and it was just my imagination working overtime. *There wasn't anyone out there, you fool,* I scolded myself, *you're just a little off balance—but it's understandable. It isn't every day you meet a family you barely knew you had two months ago.* I switched the lamp off and pulled the covers back up to my chin, and lay there, staring at the canopy over my head.

But even after I turned off the light, I couldn't turn off my brain. Random thoughts just kept running through. The storm was still raging outside, the windows rattling from the wind, every so often another burst of lightning followed by bone-shaking thunder.

But why would someone be out there? Why would someone be trying to get into my room?

It didn't make any sense. Even though my aunt Olivia had been very clear she wasn't happy I'd come to Chambord, overall things hadn't been so bad with the rest of the Legendre family. *My* family. I was being ridiculous. There was no reason anyone here would want to harm me. No, it must have been my overstimulated brain playing tricks on me, I decided, putting my hands behind my head. It had been a long, very strange day, after all.

I yawned.

After Olivia had left me alone, I'd napped for a couple of hours. I was exhausted—I'd been unable to sleep much the night before. The bed was incredibly comfortable, the sheets Egyptian cotton with a high thread count, and the comforter was soft and warm. The air-conditioning was blasting, and my room was so cold I could see condensation on the windows. I'd slept deeply and woke up feeling rested and relaxed. I bounded out of bed and removed my shaving kit from one of my suitcases. The bathroom was amazing. The floor was black and white parquet, and everything was marble. I brushed my teeth and washed my face before heading back out into the bedroom. I unpacked my suitcases, organizing my clothes in a dresser and an armoire—there didn't appear to be a closet in the bedroom. I glanced at the clock and decided to take a shower to help me wake up. The last thing I wanted to do was yawn my way through dinner with a family I'd just met.

I was nervous, but excited at the same time.

The shower was great. There was an old-fashioned claw-foot marble tub that looked big enough for two people to sit in comfortably, but there was also a big shower stall in the corner. Once I stepped inside it, I was even more delighted to see showerheads on three walls. I turned them all on, basking in the hot jets of water spraying my skin. I took a much longer shower than I usually did, scrubbing my skin until all of it was reddened by the soap and hot water. Finally, I turned off the shower and opened the steamed-up door, reaching for the enormous fluffy towel I'd hung on the wall just outside the door. I was just about to start wiping myself down when I heard knocking on my bedroom door. I wrapped the towel around my waist and slid my feet into my slippers. "Coming!" I called as I walked out of the bathroom, leaving the door open behind me so some of the steam from my overlong shower could clear.

I'd just stepped into the bedroom when the door from the hall opened and a female voice called out, "Hello? Cousin Heath? Are you here?"

"Come in," I said, reaching for another towel to wipe my face dry with. "Sorry, I was in the shower."

"So you're cousin Heath." Her blue eyes, so like my own, flashed mockingly as she stepped forward, sticking out her right hand. "I'm your cousin Ginny."

"I gathered," I replied, shaking her small, fine-boned hand, noticing the perfect French manicure. Her hands were soft and dry. I smiled at her. "Nice to meet you at last."

"Yes, well." She tossed her head and smiled at me. Her long blond hair was tied back into a heavy braid that swung with every movement of her head. She wasn't wearing any makeup, and her skin was flawless. She was even more beautiful in person than she had been in the picture my grandfather had sent. Ginny Legendre Poulos could never be done justice by a two-dimensional image that couldn't capture her energy and vitality. She was vibrant, so shimmering with electricity and charisma that I couldn't take my eyes off her. She was shorter than me by several inches, and she was wearing a light white sleeveless blouse over tight-fitting jean shorts that revealed more of her shapely legs than was ladylike, but I liked her all the more for it. She was slender, with a small waist and large, firm breasts that strained at her blouse. "Sorry about not picking you up at the airport, my bad." She bounced over to the bed on the balls of her feet and hopped up on it, crossing her tanned legs. She was wearing white sneakers and white tennis socks with a small blue ball on the back of each one. "Things got a bit intense around here last night, so I needed to get away for a bit." She flashed a dazzling smile at me. "You'll know what I mean soon enough." She rolled her eyes. "Chambord and the family can be a bit much sometimes. Getting away from it all for a while keeps me out of the booby hatch."

Holding on to the towel just in case, I wandered over to the armoire. "You don't mind if I finish drying off and get dressed? I'm dripping all over the floor." I grabbed a pair of shorts, a shirt, and underwear before walking back over to the bathroom door.

"Leave the door open a bit so we can talk, get to know each other a little bit." Her voice was friendly, almost a purr. She slid across the bed until she was sitting with her back propped up against the headboard. "I really am sorry about not picking you up at the airport." Her voice got pouty.

I left the door ajar as she instructed and started toweling myself dry behind the door. "It's all right." I raised my voice so I could be sure she could hear me. "I enjoyed meeting Charlotte Draper. She seemed really nice."

Ginny snorted in a most unladylike manner. "Please. You don't have to be so nice. Charlotte's dull as dirt. I'm surprised you didn't jump out of the car on the highway. I would have."

"She's practically a member of the family, isn't she?" I pulled on a pair of black boxer briefs and started rubbing my hair with the towel. "And it was nice of her to pick me up at the last minute." *Because you couldn't be bothered.*

"She's not family," Ginny retorted. "Our grandparents took her and her brother in out of pity because there wasn't anyone else. And look how that turned out!"

I slipped a polo shirt on over my head and pulled on a pair

of shorts. I opened the bathroom door and leaned on the frame. "How did that turn out, exactly?" I folded my arms and smiled back at her.

"You don't know?" She whistled. "You'll find out soon enough, I would imagine—but you're not going to find out from me."

I rolled my eyes. "Why does everyone in this family like riddles?"

She cocked her head to one side, a smile slowing spreading across her face. "You know, I think I'm going to like you, Cousin." She arched an eyebrow. "You ready for the shit show known as a family dinner around here?"

"Shit show?" I saw down next to her on the bed and started putting on my socks. "You must like it, though—why else do you still live here?"

"Convenience." She got up and walked over to the French doors. "I help manage the restaurant with my husband, you know. It makes my life a lot easier to be able to just walk down there. And I'd rather die than live in Avignon."

Avignon was the main town in Redemption Parish, about a ten-minute drive from Chambord. "What about New Orleans?"

"I get over there every once in a while." Her eyes looked sly. "When I get bored I head into town. But I always come back here." She looked at her reflection in the big mirror over the dressing table and started playing with her braid. "Grandpa says all Legendres are drawn back to Chambord, that it's all a part of who we are and we can never escape the pull of the home place." She laughed. "Sentimental nonsense, like *Gone with the Wind*."

"I'm a Legendre, and I never felt any pull from this place." I shrugged as I tied my shoelaces. "Of course, most of my life I didn't know this place even existed."

She turned and leaned back against the dressing table. "Is that really true? You had no idea you were a Legendre until recently?"

"I was thirteen when my father told me about my mother." I was surprised to hear my voice getting thick with emotion. "Of course I did some online research, but until Jerry Channing showed up at the airport a couple of months ago, it never even entered my mind to come here."

"Not even to New Orleans?" she asked. "When you can fly for free and the French Quarter is a mecca for gay men?"

"Well, of course I've been to New Orleans plenty of times." I sat back up. "But I never had any desire to come here." It was true. I'd come to New Orleans with friends any number of times—Halloween and Southern Decadence and Mardi Gras, sometimes just for a fun day or two in the bars of the French Quarter. There had been a few times when I'd considered renting a car and heading for Chambord, paying the admission price, and being shown around the old family estate like any other tourist. But I never did. I don't know if it was fear that kept me away—fear of being recognized as a Legendre by someone, or fear of not being recognized, of not being known, of not belonging in the storied house. I never rented the car, never suggested to any friends that maybe a plantation tour might be interesting or that it would be fun to make a pilgrimage to the beautiful old house where a camp classic gay men loved had been filmed so we could stand on the upper gallery and shout, in a terrible Southern accent, *"Git off mah propuhtay!"*

And even now, sitting on the edge of my bed in an antebellum plantation house that had belonged to my family for almost two hundred years, it didn't seem real. It was like the whole thing was just a dream of some sort, a figment of an overly fertile imagination, that I would blink and it would all be gone, and I'd be back in the bedroom of my little apartment in Bay City again.

But Ginny Poulos was all too real, and her eyes looked just like mine. We looked so much alike no one could see us and not know we were related, not even as cousins but as brother and sister. She was watching me, a curious look on her face.

"You have any advice for the lamb who's about to go to the slaughter?" I asked flippantly.

She shrugged. "I imagine Charlotte did a pretty good job of filling you in on the family and what everyone is like," she mused. "There's not really a lot of us—Grandpa, Aunt Olivia, me, you. Everyone else is dead. We're the last of the Legendres. And actually, we will be the last of the Legendres, won't we?" She said the last sentence dramatically, opening her eyes wide and drawing out each syllable, like she was introducing a horror movie on some cheesy late-night show. "You're gay, and should I ever have kids, they won't be Legendres."

"That's the second time you've brought up my sexuality," I observed. "How did you know I'm gay? Do I look gay? Is it tattooed on my forehead?"

She smiled at me. "Your Facebook page isn't private or friends only," she replied. "I looked you up." She winked at me. "Sorry about your last boyfriend."

I could feel my cheeks filling with color. But before I could say anything, she walked over to the bed and held out her arm for me to take. I got up and tucked her arm inside mine, and we walked out of the bedroom. "That's going to be really painful for Grandpa, you know. Family is everything to him." She laughed delightedly. "I'm sure he's hoping you're going to marry some girl from a good family and fill the place up with little Legendres."

Which is why he spent the last nineteen years pretending I didn't exist, I thought as we walked down the staircase. She was chattering away like a happy teenager, talking about the restaurant and pointing out things about the house itself I might find interesting. Ginny also quizzed me: What did I like to eat? What was I majoring in at college? What was I interested in? What was it like living in Florida? Did I like what I'd seen of Louisiana already? Did I think I might move to Louisiana? She never gave me a chance to answer any of her questions before she asked another, her voice breathless and excited. She talked so quickly, and was throwing so much information at me, that my head was spinning by the time we reached the doors to the formal dining room. So many paintings, so many ancestors, so much history—it was impossible to keep up or to remember everything she said. I finally just listened and hoped there wouldn't be a quiz later.

Her tanned skin felt hot against mine, and I finally realized she was as nervous as I was, her pulse pounding through her skin.

"Here we are," she said finally.

The double doors to the formal dining room were closed, and she dropped my arm and reached for the doorknob. She turned back to me and smiled. "Are you ready?"

I swallowed. "Not really." I took a deep breath. My own heart was pounding so loudly I could hear it, my mouth was dry, and I could feel my palms sweating.

I'd never been so nervous before in my life.

You're being stupid, I told myself sternly. *He's your grandfather. This is your family. You belong here.*

She turned the knob and opened the door with a dramatic gesture, saying loudly as she stepped into the dining room, "And now, Genevieve's son makes his long-overdue return to Chambord!"

I could feel blood rushing to my face and she gave me a wicked, crooked grin as she stood aside so I could enter.

There was a lot to take in as I walked into the room. The walls were painted a dark emerald green, with golden fleurs-de-lis stenciled onto them at even intervals. There was a long table that ran almost the entire length of the room, with several places set at the far end. There was a white lace tablecloth draped over it, with enormous silver candelabras holding lit green tapered candles. Overhead an enormous chandelier hung from the ceiling, but it wasn't lit, the crystal teardrops glittering in the candlelight and reflecting the colors of the rainbow. Beyond the table, the curtains over the French doors to the gallery had been pulled back, revealing a stunning view of the back lawns and the vibrant colors in the expansive flower beds. An enormous fountain danced with water.

But my eyes were immediately drawn to the man seated at the end of the table, just before the doors. He had thick gray hair, falling in curls around his ears. His skin was tanned and his face was lined. He had the same vibrant blue eyes Ginny and I had apparently inherited from him, and he was watching me closely. It took me a few moments to realize he was sitting in a wheelchair. I didn't want to stare, but his gaze was so intense I found it hard to look away from him. He was handsome, and I couldn't help but think how much handsomer he must have been when he was younger. He leaned forward a bit, his eyes never wavering from my face.

I finally tore my gaze away from him when I noticed movement on the other side of the room from the corner of my eyes. My aunt Olivia was standing at a sideboard crowded with silver serving dishes with Sterno flames burning beneath to keep the food warm. She was fitting a corkscrew into the cork of a dark green wine bottle. She turned to look at me, her eyes as cold and unfriendly as they had been earlier. She turned away without saying a word.

"Forgive me for not rising," my grandfather said with a

slight, helpless shrug of his shoulders. "I have not been well. Do not worry—I have good days and bad days, and today was more bad than good." His voice was deep, but shaky with emotion. His eyes looked wet. "I didn't think I would live to see the day when—" His voice broke and he covered his eyes with his right hand.

I stood there, not certain what to do, and Ginny whispered, "Go to him."

I walked to the end of the table and awkwardly held out my hand for him to shake. "It's nice to finally meet you in person." I paused, feeling my face flushing with color. "I—I don't know what to call you," I added lamely as he took my hand and pressed his left hand down on top of mine.

"Why don't you call me Geoffrey for now?" he said, his voice thick with emotion. His grip tightened on my hand. "It is too soon for family names, names from affection... Genevieve's son. At last...my Nina so longed for this day..." His voice broke and his hands went back to his eyes.

"It was wrong of your father to take you away from your family," Olivia said from the sideboard. Her voice was cold and cutting, her face grim as she crossed to her father's side with the wine bottle in her hand. She poured wine into a glass, which he took with a shaking hand and pressed to his lips.

That's not what you said earlier, I thought. Obviously Olivia behaved differently in front of her father, but her voice and face were no more welcoming than they had been earlier.

"My father was my family," I replied evenly. "He did what he thought was right, what was best for me." No matter how much I might have agreed with her, I would never say so aloud. It was not her place to criticize my father. "He had his reasons."

Her eyes narrowed as she glared at me, murmured something I couldn't make out to Geoffrey, who waved her away impatiently and smiled at me. "Please, sit." He indicated the chair next to his, which I pulled out and sat down in. "I hope your rooms are comfortable. Are they to your liking? It might be lonely in the west wing, but I thought you might want some privacy."

"They're very nice," I replied, shaking out my linen napkin and draping it across my lap. "A bit much for me—I'm used to a more middle-class-type existence." I smiled my thanks at Olivia as she filled my wineglass, but she ignored me and moved back over to the sideboard.

Ginny laughed. "Don't let the grandeur fool you—we're not exactly rolling in dough around here. So if you're looking for a big inheritance, you're looking in the wrong place."

"Ginny!" Geoffrey snapped, his eyes flashing angrily. "You will behave yourself, do you understand me?"

Ginny's smirk didn't fade, but Olivia looked stricken. Before anyone could say anything in the awkward silence, I said, "If you're worried about *your* inheritance, you needn't be." I smiled at her. "I don't really care about the money or any of this." I gestured around the room. "I have no family left. You all are it, for better or worse. My primary interest in coming here is to learn about my mother. After I get to know all of you, then I will decide if I'll let you be part of my life." I somehow managed to keep my voice steady. "It would be nice, of course, but I've done pretty well without you all these years. I can easily go the rest of my life without being a part of this family, too."

It wasn't entirely true, of course. The first time I'd seen the Chambord website my mind had been rocked. *All these years I've worried about money, and* this *is my mother's family?* All those long hours on my feet, smiling and being polite to all those idiots at the ticket counter? Gritting my teeth and continuing to be polite while some moron is screaming at me because I can't control the weather in New England, all so I could pay for my college tuition and my books, when all this time my mother's family had this enormous estate in Louisiana? I'd been furious at them, at my father, at my stepmother—at the entire situation. But when I'd calmed down, I'd been more pragmatic about things. Maybe they would offer to help me with college. There was a lot more going on than appeared to the naked eye—I'd even gotten the impression that Jerry hadn't told me everything I needed to know about my mother, about the family, and about whatever it was that happened when I was a kid and my father grabbed me and ran to Florida to get away from them.

But as far as inheriting the house, and the businesses? No, all I wanted was help with college so maybe I would only have to work part-time.

And I wanted to learn about my mother, who she was, what she was like, why she felt so lost and without hope that she would kill herself and leave a three-year-old child behind.

I heard Jerry's voice whispering in my head: *There are a lot of unanswered questions about your mother's death. If they covered up the truth once, why wouldn't they lie about everything?*

I pushed those thoughts out of my head as the doors at the other end of the dining room opened, and three men in the black slacks and white button-down shirts of waiters came through, carrying enormous pans of food, which they placed in the heating bins. The second two immediately retreated without a word, back the way they had come, but the first one bowed his head slightly to my grandfather and said, "Simply ring the kitchen when you are ready for dessert and coffee, sir." He then followed the other two waiters out, closing the doors behind them.

The smell of the food was tantalizing.

"One of the pleasures of having a five-star restaurant on the property is we eat extremely well," my grandfather said as Olivia picked up his plate and carried it over to the sideboard. "Of course we have a cook in the house here just for us, but we thought it might be nice on your first night to give you a taste of what we serve in the restaurant." I watched as Olivia piled a heap of white rice onto the plate and then spooned a steaming hot reddish chunky stew on top of it. She added a couple of hush puppies on the side and brought the dish back to the table. As soon as she set it down, Ginny got up and served herself. I did the same, not really sure what the chunky stew was. But as I poured it over the rice I saw chunks of onion, bell pepper, celery, and shrimp in with the tomato chunks. And it smelled amazing.

"Tonight I thought it would be just family," Geoffrey said as I sat back down and spread my linen napkin over my lap. "Tomorrow the others will be joining us for lunch."

A nerve twitched in Olivia's jaw as she sat down on the other side of the table from me. "There are some," she said darkly, "who would say those you've excluded tonight are family."

"Blood family," he replied, "is different from those we've added. Isn't that right, Ginny? Ginny agrees with me, don't you?"

"Considering you exclude her husband as well?" Malice sparkled in Olivia's eyes. "Yes, Heath, did you know that my father won't consider your spouse a part of the family?"

"Since he's gay, that's probably not an issue." Ginny smiled at me as she sat down with a plate of food in front of her.

Well, that cat's out of the bag, I thought, looking across the table at Olivia. Her face was still as rigid as it had been when she sat down, and I turned from her to my grandfather. His spoon had frozen in place, halfway to his mouth. When he saw me look, he finished putting it in his mouth, chewed, and swallowed. He smiled at me. "Do you mean to imply that I'm a homophobe, Ginny? That I wouldn't love and accept my grandson for who he is?"

He said it smoothly and calmly, and his facial expression didn't change even one iota. But he had stopped moving his spoon for that instant until he saw I'd noticed. Ginny's face turned reddish purple after he spoke, and I could see she'd hoped to provoke a different response from him.

I cleared my throat. "Thank you," I said simply.

"We've been apart too long," Geoffrey said, loading his spoon up again and not looking at me, "and I am not going to allow something so minor to come between you and your family again."

I put a spoonful of the stew and rice in my mouth. It was delicious, spicy and hot and with just a bit of tomato flavor, despite its redness and the chunks of tomato I could see. The rice texture counterbalanced the chunky stew perfectly. "This is amazing," I said, breaking open one of the hush puppies and dragging it through the stew. "What is it?"

"Shrimp creole, a standard Louisiana dish," my grandfather replied proudly. "The main problem with your typical shrimp creole dish is most restaurants make it too bland, leaving out the spices and assuming the customer will add hot sauce or pepper to liven it up. But if you don't like spicy food, you shouldn't eat Louisiana cuisine! So we make everything the way it's supposed to be made—with cayenne, white and black pepper, thyme and basil and salt and bay leaves." He took a drink from his water glass. "If it doesn't make your eyes water, it isn't hot enough."

I sipped my white wine. It was a good Chardonnay, slightly sweet but not dry. "It's delicious," I replied carefully, turning my attention back to the food.

"My husband is an excellent chef," Ginny said, her voice a little subdued. Apparently the family dynamic at Chambord was no one argued with my grandfather. He clearly dominated everyone and would undoubtedly try to do the same with me, once the honeymoon getting-to-know-me period was over. I'd worry about that when the time came, but no matter how much I wanted to go to school full-time and go part-time with Transco, it wasn't worth it to have someone control my life.

But as I finished my dinner while mindless small talk swirled around me, I couldn't help but think I could get used to this kind of life.

"Olivia, call for dessert and coffee," my grandfather said, wiping his face with his napkin and then dropping it on his plate. "We're having bread pudding in whiskey sauce, one of our specialties."

"Sounds wonderful," I replied as Olivia got up and walked over to the house phone on the sideboard. She picked up the receiver and murmured into it as I refilled my wineglass.

The conversation had been general, my grandfather doing most of the talking—about the house, the restaurant, the museum, and the grounds. He offered to take me on a tour after breakfast in the morning, which apparently was served buffet style. Or as he put it, "We just come down and eat whenever we feel like it, but it's all cleared away by nine thirty, so make sure you're up and about by then, else you'll go hungry until lunch."

"Lunch is at one," Olivia murmured, sipping her wine and not meeting my eyes. "If you have any food allergies or there are things you would prefer not to eat, you can let Cook know."

"And dinner is always at seven," Geoffrey added.

After that, conversation died down and we sat in silence, eating until we'd finished and he had Olivia call for dessert. As we waited for the dessert to arrive, we made more small talk—I answered questions about my major, living in Florida, my job at the airline, and so forth. Just as another awkward silence descended on the table, the doors at the far end opened and the three waiters reappeared, clearing our plates with silent efficiency. And then a man appeared in the doorway.

My jaw might have dropped.

He was wearing a chef's white jacket and houndstooth slacks. A chef's hat crowned his head, but some curly blue-black locks had escaped. His skin was olive brown, his eyebrows thick and black, and his greenish eyes were framed by the longest, blackest lashes I'd ever seen. His shoulders were broad, his waist narrow. He wasn't smiling at the moment—he was scowling. In his strong hands he held a large silver serving dish, steam rising from it.

"How am I supposed to run a goddamned restaurant when three of my best servers are having to run up here all goddamned night when I am booked full?" he growled, slamming the serving dish down on the end of the table. He placed his fists on his hips, and I could see veins popping out in his thick, hairy forearms. He paused briefly when his green eyes met mine. A vein in his jaw throbbed for a moment, and then he spun lightly on his feet and disappeared back out the doors, slamming them behind him—but not before I got a glimpse of small, perfectly round, tight backside.

"And that," Ginny said with a brittle smile, "is my husband, Costa."

"And that was him being remarkably well-behaved," Geoffrey added grimly as one of the waiters circulated the table, filling coffee cups. He waved off the waiters. "You heard the chef, back to the restaurant with you. We can serve ourselves."

The bread pudding was delicious, as was the coffee, but I found myself yawning before I finished my serving. "I'm so sorry," I said, covering another yawn with my hand. "It's been a long day for me." *And an emotionally exhausting one at that.*

I'd left them in the dining room, going back up the stairs and getting back to my bedroom. I sent my mother a text, letting her know I was okay, before washing my face and getting ready for bed. Despite my exhaustion, I didn't fall into a deep sleep—the combination of excitement, late-evening coffee, and the nap earlier in the day kept me in a horrible half sleep, tossing and turning in the comfortable bed until whatever it was I'd heard out on the gallery had woken me up.

It was your imagination, I reassured myself, as I felt drowsiness finally stilling my thoughts. I glanced over at the bedside clock. I was having breakfast with my grandfather in about six hours, and I needed to be awake and alert. The adrenaline from the weirdness with the door was wearing off, and the storm continued to rage around the house outside. Just to be certain, I got out of the bed one last time to make sure the French doors were locked and bolted.

As I drew nearer, I could see there was someone out there.

It wasn't my imagination.

My heart leaped into my throat as I reached for the door handle. I slipped the bolt off and pulled the door open just as lightning flared again, lighting up the gallery and the man standing there in a wet tank top that clung to his body.

"What the hell are you doing here?" Costa said, pushing his way past me into my room.

Chapter Four

The alarm on my phone went off with the foghorn sound I'd downloaded because I knew it would never fail to wake me up no matter how deeply and soundly I was sleeping.

And I'd been right. It worked every time.

I opened my eyes and reached my left hand out to the bedside table, grabbing my phone and punching in the password so the foghorn sound would stop. It always made me think of an episode of *Scooby-Doo, Where Are You!* I stretched with my phone still in my hand and groaned in pleasure as my back cracked. The storm had apparently passed in the night. This morning was all sunlight and birds singing in the live oaks outside the main house and the sound of a power mower somewhere off in the distance.

I sat up in the way-too-comfortable-for-my-own-good bed and stretched again, arching my lower back and yawning. I'd really gone into a deep sleep after whatever it was that had woken me up during the storm, and in the bright yellow daylight the very idea that someone had tried to get into my room from the gallery seemed even more preposterous than it had in the middle of the night during a thunderstorm. The time on my phone changed from 6:59 to 7:00. I had an hour to wake up and get showered and presentable before meeting Geoffrey downstairs for breakfast.

Geoffrey. It seemed odd to call my grandfather by his first name, but *grandfather* didn't roll easily off my tongue, either. My paternal grandparents had died when I was young, so the only grandparents I'd known were my stepmother's parents. They'd been great, spoiling me mercilessly when I was a kid. I was a teenager when that grandmother died of cancer, and that grandfather now lived in an assisted-living facility, since Alzheimer's stole his memories from him. I sent my stepmother another text message before getting out of the bed. I pushed the covers off and shivered—*Seriously, the temperature inside Chambord could keep meat fresh,* I thought as I grabbed a pair of workout shorts from an inside drawer of the big antique armoire and slid them on over my boxer briefs. I rubbed my arms as I walked over to the French doors, trying to get the goose pimples to go down. The doors were still locked and bolted, and I shook my head yet again at the foolishness from the middle of the night.

With a smile I unlocked the doors and pulled them open. It was like being slapped in the face with a heavy, still-wet wool blanket right out of the dryer. Sweat broke out under my arms and on my forehead as the moist, hot outside air of a Louisiana July fought for dominance with the cold inside air from the room behind me. I stepped out onto the gallery and breathed in deeply. I could feel my sinuses reacting to the pressure from the heavy air—I was going to have to take some medication or I'd be completely miserable very soon. But I felt almost drunk from the heavily scented air, redolent with the mixed smells of freshly cut grass, roses, sweet olive, magnolia, jasmine, and honeysuckle. I breathed in the heavy air deeply, stepping out onto the gallery, which was still wet from the storm. If not for the damp wood and places where water had puddled in depressions in the old gallery, there was no sign of the powerful thunderstorm of the previous night.

The sky overhead was azure, without even the merest wisp of a cloud drifting across the brilliant blue. The sun itself was bright and blazing hot—later it was going to be unbearable outside. I walked over to the railing and looked around the grounds. My room was in the west wing of the big house, which faced the enormous stone fence, the river road, and the enormous earthen levee protecting the estate from the flooding of the river. The west wing's gallery looked out over a vast expanse of lawn dotted with enormous live oaks dripping Spanish moss and the occasional fountain. The driveway was just below, opposite flower beds with roses and other flowers perfectly spaced for maximum effect and symmetry. There was also a gazebo in the shade of one of the live oaks with the brick fence just beyond it. I was high enough that I could see over the levee to the trees lining the riverbank on the other side, and a patch of brown water moving rapidly in the direction of New Orleans. I sighed and leaned on the black cast-iron railing.

It was incredibly peaceful out there. If it wasn't too hot, I could spend a lot of time out here reading. I sat in one of the wicker chairs and closed my eyes.

Seeing Costa walk into the dining room last night, and realizing he was married to my cousin Ginny, was only slightly more of a shock than having him show up outside my door last night. I winced at the memory of that scene.

"What do you think you're doing here?" he'd said, brushing past me into my room. He was wet from the rain, and dripping on my floor.

I flipped the light switch on the wall next to the French doors and closed them against the rain and wind. Costa folded his arms, the muscles in his upper torso flexing. "I was invited by my grandfather," I replied evenly. "And if you think I'm stalking you, you're even more full of yourself than I thought."

Whatever I'd been expecting to find at Chambord, the man I'd spent a glorious weekend with the previous fall wasn't it.

Spending Halloween weekend in New Orleans had originally been planned as a couples trip with a guy I'd been seeing. We were going with friends—we'd rented a two-bedroom condo on Governor Nicholls Street, just blocks away from the gay bars, and we were doing a group costume. I should have known better. Taylor and I had been on-again, off-again since we'd met, but I kept hanging in there, hoping he'd finally see the light and realize I was the right guy for him. Sure enough, about a week before the Halloween trip Taylor decided to turn the dial to off. I should have canceled out of the trip, but as always, I hoped it wouldn't turn into one of *those* trips, the way so many before had.

It did.

By the time we decided to leave the costume ball on Saturday night and head back to the gay bars in the Quarter, I was already over Taylor. We'd arrived on Thursday, and he'd been hooking up with guys left and right. Sometimes he brought them back to the condo and used the bed we were supposed to share, other times he'd vanish with a guy for hours. From the moment we arrived at the ball, he was antsy to return to the bars—probably, I assumed, to meet up with one of his previous tricks from the last three days. I managed to wrest the key to the condo from him, and with it tucked into my sock, I wasn't quite as worried about being ditched as I had been. The other couple with us were his friends, not mine, and so I didn't even have the solace of complaining to them about his behavior, and being left alone with them was a little awkward.

Once we got inside Oz, I decided I was going to have a good time and I didn't care if I saw any of the three of them the rest of the night.

I met the man I now knew was Costa Poulos on the dance floor at Oz around four in the morning. I was still high and having the most fun I'd had all weekend. I hadn't seen Taylor or his friends in a long time, and what was more, I didn't care. Guys were flirting with me, dancing with me, and I thought, *I should have done this on Thursday, fuck them, make my own fun.*

That was when I noticed the handsome guy with the amazing body dancing next to me, and smiling at me. Sweat glistened on his muscles, which were dusted with dark black hair. He was so handsome…I smiled back at him, and I wound up going back to his hotel room with him. I stayed with him until the next afternoon, cuddling and talking and, yes, having mind-blowing sex. Finally, he sadly bid me farewell, around three in the afternoon.

"Please call me," he said, writing his name and number down on a scrap of paper, "if you're ever coming to Dallas." He kissed me one more time with those thick, full lips, and I wanted to melt back into his arms again. "This has been wonderful, Heath."

I didn't know until later, of course, that the number was phony.

And I didn't know until he'd walked into the dining room last night that his name wasn't Alex Cordero, either.

"It's cute that you think I came here to find you," I said, walking past him into the bathroom and getting a glass of water. I leaned against the door frame, very aware I was just in my underwear but not really caring one way or the other. "That's just an unfortunate coincidence. But I have to ask—does my family know you're on the down-low?"

He had the decency to flush. "Ginny knows, and that's all that matters. It's no one else's business what Ginny and I—what our arrangement is."

"She doesn't care that you sleep with men?"

"No, she doesn't." He smirked at me. "Look, I'm sorry I gave you a fake name"—*and a fake phone number*—"but obviously, I can't get involved with anyone."

"So, you pick up men and have sex with them and lie to them?" I exhaled. "You know something? I thought you were a nice guy. I'm sorry I believed you." I shook my head. "I won't say anything." *Even though I want to, but the last thing I need right now is to shake everything up by telling everyone in my family I slept with my cousin's husband. That wouldn't be a smart move on my part.* "That's between you and Ginny. Now get out of my room. I need to get some sleep."

He hesitated at the French doors. "I really am sorry, Heath. I didn't mean to hurt you." He turned to go back out onto the gallery.

"Did you—did you come by earlier?" I stopped him. "Did you try to get in here?"

He looked at me like I was crazy. "I wouldn't try to get in," he said sourly. "I was getting ready to knock when you opened the doors."

"This late?"

"This late." He turned and walked away down the gallery.

I stood in the door frame, shivering in the wind as the rain started coming down harder again.

Maybe I'd just imagined the first person, or had been dreaming.

But I made sure the doors were locked before I got back into bed, and surprisingly enough, fell asleep.

A knock on the bedroom door inside brought me back to the present, so I went back in, shivering in the air-conditioning. There was about a thirty-degree difference between the inside and the outside—which wasn't usually the case in Florida, but we had the winds from Gulf blowing through. I crossed the room to the door and opened it. A young woman was standing there in a traditional maid's uniform: a black dress with a white apron tied over the front of it, dark hose, and black flat shoes. A white cap perched on top of her head. She was holding a very heavy-looking silver tray with a coffee service on it. The service looked old and incredibly expensive. She couldn't have been much older than her early twenties—a few pimples speckled her light brown cheeks. She was very slender. Her waist looked small enough for me to enclose it with my hands. She wasn't looking at me and wouldn't meet my eyes, keeping her head tilted slightly down in front of her.

Apparently, I wasn't supposed to open the door without being fully dressed—although she should consider herself lucky I'd put the shorts on. I stood there, not knowing what to say or if I was supposed to take the tray from her.

"Miss Olivia thought you might like some coffee, Mr. Heath, if you'll excuse me?" she finally said, still averting her eyes and not looking at me. I stepped aside so she could enter, holding the door for her. She placed the service down on one of the side tables near the armoire and walked quickly back to the door. She turned in the door frame and, this time, very pointedly looked me in the eyes. "She said to remind you that there's no rush, but the breakfast buffet is cleared at nine thirty." Her voice was soft, slightly accented. She looked back down again, reached for the door handle, and closed the door quickly. I stood there, listening to her footsteps receding down the hallway in the direction of the staircase.

The coffee smelled incredible, so I wasted no time pouring myself a cup while looking through what else was on the tray. There was a small silver pitcher with cream, and another one with steaming hot milk. There was a small plate with muffins and toast, and a small ceramic bowl with whipped butter. I added the hot milk to the coffee and carried it into the bathroom. I brushed my teeth and washed my face before tasting the coffee. It was delicious, hot and strong with just a hint of chicory. I turned on the shower, and while the water started getting hot, I went back into the bedroom and grabbed a blueberry muffin, then spread butter on it. It, too, was fresh and delicious.

I could get used to this life quite easily, I thought as I ate a second muffin while picking out clothes to wear when I got out of the shower. I decided on a bright yellow polo shirt and khaki shorts. I grabbed some underwear and a pair of socks and headed back into the bathroom. The old mirror was now covered with fog. I grabbed an enormous bath towel. Ten minutes later, with my skin rubbed red and my hair wet, I wrapped the towel around my waist and headed back into the bedroom. I finished drying off, got dressed, and picked up the tray. I carried it down with me to the dining room, where I set it on the end of the table nearest the door.

The only person in the room was my aunt Olivia. Her hair was pulled back and knotted into a bun at the base of her neck, and she was wearing a blue denim button-down blouse. The remnants of her breakfast were on the plate before her. She was drinking from her coffee cup. She put it down and the corners of her mouth twitched into what might supposed to have been a smile but failed miserably. "Cindy would have cleared the tray," she said.

"Sorry—I'm not used to servants," I replied, heading over to the sideboard. I got another cup of café au lait, a croissant with butter, and a plateful of fruit. I walked around the table and sat down across from her. "But it was very thoughtful of you to send the coffee up. Thank you."

"Did you sleep well?" she asked, refilling her coffee from a carafe on the table. She didn't add anything to it. "I hope the storm didn't wake you."

"I slept very well, actually, the room is amazing, thank you." I popped a red grape into my mouth. "I did wake up in the middle of the night, though I'm not entirely sure it was the storm. I could have sworn someone was trying to open the French doors from the gallery." I shrugged.

Her face drained of color, and she quickly pushed her chair back and got up. "I'm sure you were dreaming," she said, turning her back to me. "If you'll excuse me, I have things to do." She hurried out of the room.

Well, that sure spooked her, I thought as I went back to eating. I wondered for a moment if maybe I *had* been right in the first place—why else would Olivia have reacted like that? But as I sipped my coffee, reality took over from my imagination again.

It was absurd to think someone had tried to get into my room. For one thing, why would anyone want to? It wasn't like there was anything valuable in there—whereas there was plenty to steal in other places in the house. It was odd, too, that of all the rooms in the west wing, a burglar just happened to choose the only room with someone in it. Unless, of course, it wasn't a burglar but someone who wanted to harm me, which was so laughable I couldn't take it seriously. Ginny's weird comment about me being after the estate aside, I wasn't a threat to anyone at Chambord. I wasn't interested in the estate, I didn't care about any of the money, although I certainly wouldn't turn down any assistance Geoffrey might want to offer me for college.

But just because I didn't have any designs on the Legendre estate didn't mean that someone didn't believe that I did...

I shook my head. No, I was being ridiculous, of course. I've always had a bit of an overactive imagination, and here I was, letting it run away with itself again.

I was sorry she'd gone before I had a chance to ask her

about my mother. They were sisters, after all, and not many people were left at Chambord who'd actually known her.

I'd finished my meal and was getting more coffee when my grandfather walked into the room. He was moving pretty well, despite leaning heavily on a thick wooden cane with a silver tip on the bottom and a wolf's head on the handle. He smiled broadly as he saw me. "I see you're up. Are you ready to go for a tour of the grounds?" He waved his free hand. "I've already had my coffee, and I don't eat breakfast."

I sipped my coffee and put the cup down. "Yes." I stood and followed him to the gallery doors at the other end of the dining room.

"What do you think so far?" Geoffrey asked as the tip of his cane clicked on the hardwood floor. "I won't deny that I am hoping you'll consider coming to live here, with us, so you can get to know us better. I know you have a job, and school, back in Florida, but surely the airline could let you transfer to New Orleans? And there are many wonderful universities here—LSU up in Baton Rouge, Tulane in New Orleans…" He let his voice trail off.

"I appreciate that you want me here, Geoffrey, but that would be a pretty significant change," I said, opening the door to the gallery for him. At the foot of the steps sat a golf cart. "But I don't know how I feel about moving so far away from my mother—"

"Your stepmother," Geoffrey snapped. "She isn't blood."

"Maybe, but she raised me. She's the only mother I've known," I replied, going down the steps and waiting for him at the foot. "I don't remember my real mother at all. And I have friends and a life in Florida. This is all pretty amazing, Geoffrey"—I gestured with my arms at everything around me—"and it is nice to know I have family, but I'm not going to throw my entire life away when I barely know any of you. And it's not like Olivia is overly friendly to me, you know."

He laughed. "No, Olivia wouldn't be." He peered at me as I helped him into the driver's seat of the golf cart. "There's history there, you know. Your mother stole the love of her life."

I stared at him, perplexed. "Olivia was in love with my father?"

He blinked at me a few times, then threw his head back and roared with laughter. He waved me into the passenger seat, unable to talk because he was laughing so hard. When he finally got control of himself, he said, "I'm sorry." He wiped at his eyes. "Just the very idea of Olivia and David—no, it's too much. No, Olivia wasn't in love with David, Heath. She was in love with Charlotte's brother Dylan." A look of pain crossed his face. "But Dylan only loved Genevieve." He reached down and turned the key to start the cart's engine, then shifted it into gear. It jolted forward but smoothed out as he started driving down the path toward some of the outbuildings. "Olivia never forgave your mother, you know, even after your parents were married and moved to the house in New Orleans." He glanced over at me. "You don't know about the house you own in New Orleans, do you?"

"What?" I couldn't have heard that right. "Did you just say I own a house in New Orleans?"

"I should have known that David wouldn't tell you about the house," he said smugly. "The Legendres always used to keep a residence in New Orleans, in the Garden District. Alas, my father had to let that house go, but for a wedding present, your grandmother and I gifted your parents with a house in the city. Not in the Garden District proper, of course—but close enough nearby. On Coliseum Street at the corner with Felicity. The only stipulation was that it belonged solely to

Genevieve, and if anything happened to her, it would pass to her children." He pointed a finger at me as we sped past the well-kept manicured lawns of the estate. "When Genevieve died, the house became your property. I've been paying the taxes and the upkeep ever since—your father would have let the state take it back for the taxes. He hated us all so very, very much when your mother died. He blamed us for her death, of course." He shook his head as he guided the cart up to a long two-story building. He parked in front, turning off the engine. "As if what happened was our fault."

"What exactly did happen to my mother?" I asked, climbing down and walking around to help him out of the cart.

"Didn't Jerry Channing tell you?" He snorted. "I can't believe such a gossipmonger would draw the line at spilling such a juicy story to you."

"All he said was he was writing a book about what happened." I shrugged as I followed him up the steps to the front door of the building. "He was surprised I didn't know."

"And what do you know?" he asked.

"She committed suicide." I took a deep breath.

He laughed sadly. "Ah, if only that was all there was to it." He exhaled, taking a key ring from the pocket of his pants, and fitted one of them into the lock. He stepped inside and gestured for me to follow him into the dark interior. The shutters were closed on all the windows. I could make out the shape of cases, and in the light coming through the doorway I could see that they contained glasses.

Once I was inside, he flipped on a light switch and shut the door.

I gasped. Everywhere I looked, glass sparkled and reflected the light. On the walls, masks of all shapes and sizes and colors were mounted. I'd seen masks in the tourist shops in the French Quarter before, porcelain masks with white faces adorned with sequins and feathers. But they were nothing like these. These masks were works of art, made of beautiful glass in every shade imaginable, from blue to purple to reds and greens and gold. The long display cases in the center displayed remarkably delicate-looking glass goblets and champagne flutes and brandy snifters, again, either clear or in magnificent rich colors.

"This is the glass museum?" I asked, walking over to one of the display cases and looking down at champagne flutes standing proudly on top of black velvet. They were free of dust and shone in the overhead light. They looked so delicate that touching them would make them shatter.

"Chambord plantation once produced the finest quality glass in North America and did so for many generations," he said proudly. "One of your ancestors was trained on the island of Murano near Venice in glassmaking, and when he came to America, he brought the secret technique of the Venetians with him. I've spent the better part of the last thirty years tracking down and collecting the glass produced here, to create this museum and preserve the legacy of Chambord glass. This is part of your heritage, you know." He hesitated for a moment. "Are you an artist? Did the genes pass down to you from your mother?"

"I've always drawn, but I've never been trained or anything. It's just something I enjoy doing, it helps me relax," I said. It was true, although drawing had never been the passion for me that writing was. But somehow I didn't want him to know that about me, wanted to hold some information back from him. This was all lovely, and everything so far had been great—but I didn't completely trust him yet. I walked along the case, wishing I could reach inside and pick up one of the beautiful red wineglasses resting on black velvet. The cut glass sparkled like diamonds in the light. "But my father never wanted me to pursue it, said it was too difficult to make a living as an artist. I've always had some natural ability. It's a family thing?" I already knew my mother had been a painter, but I was curious to hear what he had to say about her.

"Your mother was a painter, and a very good one. She had greatness within her, you know." He leaned on his cane. "She had several shows in New Orleans, and galleries in the larger cities were interested in her work. She had just signed with a New York gallery when...when she died. So much lost potential, and such a loss to the world of art as well as a great loss for the family, of course." Again, a pained look crossed his face. "Sadly, the value of her work has gone up exponentially, of course, since she died. Have you ever seen any of her work?"

"No."

"There's some of it in the New Orleans house—in your New Orleans house," he said, closing his eyes. "After she died, it was too painful for your grandmother and me to have her work in Chambord, but we didn't want to get rid of it. It's hung in your house in New Orleans." He cracked a smile. "Since we no longer have the old house in the Garden District—well, I hope you don't mind, but whenever someone needs to stay in the city we use your house."

"What happened to her?" I stood up and faced him, crossing my arms. "All anyone will tell me about her death is that she committed suicide. Why would she do that? It doesn't make any sense to me, especially if she had just gotten an offer from a gallery in New York. She had a small child, and if her painting career was taking off... Did she suffer from depression? Was there something else going on with her? Is it something I may have inherited from her?"

"No, she wasn't depressed. She was a very happy woman. She was incredibly vibrant, full of life. She grabbed onto life with both hands. She loved to laugh more than anything, and she adored you. The sun rose and set on you. She hated being parted from you for even a moment." He sat down hard on a chair beneath a row of white-faced masks. "They always said that I spoiled her, that I didn't discipline her enough, or wasn't strict enough with her, but I didn't want to break her spirit. She had so much spirit, so much life in her...the talk was especially harsh after she died." He took a deep breath. "She was my favorite child, you know? From the moment I saw her, after she was born, she was everything to me." He rubbed his eyes. "This isn't easy for me to talk about. After all these years, you'd think it would get easier. But it never does."

"I can't imagine how hard it must be to lose a child," I replied, trying to be sympathetic.

He gave me a sad look. "I've lost two of mine. Only Olivia is left to me."

"She must be a comfort," I said, not bothering to keep the sarcasm out of my voice. "But if Genevieve"—I couldn't call her *mother,* or even refer to her that way, at least not yet—"was so full of life, why would she have committed suicide? That doesn't make sense." Maybe Jerry really was on to something.

"There is so much more to the story than you know, and you shouldn't be cruel about your aunt Olivia. She hasn't had it easy—life has not been kind to her." He exhaled. "I told you Olivia was in love with Dylan Haynes." He closed his eyes. "If only your grandmother hadn't such a big heart and insisted on taking the Haynes orphans in!"

But you and their father were friends, I thought, but didn't interrupt.

"We would have all been spared so much grief and heartache. Your aunt was older, of course. Charlotte and your mother were of an age, and Dylan was older—your uncle's age. Olivia was the oldest and always seemed to be the leader of the children. I don't know when she fell in love with Dylan, but she did. She always favored him over the others, even if he was a few years younger than she was. He was quite a beautiful child, with dark black hair and green eyes, and charm! He had charm to spare. But Dylan always only had eyes for Genevieve. Nina and I were so blind to everything, of course… We always thought of them as children, of course we did, and somehow didn't see what was going on around here until it was too late."

He grimaced. "It was Olivia who found them together, of course…Dylan and your mother. It was such a betrayal, and I, I didn't react in the best way. I sent him away." He rubbed his eyes and looked very old. "I forced him to join the military, and forbade him to contact either of my daughters ever again. So he went away. He'd always been a little wild, his grades weren't good enough for college—I thought military discipline was what he needed. And he thrived, of course. He did well, excelled, got promotions, served his country with distinction. Olivia never got over him, of course…but your mother did. She met your father, fell in love with him, married him, had you. She had everything to live for…and then Dylan returned without warning. Charlotte, of course, Charlotte had been writing to him, letting him know what was going on around here. He wanted your mother still, wanted to marry her. He believed if he came back, she would leave your father and run away with him again. Your mother—your mother didn't want that. She wanted to stay married to your father. But Dylan told him lies. He hoped if he lied to your father he would leave your mother. Your mother came here to confront him, to tell him to leave Louisiana and never come back, she would never leave your father. They struggled over a gun. It went off, and Dylan was killed. The best scenario, we figured, was your mother, horrified by what she had done, turned the gun on herself. They were both dead by the time we reached them." His eyes glistened with tears. "Your father, of course, still believed the lies Dylan had told him, so he took you and left, refused to let us have anything to do with you or with him ever again. It broke Nina's heart. She was never the same again after that. I've always believed her broken heart helped her to an early grave."

I didn't know what to say to that, so I walked away from him, over to a wall where masks were mounted inside a glass case. I knew without having to be told they were Mardi Gras masks, for the Carnival krewes, multicolored and sparkling and magnificent and inset with what appeared to be real gemstones in the overhead light. One was green, one was purple, one was gold, and one red. Underneath each mask was a little plaque with engraved letters: *Rex, Comus, Momus, Proteus, Orion...*

I froze, unable to move as I stared at the red mask labeled *Orion.*

My mind went away, there was a roaring in my ears, and all I could hear were angry voices, and people shouting, shouting loudly but I couldn't make out the words. I was terrified, scared, things weren't supposed to be like this, and I shivered as everything faded away, and then I heard a loud bang, and I saw the mask falling, like it was in slow motion, and then it landed in some dirty-looking water with a splash, resting on the surface for just a moment, rings spreading out in ever-widening circles as the red glass mask began to slowly sink beneath the surface of the water, and I couldn't take my eyes away from it, and my heart was pounding and I couldn't breathe, my breath just wouldn't come...

"Are you all right?" a deep voice asked, a strong sweaty hand grasping my forearm, and I snapped out of whatever it was I was experiencing to the present.

"Fine," I said, shaking my head and smiling weakly at the man standing next to me.

"Has that ever happened to you before?" There was concern, and kindness, in his voice, and I looked at him.

It was Costa, and even with his face twisted and black with anger he was still a handsome man. His eyes were the green of the Gulf of Mexico where it was shallow, his skin olive. There was a bluish-black shadow to his lower face, like he hadn't shaved. His lips were thick and full, and there were dimples in his cheeks. He was taller than I was, maybe almost six feet tall, and he was wearing a pair of tight white jeans and a black and gold Saints tank top. His arms and chest were thick and muscular, curly black hairs sticking out of the neckline of his tank top. I could smell his own musk beneath his cologne.

I shook my head. *Stop it—he's lied to you and he's married to your cousin.*

"No," I shook my head. "It was so weird, I don't know…I don't know what happened. That mask"—I gestured with my head, unwilling to look back at it again—"I'd swear I've seen it before."

"That collection of masks is quite famous," my grandfather replied. "The king masks, the only ones of their kind. In 1910, Chambord made the masks for the kings of the most important Carnival krewes. It was the only time in history that the masks were made from glass, and it took me a long time—and a lot of money—to bring them all back home to Chambord." He shook his head. "I've never been able to locate the masks of the queens. I suspect they are stored in tissue paper in the attics of some of the finer old homes of New Orleans." He chuckled. "They're collectibles, of course, but there really isn't much of a market for Mardi Gras collectibles outside of New Orleans."

Costa's hand still gripped my forearm, and it felt like

electricity was coursing through my body from it. I smiled at him and gently extricated my arm from his grip. He blushed and apologized, turning back to my grandfather. His face changed. "I will order the tomatoes, as you have said," he said, scowling. "But I am telling you the quality of the produce from the Thibodeaux farms is not worthy of my kitchen." He walked away purposefully, and I couldn't help but watch the curve of his tight, firm buttocks beneath the white jeans until he slammed the door behind him.

"You're certain you're okay?" Geoffrey asked, looking suddenly tired. "I think...I'm tired." He gave me a wan look. "I don't sleep as well as I should, and I don't ever want to take something to help me sleep. What if I need to get up in the middle of the night and can't wake?" He laughed. "Ah, but you're young yet. Let's go back up to the house, and I'll rest. Perhaps we can finish our tour after lunch."

"Actually," I replied, trying very hard not to look back at the case holding the masks, "I'd like to go into New Orleans and see...my house." Just saying it sounded weird to me. *My house in New Orleans.*

I glanced back over at the red mask. It was just glass, blown and shaped beautifully by a master glassmaker. The lips were slightly pursed, and several long red feathers were attached to the right side. It was outlined with sparkling red stones that looked like rubies, but might have just been cut glass. The eye slits stared emptily back at me.

He nodded. "Of course. Olivia will get you the keys and loan you one of the cars." He patted my arm. "We use it sometimes, so it's always kept up. A service comes in to keep it clean." He glanced back over at the masks, and back at me again. "You're certain you're all right?"

I nodded. "It's all been a bit much," I replied, heading for the door. "I think it would be good for me to get away from Chambord, maybe even spend the night in the city. If you don't mind?"

He nodded. "Of course not, you should see your inheritance, of course," he said as he headed for the front door. He was moving much more slowly than he had been, and I wondered if I should help him. Then again, he seemed like a very proud man.

He climbed into the golf cart and gestured at me to join him. "Come along now." He smiled as he patted the seat next to him. "You used to love to ride in the carts when you were a little boy." As I sat down beside him, he sighed. "So many lost years to make up for..."

He turned the key and the cart jumped forward.

CHAPTER FIVE

The house where my parents had lived during their brief marriage was on Coliseum Street, standing at the corner where Coliseum intersected with Felicity Street.

You have arrived, the disembodied voice on my phone's map said as I pulled the car over in front of the corner lot. I sat there, the engine running, for a moment as I looked out the passenger-side window at what was actually my property. There was an enormous stone fence, painted a pale avocado green, surrounding the lot. In some places the concrete had cracked and fallen away, revealing old red bricks underneath. It was tilted toward the sidewalk at seemed to be an alarming angle, and at various spots enormous gnarled roots from the towering live oaks on the other side of the fence had broken through, cracking the sidewalk and breaking concrete. From the car, the house appeared to be about three or four stories high, with gables breaking the slant of the roof. There was a gallery only around what appeared to be the first floor, but there were balconies on the floor just below the roof. It looked enormous—obviously much smaller than Chambord, but palatial compared to the suburban-style ranch house where I'd grown up in Bay City.

I turned off the engine of the battered Honda Accord and slipped the keys into my shorts pocket. The car was old and looked ready for the junkyard, but the engine was powerful, the air-conditioning worked, and it ran like a dream. When I'd first seen it, I thought my aunt Olivia was being a bit of a bitch, but it had started right up and handled better than my car back home.

And I felt more comfortable driving this than I would have any of the cars in the parking lot behind Chambord—Porsches, BMWs, and Mercedes.

I got the impression it was a spare vehicle used for errands that might mess up one of the nicer cars, and the slight wet-dog smell of the interior kind of confirmed that once I got behind the wheel and shut the door. It certainly stood out like a sore thumb beside the sleeker, more expensive cars around it.

Coming to New Orleans to see the house—well, if I was going to be honest—was just an excuse to get way from Chambord and try to process everything from the last twenty-four hours. My mind and emotions were already on overload. My nerves were fraying around the edges and I needed to get away from the place. I hadn't known what to expect, of course, or how I would react, but this raw feeling was something new, and I didn't much care for it.

All the way into New Orleans I'd thought about my reaction to the Orion mask.

It was spooky. I knew, somehow, that I'd seen it before; what happened when I saw it had to have been memories resurfacing from my childhood. It had upset me, more than anything else since I'd arrived in Louisiana. The angry voices, the loud noises, the mask itself falling into water—it had been so real, it could have been happening right then and there. Just thinking about it again made me shiver.

And then there was my reaction to the physical contact with Costa, my cousin's husband, a straight man.

That was almost as disturbing to me as the vision or

whatever it was of the mask I'd had just before. I hadn't been physically attracted to someone I knew was straight since I'd been in high school, fantasizing about some of the sexy jocks at Bay City High School. I'd realized even before puberty started in the seventh grade that I wasn't *normal,* that I wasn't like other boys. I wasn't into playing or watching sports the way the others were and much preferred reading by myself. I did, of course, eventually make friends with some kids who were more into reading and studying than playing sports or being popular. I was never bullied—I was lucky that way— but I knew what the other kids would do if they knew who I really was. I could hear it, every day, in the hallways and the classrooms and the gym—*gay* and *faggot* were the worst insults, what you said when you really wanted to put someone down. So I kept it all a secret, terrified someone would notice me looking at them in the locker room, changing before or after gym class, taking mental pictures I could remember later when I was alone in my bedroom.

I'd always been able to turn off my attractions for men who were unattainable.

But Costa—Costa, I couldn't stop thinking about him. I couldn't stop thinking about the bluish veins bulging in his forearms, the bluish shadow on his face from the stubble, the white teeth, the flashing green eyes, the broad shoulders, and the narrow waist.

He's married to your cousin. Forget about it.

Even now, I could feel myself getting excited just thinking about the touch of his fingers brushing against my skin, the faint smell of his masculine musk beneath the soap and deodorant, the curly black hairs poking out of the neck of his T-shirt.

So, yeah, the best thing for me to do was get away from Chambord, digest what I'd already learned, and steel myself for what was to come.

I got out of the car and walked around it to the sidewalk, leaning against the passenger side. There was a big privacy gate of cast iron, with a buzzer mounted on the fence beside it. I could see ferns and greenery through some of the spaces around the gate, but still I stood there. It was weird—maybe coming to see the house wasn't such a good idea. My stomach was churning. The house didn't look in the least bit familiar to me, nothing about it. I stood there, turning my head, looking at it from different angles, but there was nothing awakening in the deeper recesses of my mind. As far as my memory was concerned, this was my first time seeing the house.

Olivia had given me two keys—the gold one was for the gate, the silver one for the front door—and had written the alarm code down for me on a piece of paper I'd folded into my wallet. "I never go there," she'd said to me tonelessly as she handed the keys and the code to me. "It reminds me of your mother."

This is your first home, I said to myself as I dug the key ring out of my shorts pocket, *and it could be your future home. I wonder how much the house is worth?*

I shook my head. I couldn't sell the house—it wouldn't be right.

Maybe I could transfer to the New Orleans airport...

"So, there you are. I thought you were going to text me when you arrived," a voice said from behind me, making me jump.

I spun around as Jerry crossed the street, a big smile on his face, the dimples pronounced in his deeply tanned cheeks. He was holding a clear plastic cup filled with iced coffee cut with milk. He was again wearing a tight ribbed black tank top, which appeared to maybe be a size too small—his chest and shoulders seemed to be bursting out of it, and his nipples were visible. His white khaki shorts hung loosely off his hips, and the tank top stopped right at his underwear—black Calvin Kleins with a metallic-looking waistband. A black baseball cap with a gold fleur-de-lis on the front covered his bald head. Every muscle fiber in his shoulders and thick arms was visible beneath the tanned skin, and his forearms were crisscrossed with bulging veins. Each shoulder cap had a curly looking blue vein visible snaking down to the biceps.

I caught my breath. He was so attractive it almost took my breath away. *He must live in the gym,* I thought as he leaned back against the car next to me and drank from his straw. He crossed his right leg over the left at the ankle, the calf muscle flexing. I tried to keep my eyes on his face.

"I must say it was a pleasant surprise to hear from you," he said, finishing the iced coffee and folding his arms over the huge chest.

I kept my eyes on his enormous brown eyes. I'd impulsively called him from the car after leaving Chambord, hoping that seeing him would help get my inappropriate feelings for Costa out of my head. I licked my lower lip and allowed my glance to linger on the curve of his pectoral muscles.

It was working.

"Thanks for giving me a chance to explore the house and look around." He turned his head and peered at the green house. "Are you sure you don't mind me poking around in there?"

I shrugged, unable to stop watching a bead of sweat making its way down his torso from his left underarm. "Geoffrey probably wouldn't like it, but it's my house." I swallowed. "And it's—well, I just don't think I should go in by myself the first time, you know? Does that make sense? I don't know how…how I'm going to react." *And I didn't want to do it with any of the family around, either.*

He reached out and touched my right arm with his left

hand. It took all of my self-control not to shiver or melt into a puddle. He stroked my arm, his fingertips barely grazing the skin. "This must be so hard for you," he said, his voice soft and barely more than a whisper. He shook his head. "I can't imagine how you must feel, what you're going through." He made a face. "I haven't spoken to my family in years, either, but that's by choice."

"Why not?"

He gave me a rueful smile. "It's the old story: gay kid born to white trash, rural, conservative racist sexist homophobic right-wing fundamentalist Christian family." He frowned and lifted his shoulders momentarily before letting them fall again. "They caught me when I was sixteen with another boy. They beat me, locked me in a room with a Bible, told me to pray the gay away, and didn't feed me for three days." His eyes looked sad. "On the third day, one of my sisters unlocked the door and helped me escape. I've never been back there since. Of course, when *Garden District Gothic* came out, several of my relatives tried to get in touch, but not my parents. I've helped my sister out some—I put one of her kids through college—but the rest of them can burn in hell for all I care." He laughed. "I have some issues with the concept of family, as you can tell." He pushed himself off the car and stood there on the sidewalk. "You ready? Shall we give it a try?"

I nodded, my mind still wrapping itself around his story. How had he managed to go from that to successful, best-selling writer? I wanted to ask, but then figured it might be rude. If he wanted to tell me, he could. "Sure." I fitted the silver key into the lock and the knob turned. I pushed the gate open and turned back to Jerry. "Here we go."

"Thanks," Jerry said, going through the gate.

I followed, closing the gate behind me with a clang. I looked around and caught my breath.

But nothing about the house rang any bells in my memory. The yard was a lush jungle of ancient and enormous live oaks, banana trees, palm trees, elephant ferns, and other assorted plants I didn't recognize. There wasn't any grass—the ground was covered with what looked like wood shavings. The entire yard was shaded by the huge trees and ferns, with sunlight breaking through the green natural awnings here and there. The air was heavy and moist, and water dripped down from wet tree limbs and fern leaves. The tall fence seemed to close the yard off from the entire world, like it was some kind of safe inner sanctuary. The walk from the gate to the bottom of the steps was broken and tilted from live oak roots, just like the sidewalk outside. A bee buzzed past my head, and insects hummed in the silence. Now that I was inside the fence I could see that the house itself was raised about six feet or so off the ground. The house was painted in varying shades of green, the shutters a darker shade than the walls themselves. Most of the shutters were closed and latched, and there was an eerie silence and stillness about the house. It was easy to imagine that I'd somehow gone back in time to a different era once the gate was closed.

Jerry waited for me at the foot of the steps up to the porch, no expression on his face. I walked past him and climbed the steps up to the gallery. As I unlocked the front door, I asked him, over my shoulder, "What do you think you're going to find here, if anything? It's been over twenty years since my parents lived here. I would assume anything of theirs was cleaned out a long time ago." I opened the door and stepped inside the cool house. The alarm was right there on the right side of the door. I opened it, ready to punch in the code Olivia had given me, but stopped with my finger above the keypad. The green light indicated that the alarm wasn't activated. "That's odd," I said with a frown. "The alarm wasn't on."

"Maybe the cleaning crew was just here and forgot." Jerry closed the door. "As for what I'll find here—what *we'll* find here—you never know."

I flipped on the light switch just below the white alarm panel. "I imagine my dad probably left some things behind when he left," I said, slipping the keys back into my shorts pocket. "But I doubt any of that would still be here."

The first floor of the house was really just one enormous L-shaped room. There was a staircase going up to the next level. Next to it, a wall ran to the left side of the house, closing off what was probably another room from the main room. With all the shutters closed, it was dim inside even with the lights on. Ceiling fans turned overhead, with their lights on in the front part of the L. The side on the right had a few more lights that weren't on. Tables and chairs and sofas had been laid out to create different seating areas. There was a big television mounted on one of the walls, with another seating area delineated in front of it. The floor was hardwood and gleamed in the overhead light. The walls were covered with framed black-and-white artistic photographs of buildings and the river and other New Orleans scenes.

"Although," I went on, "I can't imagine Dad took anything of my mother's with him—I certainly never saw anything of hers at our house in Bay City—so I wonder what happened to her stuff."

"I doubt either Geoffrey or Nina would have just thrown everything away," Jerry said, nodding. "Nina never really recovered from your mother's death, you know."

"So you've said." I frowned. I started walking around the room. This was the place my parents brought me to from the hospital where I'd been born, where I'd spent the first three years of my life. I walked over to one of the windows. They were enormous, rising from the floor at least eight feet.

"Does it look familiar? Do you remember anything?" Jerry whispered.

"No," I replied honestly. I remembered nothing of this place. I ran my hand along the top of one of the tables. "You're right, the cleaning crew must have just been here and forgot to turn the alarm on." I held up my clean fingertip for him to see. "No dust. I'll have to mention it to Geoffrey. It's irresponsible for them not to put the alarm on."

"They may not have been the last ones here. The person who uses this place the most is your cousin Ginny," he said, "and she's not exactly the most responsible person."

How do you know she uses the house the most? I wondered but decided not to say anything. He wouldn't have been able to write *Garden District Gothic* without being privy to upper-crust New Orleans gossip. Even though he'd written a book about it, he probably still had any number of society acquaintances who fed him gossip. "I'm really not sure what to think about her," I said slowly, "but—"

A thump from upstairs cut me off in midsentence. I felt my nerves jangling and my stomach turned over. I dug out my phone to call 911, but Jerry stopped me with a hand on my arm. He shook his head and motioned for me to follow him to the staircase.

"We should call the police," I whispered, but he held up a finger to his mouth to silence me as he shook his head again.

"Someone's here," he whispered, motioning for me to follow him, "but we should make sure it's not someone with a key. The alarm was turned off, remember?"

My heart rate slowed down a bit as I realized he was right. What were the odds that someone had broken in when the alarm hadn't been turned on? And the gate had been closed—it only opened with a key.

It had to be Ginny.

I crept up the stairs behind him, and when we got to the top of the stairs I heard an unmistakable giggle, followed by another muffled thump. "Hello?" Jerry called out. "Is anyone here?"

Ginny, her hair a rumpled mess, stuck her head out of an open door down at the end of the hallway. There was a big smile on her face and she looked from Jerry to me and back again. She stepped out of the room. All she was wearing was a mesh black and gold Saints jersey that reached her knees. It was pretty obvious there was nothing underneath. "I should have known you'd want to come check out your house." She smirked at me, smoothing her hair with her right hand. "Not to worry, once Jake is out of the shower we'll be on our way and out of your hair for whatever it is you and Jerry came here for."

Jake?

I could feel my face turning red as the blood rushed into it.

"Don't be ridiculous. Jerry and I," I managed to finally say, "are just here to have a look around. But you—" I stopped talking as she ducked back into the room.

Jerry smiled at me, clearly enjoying himself. He raised an eyebrow. "There's never a dull moment with your cousin. And I think my feelings are a little hurt. Some people find me attractive."

"Stop it," I hissed at him. "You know what I meant."

Ginny reemerged from the bedroom. She was still wearing the jersey but had tied it into a knot so her flat midriff was exposed. She was buttoning up a pair of jeans and had a pair of sandals on her feet. I could hear water start running through the pipes. She brushed past us and stopped at the top of the stairs, gesturing for us to follow her. We followed her back down the stairs and around the corner into a very modern kitchen, hidden behind the wall running from the stairs to the outside wall. It was all white, with stainless-steel lamps hanging down from the ceiling and modern appliances. She opened the refrigerator and poured herself a glass of white wine from a bottle stored in the door. She poured us each a glass. "Cheers." She held up her glass so we could clink ours against hers. She hopped up on the counter and took a big drink from her glass. She gave me a wicked grin. "You could have called," she said, winking at me, "and let me know you were coming. The last thing I needed was to be caught in flagrante delicto by the biggest gossip in New Orleans." She gestured to Jerry with her free hand. "No offense, of course."

"None taken," Jerry replied smoothly. "No worries, your secret is safe with me, Ginny darling." His voice was practically a purr. I sipped my wine. It tasted expensive. He turned back to me. "Ginny has been using this house for her assignations since she was in college. It's not really much of a secret, not even from her husband, right, Ginny?"

I stopped myself from blurting out, *But she's married!*

I heard his voice in my head again, saying, *Ginny and I don't have secrets.*

Maybe I was more closed minded than I needed to be. But I always thought marriage—love and coupledom and all of that—was exclusive. You fell in love and got married and had a family and a dog and the white picket fence and all of that stuff. Like my parents—

But my mother committed suicide.

She burst out laughing and splashed more wine into her glass. "Heath, if you could see your face! I had no idea a gay guy could be so puritanical. I mean, aren't you gays all about casual sex?" When I didn't answer—I was too stunned to think of anything to say—she gestured at Jerry again. "Jerry certainly indulges whenever he feels like it, right? And I'm not judging you for bringing him here, Cuz. More power to you, I say. Jerry's a good-looking dude." She gave me a sly glance. "And given all his experience...I'm sure Jerry's a very good choice for some afternoon fun."

I realized she was more than a little bit drunk, and glanced at the clock on the wall. It was barely two in the afternoon. I opened my mouth to say something but she started talking again, cutting me off before I could get the words out. "We were finished anyway, so don't worry about y'all interrupting." Her words slurred a little bit. "And we're going down to the Fly to meet some friends. Y'all want to come?" Her voice arched up a bit at the end, making it sound a lot dirtier than the words implied.

I was saved from responding when a young man about my age came bounding into the kitchen, pulling a T-shirt over his head after giving Jerry and me a flash of washboard abs and a treasure trail leading down to the waistband of his underwear. "Hey," he said with a big smile, holding out his hand. "I'm Jake Carr. Nice to meet you." He was really good-looking, well over six feet tall and slender. His hands were big and calloused, with spots of dried white paint spattered over them and his forearms. His eyes were enormous and brown, and there was razor stubble on his face. He had shoulder-length brown hair which was styled into a fauxhawk in the center of his head.

"Come on, Jake, let's get out of here." She grabbed him by the arm and pulled him to a door, which she opened. There was a staircase leading down into darkness behind it. "Later, guys." She blew us a kiss and slammed the door shut behind her. I heard her mocking laughter through the door, and the sound of a garage door going up beneath us. An engine started, and I could hear the garage door closing.

"Well, that was kind of awkward." Jerry held his glass up to mine and clinked them together.

"So she does this sort of thing all the time?" I couldn't wrap my mind around it. "She's married to Costa, and he's gorgeous—"

"You're so young," he said with a slightly condescending yet somehow kind smile. "Costa and Ginny's marriage has never been what you would call *traditional*. And who are we to judge? As long as no one is getting hurt, what does it matter who sleeps with whom?"

I bristled. I've never liked being talked down to. "I—" He actually had a point—it *wasn't* my business.

It had everything to do with my attraction to Costa, an attraction that wasn't going to get me anywhere, no matter what the situation was in his marriage.

Even if he were single—even if he and Ginny got divorced—he'd lied to me.

How could I ever trust him?

But Costa and his marriage weren't my concern, would never be my concern, so the smart thing for me to do at this point was just close the door on that in my mind and be done with it. I exhaled heavily. "Sorry—my mind's on overload." I sat down on one of the bar stools at the island in the center of the kitchen and took another sip of the wine.

"Then don't think about things," Jerry replied. He took me by the hands and pulled me off the bar stool. "Grab your wine and let's explore the house." He winked at me. "I know there's something upstairs in the master bedroom suite you're going to want to see."

"But if you've never been here before—" I followed him back up the stairs to the second floor. I followed him down the upstairs hallway and was relieved when he opened a door to a room that wasn't the one my cousin had used. He stood there in the doorway, smiling at me. He pointed inside the room and I went in, looking at where he was pointing.

Above the mantelpiece was an enormous portrait of a stunningly beautiful woman. She was wearing a red blouse, open at the throat and unbuttoned enough to reveal a deep cleavage. She was smiling, and her features were strangely familiar. There was a rope of pearls at her neck and her long silvery-blond hair fell to her shoulders, loose and uncontrolled. It was so lifelike, I wouldn't have been surprised if she had started laughing.

And that was when I knew it was her.

My mother.

Genevieve Melissa Legendre Brandon.

My mouth opened and closed.

I started walking across the room, not aware of anything else other than the painting of the woman whose face I couldn't remember no matter how hard I tried. I stopped right beneath the painting, staring up at it in wonder. She looked so young, so alive, and the way her eyes seemed to dance and laugh had to be some kind of illusion the artist had created with his skills and oils. "She's so beautiful," I breathed out, glancing at the signature in the corner of the painting. *G Legendre,* written in black oil paint in a strong, yet feminine hand. "A self-portrait?" I asked, certain Geoffrey couldn't have painted this.

And before Jerry could reply, in my head I heard her laugh.

It had a musical quality to it, a joy and pleasure in her amusement, and I knew it was memory, a memory dredged up by this first sight of my mother. I closed my eyes and tried to remember her again…but there was nothing but that banging sound, and the sight of the red glass mask falling into the dirt, the puff of dirt displaced by its slow-motion settling…

I opened my eyes and spun around to face Jerry again.

"There's something no one wants to tell me," I said slowly. "When we met, that first night we met, you were surprised that I didn't know anything about my mother. You were shocked and almost ended the conversation. What exactly is it you wouldn't tell me? I have a right to know. And there was more to it than the murder-suicide, wasn't there?"

"You'd better sit down," he said, sitting down himself on the end of the enormous canopy bed. He looked flushed, and his hand shook a bit as he raised his wineglass to his lips. "It's really not my place—"

"Then whose place is it?" I sat down hard next to him, staring at my mother and then turning to look at him. "Do you want me to just wait until I read your book to find out what it is? You got me into this, Jerry—you owe me."

That made him laugh. He toasted me with his wineglass, his eyes dancing. "Touché, I suppose. But you should be thanking me, don't you think? After all, you were just a poor college student slaving away at an hourly wage, and now I've dropped you into the midst of a fairly wealthy family." He waved his glass around. "And you now know you own some prime real estate in the lower Garden District. You could get some serious cash selling this place, you know."

"Yes, yes, thank you," I replied impatiently. "Spit it out already."

"I told you how your mother and Dylan died, but I didn't tell you the whole story." He took a deep breath. "They weren't the only ones there, Heath, when it happened. There was actually a witness."

"Then how did Geoffrey cover everything up?" I asked, feeling the blood rush back into my face. The room was getting hotter, and somehow I knew, I knew what he was going to say before he actually said it.

"You were there that day, Heath. Your mother took you

with her when she went to meet Dylan. Everyone claimed afterward that she went to tell him to leave her alone, to get out of her life, but your father refused to believe it. He refused to believe that your mother wasn't having an affair with Dylan."

"I was there."

He nodded. "You saw the whole thing. You were the only witness, and you were only three years old." He sighed. "And you were never able to tell anyone what happened."

CHAPTER SIX

"Well, the first rule of Louisiana cooking is you have to know how to make a roux," Jerry said, placing an enormous white onion, two bell peppers, and several ribs of celery on the cutting board. He unwrapped a stick of butter and dropped it into the enormous cast-iron skillet he'd been heating over a blue flame. Almost immediately the butter began to melt slowly. "It's all about the roux." He wiggled his eyebrows at me, trying to make me laugh.

I appreciated the gesture but couldn't oblige by laughing.

I was still a bit in shock. I was feeling fuzzy around the edges, like none of this was real, like I was in the midst of some insane dream that I couldn't wake up from.

It had been about three hours since he dropped the big bomb on me, the one everyone in my family had been keeping from me since I was three years old. I still wasn't sure if I could wrap my mind around it: *My mother took me with her when she went to kill her lover and herself. She did it right in front of me.*

Little wonder Dad thought she was evil and had wanted nothing more to do with the Legendres!

When I was five years old, my father had been picking oranges off the tree in our backyard. It was an arduous task, and every time he climbed the ladder to get the oranges off the tallest branches, he complained, threatening to have the tree cut down. But my mom—*stepmother*—loved having fresh orange juice. She loved the whole process of juicing the oranges and was always finding new and inventive ways to use oranges for cooking. The tree produced far too many oranges for our own use, so once a week during harvesting season my father would drive crates of them to homeless shelters around Bay City. My job was to pick up the ones that had ripened and fallen off during the week and put them in the trash. I was never allowed to go up the ladder, and I never did anything I wasn't permitted to do.

I was a good boy.

This particular day my father was up on the ladder when my stepmother called him in to take a phone call. But for some reason that day I did climb the ladder. I still don't know why I did. Maybe there was a bird or something up there I'd seen, maybe it was a sense of challenging the rules, maybe it was nothing more than wanting to see the world from that height. But I climbed that ladder, rung after rung, until I was high up in the tree, up higher than I'd ever been before. I remember how spectacular the view was, the palm trees and the roofs of neighbors' houses, and I could see into the neighbors' yards. The teenaged girl next door who babysat me sometimes so my parents could go places they couldn't take me, Marcie Krueger, was sunbathing in her string bikini and idly flipping the page of a *Tiger Beat* magazine, lying on a large orange beach towel spread out in the lush green grass. In another yard a teenaged boy with no shirt was mowing the lawn with a push mower. A whole new world had opened for me up there on top of the ladder. There was a light breeze rustling the branches and leaves at the top of the tree, and it was a hot, humid summer day. The sky overhead was clear and blue, white wisps of clouds floating over my head, seeming to be so close I could almost reach up and grab them. I closed my eyes and enjoyed the coolness of the breeze with its slight hint of the sea.

"Heath! What are you doing up there?"

Startled, I lost my balance and fell off the ladder. It seemed to my child's mind like I was falling forever. I hit the ground and everything went black—and even when I came to, the edges of my vision seemed dark and gray and shadowy.

I felt this way now, like everything was swimming around me, and the periphery of my vision was gray and dark and shadowy. I felt a weird emotional numbness, a strange buzzing in my ears.

I'd witnessed a murder-suicide when I was three years old.

I didn't remember it.

I closed my eyes and could see the Orion mask falling again, the rubies and glass glittering and sparkling in the bright sunlight. I could hear shouting, angry shouting, but I couldn't make out any words. I remembered feeling frightened.

I opened my eyes and reached for my wineglass. I'd had a ridiculous amount of wine already—I think I kind of scared Jerry after he'd told me the truth that my family, that everyone, had been hiding from me for the last nineteen years. He'd gotten me a glass of wine and made me drink it, and then another.

Maybe I was buzzed from the wine. Maybe the wine was responsible for the numbness. Maybe the wine was why I felt like I was watching everything from some distant remove.

"Almost everything Louisiana style—gumbos, shrimp creole, you name it—they all start with a roux." He went on, expertly dicing the onion, celery, and bell peppers in record time, the knife flashing as he chopped rapidly.

"You're good with a knife," I said, over the sound of the metal knife striking the cutting board.

I was sitting in his kitchen. His house wasn't that far from—it was hard to think of it as *mine*—the house my mother had left me. It was a beautiful old Victorian, originally built in the 1870s. He'd told me it had been divided into a duplex when he'd bought it. The previous owner had rented out the other side as well as the carriage house behind, which had also been split into two apartments. "It was a termite-infested wreck, and she was old, wanted to retire to Florida"—he'd laughed as he fit his key into the black wrought-iron gate—"and didn't want to spend all the money it would require to renovate it. I had it tented, and once the termites were gone, I pretty much had to gut the whole thing." He'd turned it back into a single, and it was huge for one person. The ceilings were eighteen feet high, the floors a glossy hardwood, and the enormous windows let in lots of natural light. The kitchen was an enormous room in the back of the house and was completely modernized—"I wanted a top-of-the-line chef's kitchen so I could teach myself how to cook," he'd said as he opened a bottle of Chardonnay and poured me a glass—and I particularly liked the skylight. The glass was tinted to cut down on the sun's glare.

He smiled at me as he scooped the diced vegetables into a ceramic bowl. "I like to cook," he said, picking up his own glass of wine while still keeping a watchful eye on the melting butter. "I took some classes. It's a different way of being creative, I guess, once you've figured out what flavors and textures work well together." He measured out a third of a cup of flour, poured it into the melted butter, and stirred it with a wooden spoon until it was all dissolved. "There," he said with another smile at me, "and now we wait for it to turn brown before we put the vegetables into it." He wiped his hands on a kitchen towel and leaned back against the kitchen counter. "How are you doing? You haven't said much."

"I don't know. Besides the buzz from the wine?" I took

another sip from my glass. I was getting drunk, that was part of it, I could tell. But the alcohol was softening the edges, helping me deal with all the shocks I'd been hit with since arriving in Louisiana.

After this glass I'm going to switch back to water—the last thing in the world I need to do is get drunk in front of him.

"How should I be doing? I don't have a lot of experience with finding out that my mother killed her lover and herself— and did it in front of me." I put the glass down and took a deep breath. "It's kind of a lot to take in."

He picked up my glass and poured what was left into his own glass. "You're starting to slur your words a bit, so I think I'm going to cut you off for a while," he said, opening one of the enormous stainless-steel refrigerators. He removed a bottle of Pellegrino and twisted off the cap. He refilled my glass and dropped slices of lemon and lime into the bubbling water before handing it to me. "Look, I know it was a shock. I shouldn't have been the one to tell you, and I'm sorry I was."

"Someone had to, might as well have been you," I replied, surprised at how bitter and angry I sounded. I didn't feel that way. I felt numb and hollow, almost empty inside. Or was it the wine? "I'm so fucking sick and tired of being lied to!" I shook my head, hoping to clear it a bit. "Everyone's lied to me my whole life. It's all been a bit much. Maybe I shouldn't have come to Louisiana." I sipped the water. "Maybe I should just go home and say the hell with it."

"You have a right to know the truth." He drank some more wine and started stirring the bubbling butter-flour mixture. "But it shouldn't have been me. Your father should have told you, someone—anyone—out at Chambord." He shook his head, not looking up from what he was doing. "I was pretty sure you didn't remember anything. But you can't leave now."

"Why not? I don't owe them anything."

"You're angry and in shock—not that anyone could blame you for feeling that way." He shrugged slightly.

"I suppose they all thought they were protecting me," I said. *I should be angry,* I told myself, *but I don't feel anything. What is wrong with me?*

"You don't remember what happened. I'm not a psychologist, but my guess is the trauma was all too much for your mind to handle." He didn't look at me. The flour-butter mixture was turning a rich, dark brown. He picked up the bowl of vegetables and dumped them into the pan. He started stirring them with the wooden spoon, moving them around until they were coated with the browned mixture. "You couldn't testify, you couldn't tell anyone what really happened down there at the boathouse—"

"The boathouse?" I closed my eyes and once again saw the image of the red glass mask falling slowly through the air, hitting dark water with a slight splash.

He glanced at me and started sprinkling spices into the frying pan. First he added cayenne, white, and black pepper, followed by thyme and basil and salt. He kept stirring, the biceps muscle in his right arm flexing and bulging, the blue veins popping out even more. "The vegetables have to soften before they go into the stew pot," he said before picking up his wineglass and turning to face me. "And you still don't remember anything, do you?" He scrutinized my face. "Or are you starting to remember?"

I wasn't sure if I could trust him, so I didn't mention the image I kept seeing, the sound of the banging and the arguing voices. It might be my subconscious, unlocking memories my mind hadn't been able to handle when I was a little boy.

Or it might not be anything.

"Nothing." I sipped my sparkling water. "And how do you know so much about this, anyway?"

He smiled back at me. "People like to talk to me."

I returned his smile. "You do have a way about you. Didn't people get mad about your book?"

"No." He opened two cans of diced tomatoes and dumped them into the stockpot. "When I started writing *Garden District Gothic,* I told everyone what I was doing, and if they didn't want me to use their names, I told them I wouldn't." He laughed. "I imagine no one really thought I could write a book, let alone that it would ever get published. After all, I was just a personal trainer with a GED and a writing degree from UNO. But to answer your question, I started hearing stories about your mother's death right around when my book first came out. There were just rumors, of course, and then I was too busy for a long time to really look into anything, ask any questions. Geoffrey did a really good job covering the whole thing up." He stirred the roux again.

"But if it was all covered up..."

"How did anyone know it wasn't true?" He poured a cup of spaghetti sauce into the roux, stirring it until the roux turned orange. Then he picked up the pan, slid the mixture into the stockpot, and moved it to the burner where the pan had been. He turned the blue flame down, walked over to the refrigerator, and grabbed a plastic bag of peeled shrimp, which he also dumped into the stockpot. He stirred it vigorously before covering the pot with a lid. "That'll be ready in about an hour, give or take, and I'll start the rice in about half an hour." He wiped his hands on a black kitchen towel. "Servants always talk to other servants, Heath. It might sound classist to say, but it's true. When I was ready to start writing another book, I remembered your mother's death at Chambord and what I'd heard...so I started checking into it."

"I know Geoffrey said my mother's death was an accident," I replied slowly. "But if she killed Dylan...What was that story? I never saw anything about it online. And how did he get away with it? He lied to the police?"

He gave me a sardonic look. "Surely you're not that naïve?" He barked out a laugh. "Heath, really. Redemption Parish? You don't know how things work in Louisiana? Money and power can buy you out of anything. Then again, it's not like it wasn't an open-and-shut case. Genevieve shot Dylan and then herself. It's not like there was obstruction of justice or anything. You were the only one who could say what happened, and you didn't remember. Anyway, the story as it was given out was that it was an accident, and your mother was so overcome with grief and shock by what happened she turned the gun on herself." He rolled his eyes. "Because a mother would do *that* in front of her child. But the case was closed, and your father took you away. But, of course, people talked." He put on an oven mitt and lifted the lid on the shrimp creole so he could stir it again. "People always talk."

"So you came to find me because I'm the only witness." I blurted out the words I'd been holding in ever since he finally told me the truth, there under my mother's self-portrait.

He stopped stirring and looked at me. He took a deep breath. "I'm writing a book," he said, "one I needed to interview you for. How was I supposed to know you'd know nothing about your mother's death, or your family?" He sighed and walked over to where I was sitting, on a bar stool at the big butcher's block island in the center of the room. He stood so close to me I could smell his musk under his cologne—something by Calvin Klein, but I couldn't quite place which one. "I do like you, Heath." He put one of his big hands on my right knee. "You're a nice guy. You're smart and funny and very sweet, whether you like it or not. And I hope you know I mean that. I'm sorry about all of this. If I'd known—" He reached up and brushed my cheek with his left hand. "If I'd known then what

I know now, I would have done things differently. But I can't go back and change anything." His voice was little more than a whisper as he said those last words.

I could hear my heart pounding in my ears. He was close, oh, so close. His hand on my knee burned my skin, and it felt like the hair on the back of my neck was standing up. I could smell his breath, see the little red lines in the whites of his eyes. Salt and pepper stubble stood out on the sides of his head. I could feel the heat coming off his skin, his body.

I swallowed, not sure what I was supposed to do, what he wanted me to do.

I leaned forward and kissed him.

At first he didn't kiss me back. It seemed like I stayed there, my lips pressed against his, for an eternity, time standing still as I waited for him to respond, to kiss me back or push me away or just do something, anything other than just stand there. I could feel the blood rushing to my face. I was about to pull back away, mortified, when he put his strongly muscled arms around me and pulled me closer into his body, almost lifting me off the stool. His lips relaxed, giving a little bit, and he tilted his head slightly to one side. He was gentle at first, his hands pressing against my back, my chest pressed up against his. His muscles were firm and hard to the touch. His smell was driving me crazy with desire. I could hear him breathing through his nose, could feel the heat from his tanned skin radiating out, could feel his heart beating faster and faster as he shifted, pulling me closer, like he was trying to mold our two bodies into one. He was so strong I couldn't resist even if I'd wanted to, sliding down from the stool and my feet coming down outside of his so he was standing in between my legs. His hands slid down, cupping my butt, and he pulled me forward as his lips moved down from mine to my neck, and my head went back, it felt so good, I didn't want him to stop, and I wrapped my own arms around him, stroking the thick muscles in his back, as our crotches ground against each other. I was vaguely aware of the jazz music coming from the Bose CD player on the counter, the delicious smells of the cooking shrimp, the wind from the ceiling fan beating down from the twirling blades overhead. I couldn't believe how good his lips felt against my throat, how the strong and coiled powerful muscles beneath my hands felt, his big strong chest muscles crushing against me as I started to move my own hands down his back before—

Without warning he broke away from me with a slight cry, the spell suddenly broken as he pushed me away and cleared his throat. He said brokenly, "This isn't a good idea, Heath."

I still felt a little woozy from the wine and from the taste of his lips. I turned around and grabbed my glass, sipping at my soda water, closing my eyes. *What are you doing? Are you crazy? He wants something from you, you're the person who holds the key to the book he's writing, and now you're throwing yourself at him like a junior-high-school girl with a crush. He's so much older than you are. He could be your father.*

I knew that voice, whispering cruelly in my head, eating away at my confidence.

The voice belonged to my only real boyfriend, Aubrey Wayne.

I'd always known I was different from the other boys, even when I was in kindergarten. I didn't know how or why, I just knew. By junior high school, I knew what the difference was, knew that I liked boys the way other boys liked girls. I was deeply ashamed, wanted to be a good masculine little boy. But I liked to read and devoured old movies on the cable channels that specialized in them, staying up late to watch Bogart and Bacall, Taylor and Clift, Tracy and Hepburn,

Gable and Crawford, Bette Davis and all the other stars from Hollywood's Golden Age. I liked nothing more than to spend my Saturdays in the library, reading books and going through the shelves and examining every book, trying to decide which ones to take home in my backpack and read during the week while the other boys were playing baseball and riding their bikes and playing kick the can and computer games about demolishing things and blowing things up or gunning people down.

High school wasn't so bad, until of course my senior year when Dad died so suddenly. In high school there were a couple of jerks, but I never let on I was gay. I didn't join the GSA or hang out with the other gay kids. I used to dream every night of having a boyfriend, of having someone to hold hands with and to kiss, of someone to love and to love me and to go to the prom with.

I met Aubrey Wayne when I started going to Bay State.

Aubrey Wayne was one of those guys, the cool kids I used to watch from across the cafeteria when I was eating my lunch by myself, the guys who had lots of friends and were always laughing and having a good time. I used to sit there, watching them out of the corner of my eye, wishing I were one of them, having crushes on one or some of all of them from time to time, watching them in gym as their athletic bodies played sports well and sweated, the hair on their legs matted with sweat and damp.

I saw Aubrey from across the quad one day. I'd gotten a burrito at the student center cafeteria and was sitting on a cement bench near the fountain eating it and trying to read my psychology textbook and trying not to yawn or fall asleep. I'd started working at the airport—a friend of my mother's had helped me get the job—but with my low seniority I had to work late nights. It was hard to juggle work and school and stay on top of the assignments. I was taking a drink out of my AriZona iced tea can when I saw him.

He was short, maybe about five foot six with dark hair cut close to the scalp and pale skin. He was wearing a white ribbed tank top and a pair of jean shorts, and was built like a tank. There wasn't any fat on him anywhere, just thick strong muscle. He was handsome, with bright blue eyes and freckles spread across his snub nose, over his square jaw and his thick lips. I couldn't help staring at him, my mouth wide open, the can of tea almost to my mouth yet frozen in place. He walked with an air of confidence, like he owned the world and we were all lucky he let us live in it. He smiled at me as he walked past me, then stopped, doing a pronounced double take.

"You're in my econ class, aren't you?" he asked, his head tilted to one side as he beamed a big smile at me. One of his two front teeth was chipped, and I was barely able to focus on what he was saying, I was so dazzled. "Professor Desai, two o'clock this afternoon?"

"Um, yeah," I heard myself saying, hardly able to look away from the canyon between his enormous pectorals. *How had I not seen him in the class before?*

He sat down next to me, and we started talking. It wasn't until much, much later that I realized we only talked about him. He was from Kissimmee, over near Orlando, and he'd been a football player and a jock and loved to lift weights and he'd just broken up with his longtime girlfriend because he realized he was gay just before he left for Bay State, and did I know where any of the gay kids hung out?

And that was how it started, with me and Aubrey. He got me started lifting weights, taking better care of myself, taking pride in my appearance. He was my first, and I loved him with my whole heart. I planned on spending the rest of my life with him…until I realized he was cheating on me. Over and over and over again. When I confronted him about it, he just laughed. "I never said we were exclusive," he said, that big smile beaming at me, "and I never want to be tied down to just one guy. We're young, Heath! There's plenty of time for that when we're old."

It hadn't been easy, kicking the Aubrey habit. There were times when I thought there should be a twelve-step program for dumping someone who you love but who doesn't love you the same way. It affected everything, my confidence, my self-worth, everything. I just wanted to find someone and be with a guy who loved me. I tried to date other guys, but nothing ever seemed to work out. It was like he had some kind of radar that tipped him off when I'd met someone I liked, someone I'd seen more than once, someone who might have been right for me. Then he would show up at my door one night with a bottle of cheap wine and some grocery-store flowers, not wearing a shirt or underwear underneath his pants, and I would let him back in. Once the new guy was gone, Aubrey would be, too, leaving nothing behind but the wreckage of my self-esteem and my pride. He finally left Bay State, transferring back to UCF in Orlando, and I never heard from him again.

But I would hear his voice in my head all the time, questioning me, eating away at what self-esteem I'd managed to somehow scrape together.

Yet here I was, in the home of a successful writer, a handsome and sexy older man who'd kissed me back when I threw myself at him, and Aubrey was there again in my head.

Go straight to hell, Aubrey, I told myself firmly.

"I need to get the rice started," Jerry said, turning his back to me and turning on the water spigot. "Why don't you go wait for me in the living room?"

Stung, I stood there for a moment, staring at his back, at the beautifully shaped muscular back and ass, before turning and walking back into the living room.

Keep going, just keep walking until you get back to your house.

I ignored the voice and sat down on the black leather sofa.

I sat there alone, mortified, debating whether I should get the hell out of there and save myself the embarrassment, when he came walking in. I smiled at him.

My smile faltered a bit when he didn't sit on the couch, choosing instead to sit in a wingback chair safely on the other side of the coffee table.

He cleared his throat cautiously and offered me a very weak smile. "Dinner should be ready in about half an hour."

My stomach growled. I hadn't had lunch, hadn't eaten anything since breakfast.

"I'm sorry about before," he said hesitantly. He bit his lower lip. "Believe me, Heath, you are a very attractive young man—"

Here it comes, the big brush-off. Just keep smiling, don't let him know how much it hurts.

"—and I am very attracted to you, but it would be so incredibly unethical for me to become involved with you in any way other than as a researcher and subject until the book is finished—"

At least that's a new one, one I haven't heard before. Not Let's be friends *or* I like you but not that way *or any of the number of excuses I've heard so many times before.*

"—but I hope you won't mind waiting for me? I mean, once the book is done..." He cleared his throat awkwardly. "But in the meantime, I'd really like for us to, you know, get to know each other better and see what happens."

His face was bright red when he finished speaking, and he couldn't look me in the eyes.

He might be telling the truth. He could hardly write an objective story about you and your mother if he's sleeping with you, now could he?

"Do you believe my mother killed Dylan before killing herself?" I was surprised at how calm I sounded, that my voice didn't give away how fast my heart was racing or how much I desperately wanted to be somewhere, anywhere, else.

He looked startled then relieved that I'd changed the subject as he said slowly, "I don't like cover-ups, Heath. They make me suspicious of everything. Oh, sure, I can certainly understand why Geoffrey and Nina wouldn't want anyone to know the truth about what happened out at the boathouse that day, but I can't help but feel there's more to the story."

"It seems pretty clear to me." I couldn't look at him, so I fixed my eyes on a bookcase that held what looked to be copies of *Garden District Gothic* in many different languages. "What else could there be to the story?"

He took a deep breath. "Why would your mother want to kill Dylan?" He leaned forward. "That's what I don't understand, and that's the key to the whole story, if you ask me. But with Geoffrey and Nina paying off the parish cops out there in that little banana republic..." He shook his head. "Everyone I've talked to has said that Genevieve loved him. They dated in high school despite the age difference. And then out of the blue he joined the military and vanished, and Genevieve married someone else."

"Maybe it was an accident. Maybe there was no cover-up."

"Why did she take a gun with her when she went to meet him at the boathouse?"

"That's the second time you've mentioned a boathouse," I replied, finally getting up the nerve to look him in the face. "There's a boathouse at Chambord?" Even as I said the words, I could see the red mask falling slowly before hitting the water with a splash. "Where?"

"The boathouse is on the property, but a pretty good distance from the house and the museum and everything. You really have to go looking for it," he replied. "There's a bayou on the grounds at Chambord, and there's a small boathouse out there where the Legendres used to keep their fishing boats. There's a dock and everything. The bayou ends in a large pond, and on the other end it runs into the swamp." He took a deep breath. "It's the way the Legendres always got into the swamp to go fishing or gator hunting or frogging or whatever it was they needed to get in there for." He swallowed. "Going back to before the Civil War even. Your grandfather was never really much of an outdoorsman, but according to my sources he always kept boats, in case guests at Chambord wanted to hunt or fish. Dylan was into fishing and hunting. He used the boathouse a lot."

"So I guess it wasn't really out of character for him to want to meet my mother out there," I commented. "But why not at the house? Why not here in New Orleans?"

"That's what I'm trying to find out. None of it makes any sense."

And what does the mask have to do with any of this? I wondered, but out loud I said, "How did you find out that it wasn't an accident? That it was deliberate murder?"

"Tommy Hebert used to be the sheriff of Redemption Parish," he answered, unable to look me in the eyes as he said the words. "He was the one who covered everything up for your grandfather, looked the other way, sealed the investigation and the coroner's report for money. To this day no one can access the coroner's report—and that's not standard procedure. I tried to get a look at it, but..." He whistled. "Anyway, I knew his granddaughter"—he looked away for a moment—"and when he was dying, he wanted to talk to me. I'd tried talking to him before, but he wouldn't talk to me. But he apparently wanted to die with a clear conscience, and his priest told him he had to tell someone the truth about what happened that night at the Legendre boathouse."

"How fortunate he chose you." It came out sounding a lot more bitter than I'd intended, and he winced, his face coloring.

"Heath—"

"I'm sorry," I said, and I was. "I appreciate your ethics, actually. So what did he tell you?"

"What do you think?" Our eyes met again, but he flushed. "It was no accident. It was deliberate murder. Those were his exact words, Heath. Your mother took that gun down to the boathouse and she used it on her old boyfriend. Then she turned it on herself. And Sheriff Hebert covered the whole thing up for your grandparents."

We sat there in silence, looking at each other. I wasn't sure what to think, or if there was anything I should say, anything I could say.

Finally, I just said, "I want to know the truth about my mother. I'll help you however I can."

CHAPTER SEVEN

The sound of persistent knocking pierced down through my sleeping consciousness.

At first I just groaned and rolled over, trying to ignore the thudding of knuckles against wood. Vaguely I couldn't imagine who'd be knocking on my apartment door—no one ever did, and certainly not in the morning, and I couldn't remember any scheduled pest-control appointment. I pulled a pillow over my head as the knocking continued, resisting the urge to scream *Go away!* as awareness began swimming back up out of the fog and I remembered that I wasn't in my own bed in my apartment back in Bay City, but was at Chambord.

Chambord.

That jolted me awake, and I called out, "Just a moment, thank you," as I shoved the covers off and stretched, listening to the lower vertebrae in my back crack as I yawned. I swung my legs back to the floor and stood. My clothes from the previous day were scattered all over the floor, and I quickly gathered them up and tossed them onto a wingback chair by the dressing table. I padded, still yawning, over to the armoire and pulled on my Bay State University sweatpants and a white ribbed tank top. I headed over to the big door and yanked it open. "Come in," I said to the maid, who stood there trying to avoid meeting my eyes while holding a large silver serving tray.

She brushed past me without saying anything, set it down on the dressing table, and fled back out of the room in silence, pulling the door closed behind her.

"Good morning to you, too," I said to the door.

I sighed and went into the bathroom to wash my face and brush my teeth. I checked in the mirror to make sure I hadn't grown horns or something in the night. *Probably the gay thing—she probably is a good Southern Baptist and thinks she's never been around a gay man before. Maybe she's afraid she'll catch it from me or something.* I turned on the hot water spigot and washed my face thoroughly. It had been a while since I'd experienced anything like that, but it still happened. My Facebook and Twitter feeds were filled almost every day with news stories about gay bashings and homophobic business owners refusing service to gays and lesbians. But I wasn't hurt or offended—I felt sorry for her more than anything else. And there was certainly no reason for me to address her conduct with my grandfather. The last thing I wanted was to get her in trouble...but I couldn't help but wonder why she was acting the way she was around me.

I'd slept extremely well, which was actually a bit of a surprise. After all the heavy emotional revelations yesterday, I was pretty sure I would just toss and turn all night long. But after driving back out to Chambord, I'd been so emotionally exhausted I could barely make it up the main staircase and had tumbled into bed—and apparently hadn't bothered to turn the lights off, either. I barely could remember taking off my clothes before pitching onto the bed.

I shouldn't have driven back here last night, I thought as I started brushing my teeth. I had a slight headache, the way I always did the morning after drinking wine. I'd had a lot of wine—drank it pretty much all afternoon, but had switched to water before Jerry had served dinner. I'd also had an espresso with dessert, but even so I'd felt myself getting really drowsy as I negotiated my way back out to Redemption Parish on I-10. *I just hope I didn't make as big an ass of myself when I was tipsy before dinner as I usually do.*

Much as I loved wine, I'd made a fool of myself too many times while under the influence to allow myself to drink more often—or to drink too much.

Like at Ross Gaylord's birthday party.

I cringed at the memory as I methodically cleaned my teeth and gums. I'd barely been twenty-one then. Ross was one of my coworkers at the airport. He was in his early forties and looked amazing. He was one of those blonds whose hair turns white in the sun, and Ross's golden brown skin was evidence he spent as much time as he could outdoors. He was tall, maybe around six foot two or so, with broad shoulders and narrow hips and probably one of the most perfect butts I'd ever seen. When he was young he'd been an underwear model—the hallway of his house in the Hyde Park section of Bay City was decorated with framed images from his modeling days. Every abdominal muscle was deeply chiseled in the pictures, and his body was just as good in his forties as it had been when he was younger. He worked out three or four times a week, swam in the bay, played in a volleyball league, and went jogging on the beach. He'd started out with Transco Airlines as a flight attendant after the modeling gigs dried up—"I was washed up at twenty-five," he liked to say with a laugh—and after he tired of that he transferred to ground crew at Bay City Airport. With his seniority he always got a shift working the gates, and he actually had trained me out there when I was new. He spotted me as a gayby and kind of took me under his wing. I was more than a little dazzled by the blond muscle-god and had a bit of a crush on him, even though I knew I wasn't anywhere near good enough for him. Ross was the first person to take me to a gay bar, and he was always available for advice whenever I needed some, which seemed to be a lot more often than I would have preferred.

His birthday party was one of those events that I'd like to forget ever happened.

Ross had been living in Bay City for almost twenty years at that point and had been through any number of boyfriends. He also seemed to know every gay man in Bay City, so his birthday party was a major get-together. I worked late that night, and it was close to midnight by the time I'd gone home, showered, changed, and headed over to his house. I couldn't park closer than three blocks away, and I could hear the noise from two blocks out. I was surprised no one had called the police, but Ross was one of those charmed people bad things never seemed to happen to. The house—a four-bedroom ranch-style house with a pool and a hot tub in the backyard—was packed full of hot gay men in various states of undress. No one there seemed to have brought a shirt. The music was loud and pumping, guys were dancing everywhere, and before I'd gotten past the foyer a nubile young muscle boy wearing little more than a sequined white thong had squirted a Jello shot into my mouth. By the time I'd fought my way through the house and into the backyard to where people were jumping into the pool in bikinis, I was already feeling it.

The fact several other people had given me shots of tequila and other liquors I didn't recognize hadn't helped my sobriety much, either.

The rest of the night had been a blur. Loud music, lots of sweating bodies encased in firm hard muscles, bikinis and thongs and kissing, and one time, looking for the bathroom,

I'd stumbled into a three-way in a bedroom thick with marijuana smoke and roiling bodies and mumbled *excuse me* to no one in particular, since no one had even looked up from their business to notice me. As the night went on, I got drunker and drunker until I became obsessed with the boy in the white spangled thong who'd given me the first shot, spending the entire night stalking him and in my alcohol-induced stupor tried to kiss him—and he laughed at me. "As if," he'd said to me with a sneer and a look of total disdain on his face. "Can you imagine?" he said to another guy, in a matching thong only in red. "Like I would *ever* with you, drunk troll."

Mortified, I staggered out of the house, their cruel laughter ringing in my ears, and I'd thrown up in a flower bed, as people moved around me and made vague pitying noises.

I'd wanted to die—especially the next morning when I woke up with the Bay City Philharmonic playing inside my head.

I'd avoided Ross as much as humanly possible after that... and then I'd met Aubrey.

I turned off the spigots and stared at myself in the mirror. *He kissed you back, remember? He is interested in you.* I wiped my face dry and walked resolutely back into the bedroom. *He just wants your help with his book,* Aubrey's voice whispered in my ear. I pushed him and every other mortifying memory out of my head and walked over to the dressing table. The breakfast tray was similar to the one from the previous day— muffins and fruit and juice and a carafe of coffee, with a little pitcher of milk and sweeteners. I poured myself a cup of coffee and nibbled on a muffin.

No, I shouldn't have driven out here after the wine and being so tired, I thought with a pang, remembering how hard I'd had to work to stop from nodding off during the drive. Jerry had offered me his spare room—and there was also my own house, a few blocks from his—but stubbornly, I'd decided to drive out here.

If I was spending the night at Jerry's house, I didn't want to stay in the spare room.

And my parents' house—*my* house—was too haunted for me to stay there, at least last night, and I'd wanted to talk to my grandfather in the morning.

So, emotionally drained, I'd gotten into my car and headed back, not aware of how sleepy I was from the wine wearing off. My first full day in Louisiana had been full of shocks and surprises, to say the least. All I wanted to do was to just get back to Chambord and my bed there.

The drive from New Orleans had seemed endless, with me yawning and trying everything I could think of to stay awake behind the wheel. The traffic had been light, and eventually I'd managed to get to the Avignon exit. All the lights on the first floor of Chambord had been on when I'd pulled into the parking area in front. My aunt Olivia was sitting in one of the front rooms, reading a book. Once I came in the front door, she closed the book. "You didn't need to wait up for me," I said, stifling another yawn.

She locked the door behind me and turned on the alarm without a word. I stood there awkwardly, waiting for her to say something. She didn't. Once the alarm beeped and the light changed to red, she turned and swept away down the hallway without a word or even acknowledging I'd spoken to her. I'd been too sleepy to confront her about her rudeness, but as I climbed the main stairs, I knew I was going to have to deal with dear old Aunt Olivia, and the sooner the better.

A maid was one thing. A blood relation was another thing entirely.

I had a lot of questions for everyone in the damned family, for that matter.

It looked overcast outside, and I opened the French doors. The sky was filled with dark clouds, and the air was thick and heavy. In the distance I saw lightning fork down from the dark grayish-black clouds hanging low on the horizon. I stepped back inside just as the rain started coming down in sheets and the wind started picking up. I finished the muffin and downed a bowl of fruit before slipping on a pair of shoes and heading downstairs.

Everyone was in the dining room: Geoffrey, Olivia, Ginny, Costa, Charlotte, and a man I didn't know. No one was speaking as I walked in. Some were reading sections of the newspaper and others were scrolling through their phones. No one acknowledged me other than my grandfather, who gave me a faint smile before giving his attention back to the paper. The man I didn't know got out of his chair and introduced himself to me as I filled a cup with coffee at the sideboard. "Cole Draper," he said with a smile, holding out a big hand for a shake. "Charlotte's husband. Nice to meet you at long last, Heath."

"Nice to meet you," I said, shaking his hand. His grip was strong and firm, his hand surprisingly calloused and dry.

"How are you handling all this?" he asked, dropping his voice so no one else could hear him. He was older than Charlotte, by my best guess as little as ten years to as many as twenty. His hair was thick and a grayish silver, worn longer than most men's his age and pulled back into a ponytail. His face was lined and tanned, the skin under his chin loose. His grayish eyes were veined with red lines, and his teeth were nicotine stained. He faintly smelled of cigarette smoke. He was wearing a blue-and-white seersucker suit, with a bright red bow tie at his throat over a white shirt that clearly had an undershirt beneath. His face looked as sympathetic as the tone of his voice sounded.

He's also an outsider here.

"All things considered, not bad," I replied, giving him a small smile. "Not what I expected, but then I really didn't know what I could expect, honestly."

"I'm editor of the *Avignon News*," he went on. I must have looked confused, because he added hurriedly, "It's the parish newspaper—"

"And it's very good for wrapping fish in," Geoffrey said but took the sting out of the words with a big smile. "Now, don't look offended, Cole, you know I've been making that joke for years, and of course it's not funny—it was never funny."

"But it's always meant to be insulting," Cole muttered under his breath, turning away from me and heading back to his seat.

I sat down with my coffee without saying anything.

"So, how did you find the house?" Geoffrey said, turning his attention to me.

Out of the corner of my eye I saw Ginny squirm a little bit in her seat. Costa was focused on cleaning his plate and wasn't paying her any attention. As if he could tell I was looking at him, Costa looked up and smiled at me. I felt my heart lurch a little, and then chided myself. *He's married to your cousin,* I reminded myself, *off-limits to you. He's just being friendly, which is more than you can say for your so-called family.*

"It's beautiful," I replied slowly, turning to look my grandfather in the eye. "I don't remember living there, of course, or anything about it. You said you've been taking care of the taxes and the upkeep." I sipped my coffee. "So it's probably not really entirely mine, is that right? I must owe you a fortune by now."

Geoffrey burst out laughing. When he was finally able to speak again, he said, "Had I any doubts you were my grandson, I wouldn't anymore!" He wiped at his eyes. "No, the house is yours, Heath. I wasn't about to let the state take it for taxes and I wasn't about to let it rot and fall to pieces. It belongs to you. In exchange for the money I was spending on it, we used it as our New Orleans house. Now, of course, if you no longer want that arrangement to continue, or if you want to live in it yourself, the future of the house is up to you." He peered at me. "Of course, you're also entitled to your mother's share of Chambord and the family estate..."

Ginny choked a bit, but before she could say anything Olivia said coldly, "Which is as it should be, of course. Had she not killed herself, your mother would have had a share." Her face was without expression. "And of course, the house in New Orleans was hers." She lifted her shoulders slightly in a careless shrug.

I looked at her rigid face. "Thank you, Aunt Olivia." Somehow I managed to keep from sounding sarcastic. "While we're talking about my mother, I have a question I'd like answered. Where exactly is the boathouse? Where would I find it?"

Costa hid a grin behind his hand, and to my surprise he winked at me. But everyone was silent. The only sound was the rain outside.

"Why...why would you ask that?" Olivia finally said to break the eerie silence, her voice shaky and quiet.

"Because I want to see the place where my mother died," I replied firmly. "I know it might sound morbid, but"—I glanced at my grandfather—"I was there when she died, wasn't I?"

Geoffrey sighed and covered his eyes with his right hand. "You have every right to see it, but I am sure you can understand that I don't want to take you there. I have not set foot in the boathouse since…since the day it happened." His voice was hoarse and broken. "Why you should want to…" His voice tailed off and he pushed his wheelchair away from the table. "If you will all excuse me, I have some business to attend to." He wheeled himself out of the room without saying another word, or looking at me.

Olivia flashed a look of dark hatred at me as she got up and followed him out of the room. Charlotte made excuses, Cole said he had to get to his office, and Ginny didn't say anything before she fled, leaving Costa and me alone in the dining room.

"Well, I certainly know how to clear a room," I said to him lightly, trying to make a joke of it. "I suppose it was insensitive…"

"You've certainly got them on their heels," Costa replied, raising his eyebrows, but he didn't sound either angry or disappointed with me—he seemed more amused than anything else. He dabbed at his mouth with his napkin. "And it's kind of fun to see. The Legendre family always gets things their own way, and always have, so it's nice to see the stuffing getting knocked out of them every once in a while." His green eyes danced with merriment. "And Lord knows I've been on the receiving end of their arrogance enough times. Let me guess— Jerry Channing told you?"

"Jerry," I said, "is the only person in Louisiana who's told me anything." I shook my head. "I don't want to hurt anyone, and I don't want to cause trouble. That's not why I'm here. But nobody tells me anything." I met his eyes and felt my stomach flip. I closed my eyes. *He's too good-looking for his own good.* "I'm sure you can understand how odd this all is for me. I don't know anyone in my own family. I didn't even know how my own mother died—let alone that I was there when it happened." I took a deep breath. "It's been an interesting couple of days, to say the least."

Costa got up and walked back over to the sideboard, refilling his coffee cup. "If you want to see the boathouse, I'll take you out there," he said, turning and leaning back against the sideboard. He was wearing a gold pullover with *LSU* sewn on over his heart in purple letters. His white shorts clung tightly to his strong legs. Veins bulged in both arms. "I'm off today, got nothing to do except sit around here inside while it rains." He smiled at me. "Come on, I'll grab some umbrellas and take you down there." He walked to the door, before hesitating. "Are you sure you're going to be all right, seeing the place where it happened?" He lowered his voice. "What if—what if you remember?"

"I don't know," I replied honestly, "but I guess we'll find out once we get there."

"Is that what you want? To remember?"

"I don't know what I want anymore." As soon as I said the words I knew they were true. I wasn't sure of anything anymore.

He nodded and disappeared, returning a few moments later with two enormous purple and gold umbrellas. He handed me one and gestured for me to follow him to the French doors at the other end of the dining room. He unlatched them and we stepped through.

The rain was pouring down from a grayish-black sky. There were puddles on the veranda, and periodically the wind in blew spray from the rain, despite the roof. I shivered involuntarily and stepped away from him as he opened his umbrella. I took a deep breath and did the same, raising it overhead just as another gust of wind tried to rip it out of my hands.

"Hold tight," he shouted over the roar of the wind and started down the brick steps to the walkway.

I followed him, fighting to hold on to the umbrella. The wind was making the Spanish moss sway where it hung from the branches of the enormous live oaks. The branches themselves swayed in the wind. Lightning flashed in the distance, followed by a deafening roar of thunder. The brick path was slightly raised above the grass on either side of it, and the grass appeared to be sinking beneath water. My calves and feet were getting soaked, but at least the path wasn't underwater—at least not yet. Puddles were forming in low spots, where the ground beneath the brick had sunken, and we stepped around them. I followed him down a path through the well-manicured lawn. We walked past the museum and the restaurant and the house where Charlotte and Cole lived, the guest buildings. The wind kept trying to tear the umbrella out of my hands every once in a while, but we kept walking. I kept my head down, watching his wet calves and shoes as he walked in front of me. Finally, after we walked for what seemed like hours, the paved path turned into a dirt path running with water and mud. He stepped over onto the wet grass and I did the same. I looked up and could see a pond and a weather-beaten building at the end of a dock leading out into the center of the pond. The rain was beating a steady pattern on the rusted tin roof of the boathouse as we walked out onto the dock. He fitted a key into the padlock and opened the door, then switched on a light.

It looked like no one had been inside the structure in years. There were no boats, although there was a place alongside the dock for a boat to moor. "In the olden days," Costa said, closing his umbrella and shaking the water from it, "they used to have a speedboat and a couple of pirogues for fishing." He gestured to the mouth of the pond. "That bayou runs all the way out to the swamp, and it's pretty deep the whole way. There's all kinds of wildlife in the swamp, of course—you can hunt duck and pheasant or fish, if you'd rather." He shrugged. "Me and some of the locals fish out there—I buy their fish from them to serve in the restaurant. Catfish, bass, you name it, you can catch it out there. And fresh is always better." He gave me his catlike smile again and squatted down on his haunches, the muscles in his legs flexing.

"Yes," I replied over the sound of the rain on the roof. It was strangely soothing, and out the end I could see the rain striking the murky pond surface. I don't know what I was expecting, but after my reaction to the red glass mask the day before, I was expecting more than nothing, which was what I was getting from the boathouse interior. I walked to the end of the dock and saw the flash of a fish just below the surface. The water...it was definitely the water I'd seen in my vision or memory or whatever the hell it was I'd had in the museum. I closed my eyes and once again could see the mask falling in slow motion, the roaring sound that hurt my ears and made me wince—

"So, I understand you had an awkward moment with my wife yesterday," Costa said. He sounded amused.

I started. I'd been so lost in my own mind I hadn't noticed him coming up beside me, and I almost lost my balance and fell into the water. *How had I not noticed?* I wondered, his presence was so strong right there beside me. I could smell his breath, the Mennen Speed Stick he'd used under his arms, the strong musky male scent emanating from his body beneath the clean odors of soap and shampoo and other lightly scented body products. The raw male power from his strong body was overwhelming, and he grabbed me by the arms to steady me and keep me from tumbling into the water. His hands were scorching hot on my skin, and I felt an electric charge, like I'd somehow been struck by lightning.

"Steady there," he said, letting go and giving me a gentle smile.

"Thanks." I shook my head. *You can't have him, you don't want him, stop wanting things you can't have. He's married to your cousin, and remember—he lied to you about everything. That night together meant nothing to him. How many others has he spent the night with, given a fake name and number to? He's just another in the long list of guys you've wanted that you can't have, so don't make a fucking fool out of yourself.*

Again.

"Didn't mean to startle you," he went on, sitting on the edge so that his legs dangled over the water. "And there's no need to feel weird about Ginny and me, you know? Ginny's Ginny and that isn't going to change." He sighed, his enormous chest rising and falling.

I sat down myself next to him. I had a million questions I wanted answered but didn't have the right to ask. I wanted to know if he loved her, why he put up with her faithlessness, if she knew about the men—but then I could also hear Jerry's voice in my head, mocking my prudishness, my belief that there was no greater crime you could commit against your partner than cheating.

"It must seem strange to you," he said, looking out over the water. "Sometimes it seems strange to me, too. I wake up and I wonder, *What am I doing married to this woman?* But Ginny is a good woman, a good wife, a good friend." He gave me that dazzling smile again. "And I am busy, you know, with the restaurant…she gets bored. And you know, I prefer men."

"Well aware," I replied.

He had the decency to blush. "Her grandfather was—is—supposed to give her more control over the running of the restaurant, but he can't seem to let go. It's to be expected, but everything about the restaurant is a battle for me." He drew his two thick black eyebrows together. "Getting anything changed on the menu, trying to do something different, something besides the tired old Louisiana food he always insists the guests come to eat...But maybe more guests would come if we gave them something else to eat? Ginny agrees with me, but between running my kitchen and staying on top of everything there I don't have time to fight battles with the old man." He shrugged his big shoulders. "Your grandfather."

"He's a stranger," I admitted. "All of you are."

He put his big hand on my knee, and I felt that jolt again. I closed my eyes, took a deep breath, and pushed the feelings aside as he said, "We are not all as crazy as we seem." He glanced back out toward the pond. "The storm is passing. We should head back." He got to his feet and I did the same.

He didn't go back to the house with me, instead telling me he had some things to check out in the kitchen, day off or no day off.

I watched him go, standing under my dripping umbrella as the sun came out from behind the clouds. *You're making a fool of yourself,* I chided myself again. *He's off-limits. Get over yourself.*

I walked by myself back to the house. The air felt lighter and smelled fresher than it had before. Florida was much the same—it was always cooler and less humid after a rain, until the heat started climbing and the water started evaporating back into the air again. I entered the house through the French doors into the dining room, but the house was strangely empty. I didn't see anyone as I walked through the hallway to the main staircase, not even a maid. The house was also weirdly silent—like there wasn't another living soul inside the house. I reached the top of the stairs and was about to head to my bedroom when I realized I still had the umbrella in my hand. I turned and started down the stairs again.

I was on the third step when someone shoved me from behind, in the center of my back.

And I started falling.

CHAPTER EIGHT

I remember reading—I don't remember where—that everyone has a fear of some sort of falling; whether it's falling in love, falling from a great height, falling from grace—falling is a basic human fear. When I was a little boy, I had a recurring nightmare that I was bouncing on a trampoline. I bounced higher and higher, laughing with joy as I flew up into the air, twisting and flipping and having a wonderful time until I bounced so high that the trampoline far below me was the size of a postage stamp, almost so small that I could barely see it. Then the joy of bouncing would turn into absolute, stark terror. I always remained at the apex of the bounce, paused in terror high up in the air, until gravity's inevitable pull grasped me and my descent began, gathering speed as I fell through the air, my eyes clenched closed as I visualized myself hitting the trampoline with such great force that the springs would snap and I would crash into the ground.

I always woke up, gasping, my heart pounding, right before I landed on the trampoline.

I stopped having the dream after I became a teenager, but it was something I never forgot—that horrible feeling of being paused so high up in the air as the upward momentum began to slow before gravity began the pull back to earth.

That was how it felt in the instant after I felt the hands shove me at the top of the stairs, as I lost my footing and fell forward—that eerie, weird pause when time seemed to stand still, as though I was floating in the air. I could see, in that strange moment of frozen time, every edge of every polished mahogany stair, jutting out like serrated teeth in an almost row before finally ending at the wide expanse of polished hardwood at the very foot of the staircase. The very air seemed to stand still—

—and then time unfroze and my chest hit a step with great force, my head snapping forward and my forehead cracking on a lower step, and my vision blurred as I catapulted down the stairs, rolling over and over, an elbow cracking against wood here, a knee there, my head again hitting with a thud, and stars dancing before my crazed eyes as I revolved, far too fast for my eyes to focus as body part after body part connected in an endless cacophony of pain as I kept falling, as the few seconds it took me to go the entire distance from the second floor to the first stretched into an agonizing eternity, until finally, stunned, I came to rest on my back on the hallway floor.

Dazed, I lay there for a moment, unable to move, unable to think, my eyes unable to focus on anything except for shades of gray and dancing, cartwheeling yellow stars.

Vaguely I became aware that someone was near me, kneeling perhaps. I caught the scent of perfume—I didn't recognize it but it smelled expensive, like something from the duty-free shop at the airport. I tried to move my head but it ached so much I closed my eyes and an involuntary moan escaped my lips.

I heard a female voice over the throbbing in my head ask, "Are you all right?"

I forced my eyes open. The light seemed to hurt. Colors were blurry and objects distorted. I knew the voice but when I tried to turn my head to see her, the pain in my head intensified so much that my vision blurred again. I closed my eyes and moaned.

My head was aching but the pain seemed to be dulling a bit. The problem was my brain was getting so many messages of pain from so many different parts of my body—ribs, elbows, knees, shoulders, shins, back—that it couldn't process anything. My brain was on pain overload.

"Are you all right?" the female voice said again, more concerned this time.

I opened my eyes and focused on the ceiling. It was painted white, and there was a angry yellow water stain almost directly above me in the shape of France. Or was it Spain?

Even *thinking* hurt.

"I...I think so," I managed to croak out as the grayness in my head began to clear. "What happened?"

"You fell down the stairs."

Wincing, I managed to turn my head to look at my aunt Olivia. Her face was white and pinched, her lips a taut straight line, her eyes wide and frightened. Her tongue darted out and ran over her bottom lip.

"Don't try to move," she commanded, and in the periphery of my vision—*that's good, your vision is clearing*—I could see a woman in a maid's uniform, a woman I didn't recognize, running down the hallway toward us with a white first-aid kit clutched in her hands. "You need to be sure you didn't hurt your back." Her voice, while still firm, was softer and gentler as she said this. She reached out and touched my forehead with her fingertips, grazing them against my temple. "You may also have concussion—there's a bruise here and it looks like you're getting a lump."

I tried to sit up, but she firmly pressed against my shoulders to keep me prone on the floor. "I said don't move," she said, more sharply than before. "Shawna, give me that kit and call an ambulance, please."

"No, no ambulance," I croaked out again, but this time my throat didn't hurt, and despite the slight ringing still in my ears my voice didn't sound hollow and faraway like before. "I think...I think I'm okay." I bent my legs and moved my arms slowly without getting up. "I don't think anything's broken." I braced myself and inhaled deeply. There was an ache in my ribs, but breathing wasn't painful so I hadn't broken any. Maybe they were just bruised. "Maybe some bruises. And some aspirin?"

Olivia took the first-aid kit from the maid—Shawna—and ordered her to get me a glass of water. She set the kit down and opened it.

"Should I call for an ambulance?" Shawna asked, her voice timid.

I looked up into her concerned face and gave her what I hoped was a reassuring smile. "I don't need an ambulance," I replied. I started to sit up. I closed my eyes as a wave of dizziness swept through my brain, but I managed to do it without more pain. I exhaled.

"You have a sizable lump on our forehead, and I can see one on the back of your head," Olivia pointed out evenly. "I'm worried that you might have a concussion, and those are dangerous." Her lips compressed into a tight line. "Maybe not an ambulance, but I think we should take you to the parish hospital for X-rays, at the very least. Just to be on the safe side. You won't object to that, surely?"

"Fine. Whatever. As long as I don't have to drive." What I really wanted to do was go back to bed and lie down, but I could tell she wasn't going to take no for an answer.

The corners of her mouth twitched in what might have been an attempt to smile. She tore open an alcohol wipe and rubbed it over some raw skin on my left shin. "I'll just clean those open wounds first," she said as she tore open another. The alcohol stung, and I tried unsuccessfully not to wince. Shawna pressed a glass of water into my hand and a couple of blue tablets. I washed them down with the cold water and winced again as Olivia applied yet another alcohol wipe to my knee. She crumpled it into a ball and handed the trash to Shawna before getting to her feet. "Can you stand on your own?" she asked.

"You'd better help me," I replied, gritting my teeth as I gave her one hand and tried to get my feet underneath me. My left knee screamed a bit, but I managed to get to my feet without collapsing or any dizziness, which was a good sign. I took a few tentative steps, and the knee was sore and so was my right ankle, but neither seemed to be swelling, and I seemed to be okay. My back and my neck both felt fine, just a little bit sore.

Or maybe it was just the aspirin kicking in.

She helped me down the hallway and out the front door. "I'll get the car," she said, removing a set of keys from the pockets of her long jean skirt. "You have your insurance card?"

"In my wallet." I nodded, leaning against one of the enormous round columns on the gallery.

I watched her hurry down the front steps and out to the parking lot. The lights of a gray Mercedes blinked on and off as she approached it, and within a matter of moments she'd brought the car around to the foot of the steps. The passenger-side window moved down. "Can you make it down the steps?" she called, concern on her face.

I gritted my teeth and nodded. There were no railings, and there were a dozen or so steps for me to navigate. I moved as carefully and slowly as I could, wincing each time my weight came down on one of my feet as pain shot through my head. *I'm going to need painkillers,* I thought as I slid into the passenger seat of the Mercedes and clicked my seat belt closed.

"I can never get used to the gates always being open," she commented as she steered the car down the driveway toward them. "They were always closed when I was growing up. I hate having to have security guards."

"I can't imagine," I said as she waved at the guard shack.

"You can't," she agreed as she stopped at the foot of the driveway, where it bisected the river road. On the opposite side was the towering levee, with grass and flowers grown into the side. "It's like we're prisoners in our own home." She turned right and the Mercedes got up to speed so quickly it was almost like flying.

Put my old secondhand Toyota Camry to shame, that's for sure.

"The tour days are the worst," she went on. "Of course they don't have access to the wings where our rooms are—they only tour the main part of the house and the grounds, but it always makes me feel like we're whoring out our home."

"Then why have the tours?" I asked, wincing as she hit a pothole and my head jostled to one side. "Isn't there enough income from the restaurant and the museum and the overnight guests and so forth to keep the place going?"

"There's never enough money," she replied. "You have no idea how much it costs to keep Chambord operating. We have to take every penny we can squeeze from the tourists."

I glanced at her out of the corner of my eye. Was that her way of telling me there was no inheritance for me to pin my hopes on? I thought about telling her all I wanted out of the Legendre legacy was maybe some help with my school expenses, but decided not to. She'd taken a clear dislike to me from the moment I arrived, and asking for any kind of financial help wouldn't make things any better.

She didn't speak again, which was fine with me. I wasn't sure what to make of my aunt Olivia, but this concern and kindness in taking me to the emergency room couldn't be mistaken for a softening of her attitude toward me. She'd made it very clear she'd hated my mother, and she wasn't exactly overflowing with the milk of human kindness for me, either.

The drive only took about fifteen minutes, and before I knew it we were driving over a small bridge with rusty trestles and heading into a small town. She took a right and pulled into a parking lot at a small hospital just after the city limits sign: *Avignon, Population 14,321.* There weren't many cars in the parking lot, and the hospital itself was a three-story building of cement and brick in that unmistakably hideous style that was enormously popular for public buildings in the 1950s. She turned off the engine and unbuckled her seat belt. "They can handle emergencies here," she said without a smile, "but if it's anything serious they'll have to send you to either New Orleans or Baton Rouge."

My head was still throbbing but pretty much the rest of my body was doing much better. There was some residual soreness, but I didn't think anything was sprained, broken, or even out of socket. "I don't know, maybe this isn't necessary," I said slowly. "I'm feeling better other than a headache."

"You don't get to decide. You might have a concussion," she replied, opening her car door and swinging her legs out. She walked briskly across the parking lot. I followed her, moving slower because of the aches. She went up the sidewalk and through the electric doors for the emergency room. By the time I made it through the doors she was explaining to the duty nurse what had happened. As I made it up to the counter, I heard her say I'd fallen down the stairs.

I remembered the feeling of being shoved from behind.

I'd been *pushed.*

Someone at Chambord had tried to kill me.

A wave of nausea swept through me and I could feel myself start trembling, but I forced it to stop before the nurse, whose name tag read *Becky Stroud,* could notice. She handed me a clipboard in exchange for my insurance card and driver's license. "Fill these out," she said with a courteous smile, "and we'll get you taken care of."

I sat down in an uncomfortable chair with scarred wooden armrests to fill out the requisite paperwork. I was on autopilot as the cheap pen Nurse Becky had given my flew over the form, filling in spaces and checking boxes when necessary (*mumps* no, *measles* no, *pneumonia* yes, *whooping cough* no), the dull throbbing continuing in my head while my mind tried to wrap itself around the truth that my fall had been very deliberate.

Someone tried to kill me. It might have even been Olivia.

I glanced at her out of the corner of my eye. She was seated next to me, her legs crossed at the ankles, reading an old issue of the *New Yorker* she'd taken out of her enormous black leather purse with the Chanel logo clasp.

Where was she when I was pushed?

I tried to remember the hallway at the foot of the stairs, but I couldn't remember if she'd been down there. The upstairs hallway had been empty, that much I was sure about. But I hadn't been paying attention—I'd been lost in my own thoughts as I started down the stairs. *Wool-gathering, your head in the clouds,* my parents had always said when I was lost in my imagination.

But I hadn't imagined the feel of the hands in the center of my back.

What I need to do is have her drive me to the goddamned airport in New Orleans and go home, get the hell away from Chambord and forget I'm related to these people.

But my natural stubbornness rose up. *The hell I will, I*

belong here just as much as any of them. I just have to be careful, that's all—and not trust any of them. They won't run me off.

There was no point in going to the police. I had nothing to tell them.

I'd reached the part on the form where it asked about family history.

"Do we have a family history of heart disease?" I asked, tapping the clipboard with the pen. "Dad's family didn't."

Olivia didn't look up from her magazine. "No."

"You know, I've been filling these forms out incorrectly all my life," I said casually. "What about cancer? Stroke?" I started rattling off the hereditary diseases rapidly, like I was firing a machine gun.

Olivia closed the magazine and held out her hand. "Give it to me," she said.

I handed it to her and she checked off a few boxes—*kidney disease, diabetes, blindness*—and handed it back to me. I was about to ask her another question when Nurse Becky came toward us, pushing a wheelchair. I handed her the clipboard, which she slipped under her arm, and sat down in the chair. Olivia rose and walked alongside as I was wheeled back to an examination room. "Dr. Lippert will be with you shortly," Nurse Becky said with a faint smile as she left the room.

Olivia cleared her throat. "You gave me quite a fright, you know," she said softly. "When I heard...when I heard you fall, it reminded me—" She closed her eyes and wrapped her arms around herself, shivering. She took a deep breath. "It reminded me of when my mother died. Your grandmother. She fell down those very same stairs."

"I thought—" I tried to remember exactly what Jerry had said. "I had the impression she had a long illness."

"That was the irony." Olivia lifted her shoulders in a slight shrug. "She had breast cancer. But just a few days earlier she'd been told she was cancer-free, after several years of fighting it. The surgeries, the chemo"—she shuddered—"and then to trip on a staircase she must have gone up and down thousands of times. I heard her fall. I will never forget the sound of her scream, the thumping. Her neck was broken. So when you fell, my heart went into my throat."

Before I could question her, the doctor came bustling into the room. She was older, maybe in her late fifties, with streaks of gray in her brown hair. She was short and stocky but had a pleasant face that clearly was used to smiling. "So, I hear you took a tumble?"

"He fell down the staircase," Olivia said before I could say anything.

"Did you see what happened?" The doctor, whose name tag read *Norma Lippert, MD,* asked. "Can you hop up on this table for me?"

"He fell down the staircase," Olivia repeated as I hopped up as instructed. I glanced over at my aunt. Her face was set, her forehead wrinkled, her arms folded in front of her.

I let the doctor shine a light into my eyes and ask me a barrage of questions. She examined the bumps on my head, and had me wheeled off for X-rays, which I submitted to complacently. Olivia wasn't in the examination room when they wheeled me back in. After a few moments Dr. Lippert returned with a smile. "Okay, nothing broken, nothing out of place. You don't seem to have a concussion or any skull damage, but if you start to have double vision, or start throwing up, come right back here." She handed me a prescription. "This is for some painkillers. Take them if you need them. And come back in after a couple of days for a follow-up, just to be on the safe side." She smiled. "And be careful on the stairs from now on."

I bit my tongue as Nurse Becky wheeled me back out into the waiting room. Olivia stood up, folding her magazine and shoving it back into her purse. "You'll live?" she asked, her face expressionless.

I nodded as Nurse Becky pushed me out the electric doors. "I'll get the car," Olivia said, pulling the keys from her purse and heading out to the parking lot. A few moments later I was in the car. "Since we're in town I might as well run some errands, since you aren't dying. I'll drop you off at the drugstore to get the prescription filled. There's a coffee shop where you can wait for me when you're finished there." She backed out of the spot and drove out of the parking lot.

"I wish I'd known my grandmother," I said as she turned in the direction of the town.

"It was wrong of your father to take you away and keep you from her all those years," Olivia replied. "I expected better from your father. I thought he was a better man than that."

"He was a good man," I retorted, as the brief window of closeness I felt for her slammed shut immediately.

"He should have never married your mother," she said darkly.

"What was my mother like?"

"Like?" She laughed bitterly. "Genevieve was spoiled from the day she was born. She was a little princess, and we all existed simply to serve her and make her happy. She was our parents' favorite, almost from the day she came home from the hospital." She stopped at a light. "We all spoiled her, though— it wasn't just Mom and Dad. If we'd only known what the spoiling would turn her into…" She whistled. "Well, what she became."

"What did she become?"

"Selfish. All she cared about was herself." Olivia spat the words out as she pulled into a parking spot in front of a Rexall

Pharmacy. There was a CC's Coffee Shop next door to it. "As long as she had what she wanted, she didn't care about who she had to hurt to get it."

She was in love with Dylan, I remembered Jerry telling me, *but Dylan loved my mother.* "Is this about Dylan? You let your feelings for a man interfere with your feelings for your sister?"

"Sister." Her face twisted with contempt. "Genevieve didn't have family feelings toward me, so why should I have cared for her?" She was gripping the steering wheel so tightly her knuckles turned white. She turned and glared at me. "She was your mother but you never knew her," she hissed. "And if her idea of being a mother was anything like her idea of being a sister, you're lucky she shot herself."

I was so shocked I just stared at her.

And the anger visibly drained out of her, like a punctured balloon, and she sagged against the steering wheel. "It isn't your fault," she muttered, "you just look so much like her..." When she looked at me again, there were tears in her eyes. "Why did you come here? Why don't you go back home, where you belong, and leave us all alone?"

Wounded, I opened my car door. My voice shaking, I replied, "Because I stupidly thought it might be nice to get to know the only blood relatives I have," before slamming the door closed and going into the pharmacy. I dropped off the prescription and went into the coffee shop. My hands were trembling, so rather than ordering, I went into the bathroom and turned on the cold water spigot. I splashed the water into my face while I tried to get my heart rate and breathing back under control, to stop the shaking. I looked at myself in the mirror—the ugly purplish-yellow bruise on my forehead where it must have hit a step, the fat lip, the dark circles under my eyes, the red streaks in the whites of my eyes. *You just need to get to the airport in New Orleans and get on the next plane out of here.* One of the benefits of working for an airline was the ability to get on a flight at any time as long as there was a seat. *Just head back to the house, pack everything up, get Charlotte or someone to drive me back to the airport. They can all go to hell—I don't need them. Then put the damned house in New Orleans up for sale. I didn't come here to be insulted, or to have someone try to kill me…*

I couldn't help it. I started laughing.

Drama queen.

Did someone shove me down the stairs? That was how I remembered it, and I would have been willing to swear at the time I'd felt someone give me a good push. But now, now I wasn't so sure. And what was I going to do about it, even if it was what happened? I couldn't exactly go to the police and say, "I think someone pushed me down the stairs at Chambord." They'd think I'd lost my mind.

Maybe the Legendre family hadn't exactly welcomed me with open arms. My aunt resented my mother—maybe had even hated her, from the way she talked about her. My first cousin, my only cousin, was in some kind of weird marriage and blew hot and cold when it came to me. But none of that really mattered in the long run. My grandfather wanted me there, and as long as he wanted me to stay I wasn't going to let the others chase me back to Florida.

I dried off my face and walked back out to the counter where I ordered a cappuccino to go. There wasn't anyone else in the coffee shop, other than a tall young man in a deputy's uniform sitting at a booth in the back corner, scowling at the screen of a laptop computer. Once I had the cappuccino, I walked back to the pharmacy, paid for my prescription, and went back out to the sidewalk and took a look around.

Avignon looked like a nice enough town. There was

a town hall down the road, and any number of small shops, mostly antique stores, from the looks of things, and some other businesses—dry cleaners, Laundromat, diner, toy store, bookstore—the usual small-town type storefronts. But just on the other side of the dry cleaners I saw the sign for the *Avignon News.*

I had my phone, so if Olivia came looking for me at the coffee shop and didn't find me, she could call me. If worse came to worst, I could also catch a ride back to Chambord with Cole.

I walked down the sidewalk and went into the newspaper offices. "Hello," I said to the older woman painting her fingernails at the receptionist's desk. "Is Cole free?" I asked with a bright smile.

She smiled back at me. "He's in his office. You can go on back." She waved with her hands, and I wasn't sure if she was gesturing for me to go back or drying her nails. I thanked her and walked through the open door into the back hallway. I could see Cole sitting at a desk through an open door at the end of the hallway, typing on a keyboard. He looked up when he saw me coming and smiled.

"Come in, have a seat," he said, not getting up but turning his attention from the computer to me. "This is a pleasant surprise." He frowned. "What happened to your forehead?"

I reached up with my free hand and patted the place where the bruise was. "I tripped and fell down the stairs," I said with a self-deprecating smile. "I'm kind of clumsy. You can only imagine how embarrassed I was. Olivia insisted on taking me to the emergency room for X-rays." I shook my head. "She's running some errands and dropped me off at the coffee shop, but when I got out of the car I saw your office down here and thought I'd come in here and ask for your help with something."

"Anything."

"Do you have back issues here?" I forced a smile on my face. "I'd kind of like to go back and read what was in the paper…" I took a breath. "About my mother's death."

"Are you sure you want to do that, Heath?" he asked, taking off his glasses and placing them on the desk. "It might reopen some old wounds."

"I don't even remember her, Cole," I replied. "I didn't even know what she looked like until I got here." I took a drink from my cappuccino. "It's amazing how little there is about her on the Internet."

He smiled faintly. "Yes, I'd never really thought about that, but I suppose that would be true." He spun his chair and rolled over to the big bookcase in the corner behind his desk and pulled out a very thick bound book which he handed across the desk to me. I tried taking it with one hand but it was heavy and I almost dropped it. "That is the index of all issues of the *News* from the 1960s through the year 2000," he said. "Every mention of your mother during her lifetime in our paper would be listed there." He got up and led me out of his office and opened a door, which contained a staircase. "Up those stairs is the morgue, where copies of every issue of the paper are kept, in order. No one is allowed to take anything out of there, and I do expect everyone who accesses the archive to put everything back where it goes. Can I trust you?"

"Of course." I started to climb the stairs, but on the second step I turned back. "Cole, is it true my grandmother's diaries have disappeared? Jerry Channing mentioned yesterday he was looking for them."

Cole stared at me for a moment, then burst out laughing. "Nina's diaries? They're hardly missing." He shook his head. "Nina always kept them locked up in her strongbox while she was alive, but after she died—I believe Geoffrey has them in his bedroom and reads them periodically to feel closer to her."

"But why would Jerry think they were missing?"

"I can't imagine Geoffrey would hand his wife's diaries over to someone who intended to write a book about the family, a book that might not necessarily be complimentary to the Legendres, and say, *Have fun!*—do you?"

That made sense—certainly a lot more sense than Jerry's theories about what happened to them. I said thank you and started climbing the stairs. The second floor of the building was just a large open space, with racks and racks of long boxes with dates written on labels on the front of them. I sat down with the index book and opened it up, flipping through until I reached the page where I found my mother's name. I picked up a piece of scratch paper and made notes of the issues in which she appeared, and the page numbers. There were surprisingly few entries, and from the dates given with the issues I assumed they included her birth notice, high school graduation, debutante ball, marriage, my birth, and her death. I checked the papers to make certain, and I was right. A few of the dates I couldn't quite place included her being named homecoming queen at Redemption Parish High School, and another was an announcement of a gallery show for her paintings held in New Orleans. I made a note of the address, the name of the gallery, and its owner. The wedding picture of her and my father took me by surprise. They both looked so incredibly young, and they looked so happy.

And neither had any idea of the tragedy that would end their marriage in a little over four years.

The final article was, of course, the death announcement.

There was no mention of how she died, or what caused her death, just that it was sudden and there would be no memorial service, per her wishes. I paged through the yellowed paper just to make sure, but there was nothing whatsoever about Dylan's death. I opened the index and looked him up, but as far as the *Avignon News* was concerned, Dylan had never existed.

I didn't even know what he looked like.

I had just finished putting the newspapers away when my cell phone began ringing. I pulled it out and grimaced at the name on the screen. "Aunt Olivia."

"You aren't at the coffee shop."

"I'm actually at the newspaper office just down the street," I replied cheerfully. "I was looking my mother up in the archives."

There was a sharp intake of breath, and after a brief pause she said, "I must apologize for earlier. You must understand I was very worried about you."

Were you really? "I'll come meet you at the coffee shop," I said, heading down the stairs. I dropped the book off and thanked Cole before exiting.

Olivia was standing on the sidewalk in front of the coffee shop, talking to the young deputy I'd seen earlier. Before I reached them, he touched his forehead and walked the other direction. When she saw me, she frowned. "You shouldn't spend time with Cole. He cannot be trusted."

"What do you mean?" I asked as I got into the car.

"Cole..." She started the car and backed out of the spot. "My father bought the newspaper for him, you know. He wasn't always the owner."

"Is it because he kept the truth about my mother and Dylan out of the papers?" I asked. "Was that his reward?"

"I don't know," she replied as she drove across the little bridge on the way out of town. "My father doesn't consult me on those things. He never has."

"Did you hate my mother because of Dylan?"

She laughed. "Dylan. Dylan wasn't worth hating my sister over." She glanced at me out of the corner of her eyes. "I thought I loved him…but in the end he wasn't worth my love. Or Genevieve's."

"Was she going to leave with him that day he came back for her?" I asked softly.

"If she was going to leave, why did she take the gun with her?" She gave a slight shrug of her shoulders. "This all happened so long ago, why can't you just leave it alone?" We passed through the big gate. "You're very young, Heath, and I've maybe not been the friendliest aunt to you since you arrived here. I didn't want you to come. I was against it from the beginning." She pulled into a parking spot in front of the house. "I didn't want any of this dredged up again. Let the dead rest, Heath." She sighed. "Our wounds have only recently begun to finally heal from that horrible day nineteen years ago. Please don't tear the scabs off just yet."

Chapter Nine

W hat are you reading?"
    I looked up and smiled at my cousin Ginny. I held up the book I was reading so she could read the spine.

"*Garden District Gothic,*" she said slowly, sitting down in the wicker chair on the other side of the table from me. "Jerry's book. I thought you had already read it."

"I have, it's just been a while." I placed a bookmark in the book and snapped it closed. After Olivia had brought me back to Chambord, I'd gone into the library to look for something to read. Oddly enough, Jerry's book was sitting on the table there, so I picked it up and went back to my room with it. I'd called down to the kitchen to have some iced tea sent up and had gone out onto the gallery to enjoy the cool breeze from the river and reread the book. "I figured since he's writing a book about my mother, I should probably reacquaint myself with his writing style."

"And what do you think of it, now that it actually will have some impact on your life?"

I glanced over at her, but there was no malice on her face. She looked genuinely interested. "I don't know," I said after a few moments. I wasn't lying to her, either. I honestly wasn't sure what to think. When I'd originally read *Garden District Gothic* back when I was a teenager, the book had already been out for almost ten years. I didn't want to admit to Ginny that I'd read the book for the first time after I'd found out that the woman I'd always thought of as my mother was really my stepmother. I'd gone to the library and looked up every book I could find on Louisiana, and New Orleans. The librarian had recommended it to me; she said it was one of the most popular books ever written about New Orleans. I was vaguely familiar with the case Jerry had written about in the book; the murder of child beauty queen Delilah Metoyer was one of the most famous unsolved cases in the country, and the fact Jerry's book was a perennial seller was proof that there was still a lot of interest in the case. Every so often, on the anniversary of the murder, one of the news networks or a tabloid would do a retrospective.

It was impossible not to know who Delilah Metoyer was, unless you didn't own a television and you never went into a grocery store.

I'd been fascinated by the book the first time I'd read it. I hadn't been able to put it down. It never ceased to amaze me how Jerry got all those New Orleans society people to actually give him permission to quote them, not just about the case itself but about other things you'd think they wouldn't want put into a book. Rereading it now, I could hear the words being said in his voice as I read along, and I was becoming more and more leery of his proposed book about my mother's death.

"You know he's going to write about you," Ginny said, pouring herself a glass of tea from the sweating glass pitcher on the table between us. "It's kind of why I've been keeping my distance from him since I found out about the book." She sipped the tea. "Mmm, that's good." She leaned back in the chair and crossed her legs. "I mean, it's been so long since it happened no one even thinks about it anymore. Olivia says even at the time no one really did, because of all the publicity about the Metoyer case." She lifted her glass to me ironically. "Whoever killed Delilah Metoyer did our family a big favor."

I made a face. "Really, Ginny?"

"I know, it's in poor taste, but that doesn't make it any less true, my dear cousin." She sighed and peered at me. "That's a rather nasty bruise on your forehead. I understand you had an accident." Her voice didn't sound concerned in the least. There was actually an undertone of amusement, as though she liked the idea of me tumbling down the stairs.

"I can't tell you how touched I am by your concern for me," I replied sarcastically. "But whatever Olivia told you is wrong. It wasn't an accident. Someone pushed me. Someone deliberately tried to injure me—maybe even tried to kill me."

Ginny's jaw dropped, and I didn't think she was acting. She was honestly shocked. "But why? Why would you think anyone would push you?" she choked out the words, waving her hand as a horsefly buzzed around her head.

I raised my eyebrows. "Olivia said that was how our grandmother died, falling down that very same staircase."

"You don't think it's a coincidence? Olivia said you tripped."

"I didn't trip. I was pushed." I looked out over the lawns. "Whether you believe me or not doesn't make it any less true. I thought it might have been you."

She gasped. "Why would you think that? Why would you think I—or anyone—would want to hurt you?"

I shrugged, probably more delighted at wrong-footing her than I should have been. "You tell me, Ginny. I don't really know any of you all that well, and I *know* I was pushed. I didn't imagine it. I can't prove it, but I know."

Her face was grim. "I don't think you're making it up."

So it wasn't her. Or she's playing me. "Besides, outside of Geoffrey, it's not like anyone is exactly glad I'm here."

My gaze never wavered. "Everyone seems determined to make sure I don't feel welcome. If I had a dime for every time Olivia's told me to go back to Florida, I could quit my job. I mean, I get it—she hated my mother and I look like her, so I'm an unpleasant reminder, but it doesn't exactly make me feel good, you know?"

"Yes, I can see that, but don't you think you're being a little dramatic?"

"You've not exactly been friendly," I replied. "Are you afraid I want to inherit Chambord, or Geoffrey's money? I'm not interested in that." I took a breath. "I won't lie, it would be nice to have some help with my college expenses so I don't have to work full-time and go to school part-time, but as for Chambord? It's all yours. I'm not interested."

She shook her head. "You're entitled to a share," she said, surprising me—that really wasn't what I was expecting to hear from her. "We all are—you, me, Olivia. We're Grandpa's heirs, and we should inherit equal shares in the estate, if it comes to that." She poured herself a glass of iced tea. "I've always thought—I mean, even before you got in touch with Grandpa—I mean, I remembered you. I was a kid, but I remembered you. All of us did, it's not like your dad grabbed you and ran off to Florida and you ceased to exist to us. I actually thought about you a lot, honestly." She got a faraway look in her eyes. "It would have been nice to have another kid around, you know? I was lonely. And most of the kids at school—I never could be sure if they were really my friends or if it was the Legendre name." She gave me a sad smile. "At least you never had to worry about that. Your friends liked you for you."

But you've never had to really work a day in your life. "So why didn't you reach out to me? You could have skipped the adults and gone directly to me."

She had the decency to blush. "Your mother is a forbidden subject around here, and always has been." She took a deep breath. "I remember the day she died, you know. I was six, or seven, I don't remember which." She looked out over the lawns. "I loved Aunt Genevieve. She never treated me like a child. She was always laughing, always in a good mood, always happy to see me. She was never too busy to play or talk to me, and she was always bringing me presents." She laughed. "I suppose it just goes to show that I could always be bought. I was so jealous of you..."

"What about your mother?"

"My mother? No one's ever asked me that before." She finished her glass and refilled it. "My parents were good parents, I suppose, but I don't know. They weren't very affectionate. I guess they loved each other so much they didn't have time for me. They certainly didn't have any other children, did they?" She gave me a look. "And then, well, they died when I was five. Not much older than you were when your mother died. Has anyone taken you to the cemetery?"

"The cemetery? No."

"No one's shown you your mother's grave?" She looked shocked. "Are you okay to walk, or should we take a cart?"

I pushed myself to my feet and took a deep breath. "Maybe a cart would be smart," I replied. The mild painkillers prescribed had taken the pain away but hadn't made me loopy, which was what the ones I'd used after having my wisdom teeth removed had done.

She popped up out of her seat. "I'll meet you on the back gallery."

I took my time and made sure I had a firm grasp of the railing as I made my way down the staircase where I'd fallen. I breathed a huge sigh of relief when I reached the bottom of the stairs, though, and then walked down the hallway to the

French doors leading out to the back gallery. At the bottom of the stairs Ginny waved to me from behind the wheel of one of the golf carts. She glanced over at me when I slipped into the passenger seat beside her. "Are you okay? You look pale."

I laughed bitterly. "I've been on a bit of an emotional roller coaster the last couple of days, in case you haven't noticed." She put the cart into gear and it jerked into motion. I pointed to my bandaged knee. "Not to mention a trip to the emergency room." I leaned my head back against the headrest and closed my eyes. "And now I'm going to go see my mother's grave for the first time. Forgive me for not being cheerful."

She bit her lower lip. "Sorry, Heath. We're all so wrapped up in the little dramas of our own lives, I guess, we don't ever stop to think about how other people feel, or what they're going through."

"Yeah, well." We were heading down the path past the museum and the guesthouses.

"No, I'm really and truly sorry about how I've been behaving." She laughed. "Costa tells me I'm a selfish bitch, and he's right...I'm spoiled and used to having my own way and not caring what other people think." Her voice sounded melancholy and sad.

"There's something to be said for not caring what other people think," I replied. "Maybe someday I'll get there. But I always want everyone to like me—I guess it's because I've always felt like an outsider because of being gay. I don't know what I was thinking when I came here. I'm just as guilty, I suppose. I thought I would finally feel like I belong somewhere."

She glanced over at me as we passed the last guesthouse. "And we haven't exactly made you feel like you belong, have we?" She turned left onto another path and sped up. Overhead, long beards of Spanish moss hung from enormous live oak branches. I looked back as we went over a hill and no longer could see the main house.

"To be fair, it's not exactly a normal situation for anyone, is it?" I slapped at a mosquito on my calf. "It is what it is, I suppose. It's funny, after I found out about my mom—about Genevieve—whenever I would get in trouble, or whenever I had my feelings hurt, or I was mad at my parents for whatever reason, I used to go into my bedroom and shut the door and pull up the Chambord website and imagine what my family was like. Dad didn't really have any family, and Mom—my stepmother—she had some relatives in Bay City, but they never really felt like family to me. I used to lie in bed and fantasize what it would be like to grow up here at Chambord... fantasies. And so I guess that's what I was thinking when I came here, that all of my dreams were coming true, that I was going to have a family and everything was going to be all right from now on." I sighed. "Fantasies."

To my surprise, she reached over and put her hand on my knee. "I used to do that, too." She laughed. "Something we have in common."

I put my hand down on top of hers. Maybe...maybe Ginny and I could be friends.

The cart went up another rise and once we reached the top I could see the cemetery at the foot of the hill. To its right ran the bayou that also led to the pond where the boathouse was located. It was surrounded by a black wrought-iron fence about four feet high, and there was an enormous gate with a padlock on it at the end of the paved path. There were headstones evenly placed throughout, and several weathered-looking tombs. Enormous marble statues of angels were also placed at intervals throughout, and the largest tomb had two angels facing each other in front of the door, their wings making an arch over it. Two enormous and ancient live oaks, their branches dripping with the gray ringlets of Spanish moss, cast shade over the dark emerald-green grass covering the graves.

Ginny pulled the cart up to the gates and turned off the engine. "This place used to give me nightmares when I was a little girl," she said, getting out and pulling out a ring of keys from the pocket of her shorts. She unlocked the padlock and the chain dropped away, and she opened the gates. I rather expected them to squeal, but the hinges were well oiled and silent. "But the slave cemetery is spookier." She gestured off into the distance. "Those graves are only marked with small flat stones and a name, and it's down by the bayou. When the bayou floods it floods. If and when Chambord is mine"—she glanced over at me—"or ours, I suppose, I want to have the slave cemetery moved to higher ground." She shivered. "They suffered enough in life, you know? Their graves should be treated with more respect."

"I wouldn't have a problem with that," I replied, following her inside the gates.

It was silent there in the cemetery, the only sound the wind whistling through the heavy branches overhead and the buzzing of insects, the humming of cicadas, and the steady chirping of crickets. "Genevieve is in this tomb," Ginny said, leading me to the enormous mausoleum with the angel wings making a canopy over the door. "The tomb looks older than it really is. The original tomb is the one over in that corner. Once it was full, they started burying the family in the ground. But our great-grandfather built this…monstrosity, and it's been where everyone is put ever since." She stroked the door before putting a key into the lock. Her voice broke. "My parents are in here, too."

I rubbed her shoulder. "I'm sorry."

"I was supposed to be with them, you know." She turned and gave me a look full of pain. "But I was getting over the flu.

I cried and cried about being left behind, begged them to take me, but they took the trip without me." She wiped tears out of her eyes. "Their neglect saved my life."

I put my arm around her. "It wasn't your fault."

"I know that—but it doesn't help the way I feel." She gestured to the left. "There's your mother."

I took a deep breath and turned to face the drawer with my mother's name carved in marble on the outside: *Genevieve Melissa Legendre Brandon*. Beneath her name were the dates of her birth and death, and beneath that the words *Daughter Sister Wife Mother.*

I felt the hairs on the back of my neck and my arms stand up as I slowly took the few steps to the stone with my mother's remains behind it. There were two empty space below her, and the stone was about five feet above the ground. "Mother," I whispered, not caring if Ginny heard me. I reached out and touched the stone, tracing her name with my index finger. I felt strangely moved, tears coming up in my eyes. It didn't make sense. I didn't remember her, hadn't even known she'd existed until ten years or so ago, but this overwhelming sadness…I couldn't turn it off. I rested my forehead against the cool marble and closed my eyes, tears trickling as my lids came down—

—and I remembered the feel of my little hand in a bigger one. We were walking fast along the path, and I could see the boathouse in the distance, that's where we were going, and in my other hand was a stuffed lamb, it was my favorite toy and its name was Lambchop, and it was a hot day, stiflingly so, the humidity hanging over us like an oppressive blanket that couldn't be kicked off, and I could tell, even in my childish brain, that she was upset, she wasn't happy, and I wondered if it was me she wasn't happy with—

I opened my eyes, my heart pounding.

Another memory.

I became vaguely aware that Ginny was speaking.

"So, anyway, the day she died…that was a terrible day." I turned and looked at her. She was wringing her hands, her eyes open wide and her face pale in the shadows inside the tomb. "My memories aren't as clear as they should be, but I remember that whole day as being kind of tense. You know how kids can sense something is going on with the adults, even if the adults don't want the kids to know? The kids always do…Anyway, the whole day was, I don't know. I remember my parents were upset about something, and so was Olivia. I walked in on them having a very heated argument, which of course stopped as soon as they saw me. The last thing I remember hearing before they noticed me was my mother saying something about Dylan and Genevieve, that if Dylan ever knew the truth, he would never stop even if it meant tearing the family apart."

I stared at her. "What did she mean by that?"

"I don't know. They stopped talking when they noticed me. I just know they were all upset, and Olivia said that it was up to Genevieve to handle it, and she would handle it however she thought was best, no matter what the cost." She frowned. "Those were her exact words—*no matter what the cost.*"

"And you never asked Olivia what she meant?"

"I told you—the subject was forbidden around here. Anytime Genevieve's name came up, the subject was changed." She gave me a weak smile. "But as I was saying, I never forgot you. You know you used to follow me around, like a puppy dog. You were a very sweet little boy. I was terribly sad when you went away." She shook her head. "You're right, though—I should have reached out to you. I do know that Gram used to write to your father all the time, begging him to bring you back to Chambord, but the letters were always returned unopened.

Grandpa didn't know she was doing that, you know. He would have forbidden it."

"What was she like?"

"Gram?" She sighed. "Gram was one of the kindest and most loving people I've ever known in my life. When she died, it was like a light went out here at Chambord. She never lost her temper, never raised her voice. And they adored each other—Grandpa and Gram, I mean. They had a perfect marriage. I always hoped I'd have one like theirs when I grew up. Instead I married Costa."

As curious as I was about her marriage, I decided not to pursue that. Instead, I asked, "Do you know what happened to Nina's diaries?"

That startled her. She recoiled as though slapped. "Her *diaries*? Wow, I hadn't thought about those in years. How did you know about her diaries?"

"Cole told me about them." I scratched my forehead. "Actually, Jerry Channing was the first to mention them, and then Charlotte's husband mentioned them again this afternoon when I was at the newspaper office."

"What...what were you doing at the newspaper office? And why would Jerry—how would he know about the diaries?"

He hadn't sworn me to secrecy, so I plunged ahead. "Why wouldn't he know about them?" I replied. "And of course he'd want to see them—he's writing a book about my mother's death. What better source could there be than her own mother's diaries?"

"Yes, well. Good luck getting Grandpa to let Jerry look at them." She laughed. "Grandpa isn't exactly thrilled about his book. That can't come as a shock to you—nor could the fact that Grandpa doesn't want all that personal family information exposed in a book. He'd rather die than let Jerry see the diaries." She shook her head. "He doesn't even let us see them, you know. They're locked in his personal safe." She gave me an odd look. "You didn't mention to Costa that you…what you saw in New Orleans yesterday?"

"Of course not. It's none of my business."

She gave me a lazy smile. "That's right, it isn't." She narrowed her eyes and examined the look on my face, which must have made her uncomfortable, because she went on, "Costa and I have an arrangement that suits us both very well." She nonchalantly shrugged. "As long as we both are getting what we want, what business is it of anyone else's?"

She was right, of course—what went on with her and Costa wasn't any of my business. But I couldn't stop wondering about them. Costa seemed like such a nice guy, and he was pretty damned sexy, too. It wasn't any of my business…but my grandmother's diaries kind of were.

She looked around and shivered. "Can we get out of here now? Or do you want to stay? This place—it always gives me the creeps. I can leave the cart for you, if you like."

I shook my head and followed her back out to the cart, waiting while she locked the tomb and the gates. We rode back to the house in silence. "Thank you for taking me," I said when we reached the back steps of the house.

She gave me a wan smile. Apparently whatever moment of closeness we'd had at the tomb was over. She drove the cart away and I walked back inside and shut the doors behind me. I walked down the hallway. The door to my grandfather's office was open, and he was sitting at his desk in his wheelchair, reading. He looked up as I walked in. "How are you?" he asked, pushing his reading glasses up and peering at me. "Olivia told me about your fall."

"I've been better," I replied, sitting down near him in a very comfortable wingback chair. "I'll be sore for a few days, but I can live with it. They gave me some mild painkillers. That'll help a lot."

"I'm so sorry," my grandfather said, his voice sympathetic. "This trip has been terribly hard on you, hasn't it?"

"I didn't think it was going to be easy," I replied. "But I didn't expect to be pushed down the stairs."

"*Pushed?*" His eyes widened. "You don't mean that."

"I was definitely pushed down the stairs," I replied grimly. "Trust me. I know what two hands shoving me in the back feel like. The only question is why? Why would someone want to push me down the stairs, Geoffrey?" I hesitated before adding, "Someone must be afraid maybe I'm going to remember what happened down at the boathouse when my mother died."

His jaw set. "Your mother—I know this is hard, Heath, but it's the truth—killed a man and turned the gun on herself. I don't think she intended to kill Dylan. I don't know, maybe they struggled over the gun and it went off, but everyone who knows is dead—"

"Not everyone."

"No, not everyone," he said softly. "But you've never been able to remember, have you?"

I closed my eyes and saw the Orion mask falling into the water again, the beautiful deep-red glass hitting the green-black water, the sun's rays reflecting and shining off the red.

"Ginny says you have Nina's diaries, locked in the safe."

His entire body sagged. "Yes, I do. But why would you be asking about her diaries?"

"Jerry mentioned them."

"Yes, he asked me." Geoffrey sat up rigidly in his chair, his eyes flashing angrily. "As if I would allow a stranger to paw through my Nina's memories! So that he could write about them in a book for everyone to see." He shook his head. "The nerve! I ordered him out of here and told him he was never welcome here again." He smiled at me. "Although I should be grateful to him and his damnable book, since that's what brought you here." He peered at me shrewdly. "You do know Jerry is only interested in you because you were there. Even if you don't remember."

The words stung, maybe more than they were intended to. Geoffrey couldn't know that I was attracted to Jerry, or that I'd seen him in New Orleans—unless, of course, Ginny had told him. But Geoffrey didn't run my life, thank you very much, and I would see whomever the hell I pleased, whether my grandfather liked it or not.

But I wasn't about to have that conversation right now, either.

I raised my chin. "I'd like to read the diaries."

He licked his lower lip. "Are you sure? You might not like what you read—about your mother, about your father." He paused. "Nina was a very lovely woman. She was kind to everyone. But in her diaries, she wasn't so kind. She was honest, and when she was upset, she chose to share her feelings with her diaries. I have kept them all these years because… because they make me feel closer to her again, when I read her words, I can see her, I can hear her voice, I can smell her perfume…"

"You have your memories," I said. "I don't even have that."

He wheeled himself over the fireplace and pushed himself up to his feet. With one hand on the mantel, he swung the painting of Louis Legendre aside, exposing a safe door. He spun the dial quickly in one direction than another, then back the other way again. He turned the handle and pulled the door open. He sat back down in the wheelchair, hard. "They're all inside the safe," he said heavily, pushing himself away from the fireplace. "Help yourself."

Uncomfortably I walked across the room and reached inside the safe. I pulled out the stack of books, all bound in cracked and fading red leather. On the front cover, in the lower right hand corner of each, was stamped *Nina Legendre* in gold leaf, and a year followed the name.

"She burned the ones from her childhood, just before she died," my grandfather said from the other side of the room. "When we were married, she started having the books specially made in New Orleans and bound in red leather. Red was her favorite color," he added as an afterthought, as though it made any difference one way or the other.

I started going through the stack on the desk. "Two years are missing," I said with a frown.

"Impossible," he replied, rolling back over to the desk. "No one has access to that safe but me, and they were all there."

"Could you have left them out?" I asked. The missing years were the year my mother died, and one seven years earlier. "And someone else picked them up? And no one has the combination besides you?"

"No one." He stared at the pile of leather-bound books. "They've been in my safe ever since Nina died. They were in her desk, which she always kept locked." He rubbed his eyes tiredly. "Maybe they've always been missing, and I just never noticed."

You never noticed that the diary for the year my mother died was missing?

I didn't believe that for a moment but his distress seemed genuine.

I picked up the stack of books and replaced them in the safe, except for the one for the year I was born. I closed the safe, turned the handle, and spun the combination dial before swinging the portrait closed. I picked up the book and turned to my grandfather. "I think I'm going to drive into New Orleans and maybe stay at the house for the night. I want to be alone and think. Do you mind if I take the diary with me?"

He waved his hand tiredly. "Just be careful with it. And don't let Jerry Channing get his hands on it."

Impulsively, I walked over to him and kissed the top of his forehead. "Thanks, Geoffrey, I really appreciate all this." I paused. "It means a lot to me, being here, getting to know you and everyone else in the family. And my grandmother."

He didn't answer, just buried his face in his hands and gestured for me to leave him. So I walked out of his sitting room and walked down the long hallway back to the main staircase. Olivia was standing at the top of the stairs, her face an expressionless mask. She stood there, watching me as I came up the staircase, and her expression never faltered. "I'm going into the city," I said when I reached the top of the stairs, turning and leaning against the newel post. "I won't be back tonight. Right now, I'm planning on coming back out here in the morning, but I may change my mind."

"Is that one of my mother's diaries?" Her eyes flicked down to the book clutched in my right hand.

"Yes, Geoffrey gave it to me to read, so I can get a better idea of who my grandmother was." I held it up. I started to walk down the hallway but stopped and turned back to look at her. She hadn't moved, was still standing there watching me without expression. "Did you know that some of the diaries are missing?"

"Missing?" She didn't flinch.

"Yes. The diary for the year my mother died is missing, and so is one from seven years earlier."

Her face drained of color. "That—that cannot be," she said hoarsely. Her right hand grasped the banister so tightly I could see her knuckles turning white. "There must be some mistake."

"No, there isn't. They aren't there."

She said nothing, just turned and walked hurriedly down the staircase. I stood, watching her as she continued down the hallway to Geoffrey's sitting room. She went inside and shut the door behind her.

Interesting, I thought. What could be so important about the diaries that would make her so upset they were missing?

I went into my room to pack an overnight bag. I needed to get away from this house for a while, to clear my head and read the diaries. What better place than my house in New Orleans?

CHAPTER TEN

It was starting to rain again as I climbed the steps to my house.

The sunny day had turned dark and cloudy as I drove into New Orleans, and I'd almost made it without getting rained on. I shifted my overnight bag on my shoulder as I tried to get the front door key maneuvered into position. Sweat was running down the side of my face, and my armpits had already soaked through my T-shirt. Hopefully the rain would break the hideous humidity—it was like walking through a thick soup. I dropped my keys and put my bag down with a sigh. I wiped the sweat from my forehead with my T-shirt before it could get into my eyes. This heavy, wet, stagnant air was absolutely horrible. I swallowed and managed to get the door unlocked, tossing my bag inside and shutting the door behind me just as the storm broke.

I punched in the alarm code and once the red light turned green, indicating the alarm was disarmed, I flipped the light switch just inside the door. With most of the shutters closed and the sun blocked by angry clouds, it was dark as night inside the cool house. I actually shivered—it felt like it was about fifty degrees inside. I leaned back against the door and closed my eyes.

I was still having trouble wrapping my mind around the fact this house actually belonged to me. It seemed like I'd locked up my apartment in Bay City and headed for the airport a million years ago, like that had been someone else. I owned a house! *Maybe it isn't such a crazy idea to put in for a transfer to the airport here, check into enrolling in one of the local universities—Loyola and Tulane are probably out of my price range, but maybe UNO? Cutting out the expense of having to pay rent would be a huge help, although the utility bill on this place is probably outrageous...Is it necessary to keep it at the temperature of a refrigerator?*

It was all a bit much to take. I shook my head. *Don't forget someone tried to kill you earlier today, Mr. Rocket Scientist.*

That thought brought me right back down to earth.

I'd called Mom while I was driving in on I-10. To say she'd been taken aback when I told her I owned this house was an understatement. Whatever it was she'd been expecting to hear from me, it wasn't that I was the proud owner of a house I'd inherited from my birth mother. She'd listened to what I had to say—I censored out the parts about me being a witness to my own mother's death and being pushed down the stairs, as I didn't see any need for her to worry. All she had told me in response was that she loved me, and a reminder that I needed to be careful with the Legendres.

"Your father didn't trust these people as far as he could throw them," she said before hanging up, "and he didn't just make that up, you know." She hesitated. "Please be careful, Heath. And call me every day, okay?"

I know I wasn't imagining the worry I heard in her voice, either.

You don't know how right he was, Mom.

I locked the door and headed for the kitchen. Outside

I could hear the rain pelting down, and through one of the kitchen windows I could see a line of crepe myrtles bending and dancing in the wind, as though choreographed. The rain was coming down in thick fat drops, slapping against the roof of the gallery outside with loud splats. I flipped on the lights in the kitchen—*my* kitchen. The kitchen in my apartment back home was about the size of the walk-in pantry in this one.

Yes, I could make myself at home here quite easily.

I opened the refrigerator and smiled to myself. The bottle of white wine from yesterday beckoned to me, half-full, and I grabbed it by the neck with a sigh of relief. I removed the stopper and grabbed a glass from the rack hanging above the sink. I poured myself a healthy splash and closed my eyes as I took a big sip. It was perfect, one of the best Chardonnays I'd tasted in my limited experience with wine. I carried the glass with me back into the living room to retrieve my bag and headed upstairs.

I tossed my bag into the bedroom suite across the hall from the one Ginny had used with her lover—there was no way I was sleeping on *those* sheets.

I walked over to the window. This suite didn't have a balcony, but the gallery roof was only a few feet lower than the sill. *I'd like to make another gallery for the second floor, only uncovered,* I thought as I looked out over the yard. It really was like a jungle out there, and with a moment of sad clarity I realized that the upkeep on this house would probably cost me more than my rent in Bay City. The yard had to have been kept up by a team of professionals, and I didn't know enough about horticulture to maintain it myself. Geoffrey had also mentioned housekeepers, which would explain why there wasn't any dust anywhere, why the floors shone like the surface of a mirror. I sat down in a chair next to the window and took another sip of the wine, watching as the heavy drops of rain splattered against the window and ran down to the sill. The gutters in the street were filling with water.

Apparently, New Orleans flooded in every heavy rain.

As I sat there watching, the rain started falling heavier and harder.

Living here was obviously not a possibility for me, certainly not on my airline salary.

I got up and walked back downstairs, looking around for something, anything, that might trigger any memory of having lived here as a child, any memory of my mother.

But there wasn't anything, which I should have expected. For all I knew, this wasn't the same furniture my parents had.

I went back upstairs and sat down in one of the big easy chairs facing the portrait of my mother. I toasted her with my glass. "Thank you for the house, Mother," I said in the silence.

I closed my eyes and tried to recall the flash of memory I'd had at her grave. Had that just been my imagination? It had been so vivid, though—it had to be a real memory. But beyond the site of the boathouse, and my mother's hand holding mine as we walked hurriedly, and that strange sense that she was upset and worried, there was nothing.

Frustrated, I opened my eyes and stared back up at her painting.

Why did you kill him, Genevieve? And why did you take me with you? What kind of woman were you?

It didn't make any sense.

From what Ginny had said, she'd been a good mother, so much so that Ginny had been jealous that she'd been my mother instead of hers.

A good mother wouldn't put her child in danger.

A good mother wouldn't take her child with her if she'd been planning on killing her ex-lover.

Ergo, it stood to reason that my mother had no intention of killing Dylan when she went to the boathouse that day.

What if my mother didn't kill Dylan? What if she didn't kill herself?

I sat up.

It was so obvious that I couldn't believe it hadn't occurred to me before.

Jerry was right. There was definitely more to the story than had ever been allowed to come out.

Or you're being overdramatic. No matter how much power Geoffrey wielded in Redemption Parish, why would he cover up a double murder?

He wouldn't have.

No, she had gone down there to kill Dylan. She had clearly not been in her right mind—a sane person wouldn't commit murder, after all—which was why she had taken me with her instead of leaving me behind in the house.

I closed my eyes and relaxed into the chair. It was really comfortable. I could easily go to sleep right there. I took another drink of the wine and looked around the room. I was falling in love with this house. Even if I didn't remember ever living there, I still somehow felt connected to this place. Maybe it was because I knew I'd lived there as a child, but it kind of felt like I was at home.

It also felt good to be away from Chambord, away from my family, away from all the people and servants, and just be able to relax and think. One of the reasons I loved my little apartment back in Bay City so much was being able to get away from other people and just relax by myself.

I took a sip of the wine, which tasted very expensive. I should, of course, have expected that—Ginny didn't strike me as the kind of woman who would drink anything cheap. But the rain and the wine were lulling me into a place of utter and total relaxation, which felt really nice. I hadn't realized how tense I'd been since getting to Louisiana.

I put my feet up on a hassock and took another sip of the wine. My mind began to wander again.

It was odd that those two diaries were missing, and I didn't believe for a minute that Geoffrey had never noticed that two of his beloved wife's diaries were missing. He couldn't have known I would ask to see them—and again, he could have said no. I relived the moment—had he been surprised or startled? Or had the diaries been destroyed because of what they contained?

What could Nina have written in her diaries that needed to be concealed?

What if my earlier thought had been right, and my mother hadn't killed Dylan?

It was entirely possible, not as far-fetched as I'd thought earlier, now that I thought about it some more. It was possible it was just wishful thinking—I didn't want to believe my mother was a murderer, that she'd killed with me there to witness her crime.

But I couldn't deny that the accepted story, the one for public consumption, was an utter and total lie. According to the official story, Dylan hadn't even died at Chambord, and my mother died in a tragic accident. But I knew that story was bullshit. If the accepted story was bullshit, it stood to reason that the story told inside the protective conclave of the Legendre family could also be a lie.

Maybe that was what Nina had written in her diary. Maybe that was why no one could ever be allowed to see that volume.

Yet why would the one from seven years earlier also need to be hidden away?

I finished the wine and went back into the kitchen to refill the glass. I sat back down, picked up Nina's last diary, held it in both hands for a moment, thinking.

Seven years before my mother died, she had been sixteen, a high school student, a cheerleader and homecoming queen.

That was the year Geoffrey had forced Dylan to go into the military.

Something else went on that year. Something Nina had recorded, something that needed to be kept a secret.

Dylan and Genevieve, Genevieve and Dylan.

What secrets did they—and my grandmother—take with them to the grave?

I took a deep breath, had another big gulp of wine, then opened the diary and began to read.

January 1

Chambord is filled with guests. Every one of the cottages is rented, and the restaurant is booked full for the entire day. Everywhere I look, everywhere I turn, there are strangers roaming the grounds. They are everywhere, even though it's cold out there—we had a frost warning last night, and I am worried it may have killed some of the elephant ferns—but that isn't stopping them from looking everywhere. I swear if not for the security guards they would probably come onto the gallery and press their faces up against the windows trying to see inside. I always feel like a prisoner inside my own house, and I hate having the downstairs shutters closed—it always makes the house feel like a cave, with us all huddled inside and shaking with fear that whoever is out there might somehow get hold of us or get inside.

Geoffrey hates it and, like always, is grumbling

and hiding out in his sitting room with the door locked. If I am still here on the next New Year's, I am going to insist we close the restaurant and not allow any guests in the cottages. Reopening to the public so soon after Christmas always seems to shorten and cheapen the holidays.

And why aren't we allowed to have our privacy at least for the holidays? At least Geoffrey changed his mind about decorating the trees and charging admission at night for people to ooh and ahh over the lights. I wasn't kidding when I told him I would leave him. I am tempted to drive into the city and stay at the house there, but it always seems so haunted at the holidays, and I don't want to break my own heart again. Every time I go inside that house I hear Heath's laughter, and it's like he and Genevieve are always in my peripheral vision, just out of the edge of my sight, and if I turned my head fast enough I might actually be able to see them...but I know that's not true. She is dead, and he is gone. My grandson. Just thinking of him makes my heart heavy.

Much as I hate respecting David's wishes, I stay away from my grandson. It would only hurt Heath more if we fought over him.

Losing my grandson makes the loss of my own children hurt all the more. I used to dream of having a house full of children again. But Olivia has made it clear she will never marry, and so there are only the two grandchildren, all there will ever be, and one is lost to me.

At least Ginny is here at Chambord for me to fuss over and spoil the way a grandmother is supposed to, and I can only pray that someday I will be able to do the same for Heath again. He was such a beautiful little boy, so happy and so like his mother when she was a baby it always made me catch my breath a little bit. I wonder if he still looks like her. I wonder if he's happy, I wonder if he remembers me at all...

The present I sent to Heath sits on my desk. I haven't had the heart to remove the wrapping paper. The big black letters Return to Sender glare at me and break my heart. I can understand why David would take Heath away, why he wouldn't want anything to do with us after everything that happened, but that doesn't make my heart ache any less. It doesn't assuage the loneliness I feel at Christmas when the family gathers and my only grandson isn't there.

I wonder how he is, what he is like, what kind of man he is growing up to be. Is there any of Genevieve in him? A parent isn't supposed to outlive her children, but I've buried two of mine. Only Olivia is left, and only my darling Ginny...I dreamed of a house filled with children and grandchildren during holidays, of turning gray and getting wrinkled and being surrounded by the love of family. Instead, I have two children in the grave and a grandson I may die without ever seeing.

David is bitter and hates us. Who could blame him? We lied to him. Genevieve wanted him to know the truth, but we wouldn't allow it. Some secrets are best left alone, but I have to wonder, had we told David the truth, had we let Genevieve be honest, would the tragedy have been averted? Might not my children be alive today? Would Heath be here with us now this holiday season? But we thought we were doing the right thing—how could we have known how it would

turn out? With dead bodies and more lies upon lies,
perhaps it is no more than we deserve.
  Cold comfort on this new year...

I picked up my wineglass again and took a sip. *Lies.* What lies was she talking about? *Lies upon lies.*

And they were still being told, the secrets still being kept.

Was that why someone had pushed me down the stairs? Maybe my return to Louisiana had put things into motion. The secrets were bubbling up to the top.

I put the diary down. I didn't want to read anymore. It made me sad, made me resent my father for taking me away and keeping me from the grandmother who'd ached for me, who'd cried over my loss, but had accepted it as the cost of the lies that had been told.

I got up and started pacing. The wine was starting to make me warm and fuzzy, or maybe that was just the alcohol combining with the painkillers.

The rain was falling even harder now, and it had gotten dark as night outside. I could hear cars driving by slowly on Felicity Street. I looked out the window. The street was filling with water, which was probably why people were driving so slowly. The elephant ferns and palm fronds were swaying in the stiff breeze, and it was getting darker and more gray outside with every passing minute. I walked over to the fireplace and stared up at the self-portrait of my mother. She looked back at me, unblinking, her lips pursed in a slight smile, her right eyebrow cocked just a little. She looked serene and happy in the painting—but then, would she really do a self-portrait of herself looking miserable? I moved over to the wall of photographs between the fireplace and the outside wall.

I didn't recognize some of the people in the pictures, but it was safe to assume that the woman in a wedding dress posing with a much younger version of my grandfather in a tux was Nina. She was looking at him adoringly. I glanced from the picture back to the painting and smiled. My mother had my grandfather's eyes, but other than that she looked a lot like her own mother. Nina was a beauty, and there was also a very strong resemblance between her and Ginny and, much as I didn't like to admit it, me as well.

The only thing I had in common with my father was my hair. We both had thick, curly dark brown hair. When I was a kid, it used to bother me that I would look at my parents and not see any resemblance to me at all in their faces. It now made sense, of course—I looked very much like my mother. I had her heart-shaped face and a strong, pointed chin—mine was more square than hers, more like Geoffrey's—and the same nose. We had the same brows, and the same eyes, the same cheekbones.

It must have driven my father crazy to look at me and see her.

It made me love and miss him all the more. No matter how he felt about my mother, he had always been a good and loving father to me despite the fact that every time he looked at me he had to have seen the woman who'd caused him so much pain. But he'd never once given me any indication that I was a painful reminder of his first marriage, and for a moment I felt an almost overwhelming sadness.

It might have been almost six years since he died, but I doubted I would ever really get over it.

I blinked back some tears and focused on looking at the family photographs on the wall. One of the things that struck me as odd about Chambord was the lack of anything that would make the place homey—family photos, souvenirs, trophies, that sort of thing. Just enormous oil paintings of long-dead ancestors mounted on the walls, glaring unhappily out at anyone passing by.

The ringing of the front doorbell startled me so much I almost dropped my wineglass. I set it down, ran down the steps, and headed to the front door, pulling it open. I couldn't believe my eyes. "Costa! What are you doing here? Come on, get inside." I stood aside so he could enter. "Why did you ring the bell? Don't you have a key?" *Your wife does, after all.*

"I saw your car out front, and I was worried if I just let myself in—well, I didn't want to scare you." He was drenched from head to toe. He was wearing a white ribbed tank top that clung to his torso like plastic wrap. The rain had soaked it through to the point where it was practically see-through. There were goose bumps on his arms, and he was shivering as water ran down his face and dripped from his chin. His teeth started chattering. "It's freezing in here…"

"Let me grab you a towel before you catch cold," I said, letting him stand on the mat while I dashed over to the downstairs bathroom. There were some towels in the linen cabinet, and a men's robe was hanging on a hook inside the door. I didn't know who it belonged to, but I grabbed it. I handed it and a fluffy white towel to him. "Go into the bathroom and get out of those wet clothes," I instructed, "and give them to me to put in the dryer."

Shivering, he nodded and walked down the hall, going into the bathroom and shutting the door. I used another towel to wipe up the water he left behind. I went back into the living room and grabbed an orange-and-brown afghan from one of the reclining chairs. When he came out of the bathroom with the robe on, carrying the wet clothes, I took them from him and walked into the laundry room, tossing them into the dryer and turning it on. "Would you like some wine?" I called, almost jumping out of my skin again when I turned and saw him standing there, smiling at me.

"Some wine would be great," he said, draping the afghan around his shoulders. He was still shivering.

My heart was thudding as I walked into the kitchen. Just being around him was too difficult, I thought as I filled two glasses. *I can't stay in Louisiana, feeling the way I do about him.* I'd hoped that being with Jerry might help me forget, but obviously it hadn't. I took a deep breath and walked back into the living room. I handed him a glass. "What are you doing in New Orleans, anyway? And out in the rain?" I wanted him to say he'd come into the city to see me, but I knew that wasn't what he was going to say.

"I actually was having a coffee with a friend of mine at District Donuts, down at the corner of Jackson and Magazine." He sipped the wine and gave me a look I couldn't decipher. "My car was parked on Jackson, and then I thought you might be in town. I thought…I thought maybe we could talk, and better to do it here than out at Chambord." He shook his head, little drops of water scattering in every direction. "On the way here, I got caught in the rain. I'd thought I could get here before it started raining, but no such luck." He shrugged. "Of course by the time I got to the gate, I was soaked, but I was glad to see the lights on, so I knew you were here." His face broke into a big smile. "I can't tell you how glad I am that you *are* here." He shivered. "I don't blame you if you don't want to talk, but you don't mind if I wait out the rain, do you?"

I laughed. "Well, you're not going anywhere until your clothes dry, at any rate. And it would be stupid for you to go back out in the rain after drying them, wouldn't it? Besides"—I swallowed and looked away from him—"I'd enjoy the company for a bit. And we do need to talk."

"Thanks," he said, sitting in a wingback chair and propping

his rather large bare feet on the coffee table. He crossed his legs and smoothed the robe down.

I rather pointedly looked away. His robe was open at the chest, and I could clearly see the inside cleavage of his impressive chest. Striations of muscle rose from the deep valley on either side, and he had an almost smug look on his face.

He knows I'm attracted to him, I thought, taking another gulp of the wine, *and it's almost like he set this up—but he couldn't have known he'd get caught in the rain, or that I'd let him ride out the storm here, could he?*

"So, why did you marry my cousin Ginny, anyway?" I asked casually, crossing my own legs in what I hoped was a nonchalant manner. "Are you bisexual, Costa?"

"Bisexual?" Whatever he thought I was going to ask him, it wasn't that. He looked completely surprised. He closed his eyes and leaned his head back. "It's a long story. And I'm afraid it doesn't make me look very good. But I want to be honest with you."

"I would appreciate honesty this time," I said, pleased to catch him off guard for a change. "I mean, I thought you and I"—I gulped down some wine—"I thought we'd connected when we met, Costa. You can't imagine how much it hurt to realize that you'd lied to me about everything. Do you have any idea how cheap that made me feel?"

"I'm sorry," he said softly. "I really am."

"Go on, tell me about your wife. My cousin." I cut him off brutally. Much as I hated to admit it, it still hurt.

"I met her when she was going to Tulane," he said, scratching his head and leaning back in the chair. "My God, that was a long time ago! I actually met her in a gay bar in the French Quarter—at Oz." He smiled faintly as he remembered. "She spilled her drink on me on the dance floor—she was pretty drunk. She apologized, and from there we just started talking. She was a lot of fun. We hung out together most of the night, we exchanged phone numbers, and things just kind of picked up from there. I had no idea who she was—Legendre is a pretty common Cajun name, if you didn't know that already—so I never made the connection between her and Chambord until months later." He took a deep breath and wouldn't meet my eyes. "My parents are Greek immigrants who moved to New Orleans from the old country because they had relatives here. They opened a restaurant, and it was kind of successful. I grew up around restaurants. I was an only child, like Ginny—I had an older brother who died young. It was my father's dream that I would become a famous chef, and so he sent me to the Cordon Bleu for training. Unfortunately, when I came back to New Orleans, my parents and I had a bit of a falling-out. They're deeply religious." He sighed.

"What does that mean?"

"They're Greek, but they had a problem with my interest in boys. It's a sin, you know." He looked at me, his eyes glittering with tears. "Despite what people think, devout Greek Orthodox Church members aren't very keen on the old ways. They can be just as rigid as Catholics."

"Wait—what?"

"You heard me." He shrugged. "Me and Ginny really hit it off, and when my father had a stroke, and Ginny needed a husband and she was heiress to Chambord, so…"

My head was spinning. "Are you telling me you married her for the *restaurant*?" I felt a little nauseous. I hoped my thoughts didn't show on my face.

"And everyone was happy. My parents, your grandparents…my and Ginny's marriage was the perfect cover for everything. We run the restaurant and we've done a good job. And the marriage—well, the marriage is a cover for both of us. She can do what she wants, I can do what I want, and nobody ever gets hurt."

"That's not true. Some people get hurt," I replied and was mortified to hear the quiver in my voice.

"I'm sorry, I really am. I never meant to hurt you." He shrugged. "I'm sorry I lied to you. I'm sorry." He got up and walked over to where I was sitting. The afghan fell from his shoulders as he knelt between my legs. He reached up with one hand and cupped my chin. "I do care about you, Heath. I never stopped thinking about you, and then when you showed up at Chambord, I dared hope…" He stroked the side of my face, sending a shiver through my body.

"You're not just saying—" But he cut me off, putting a finger against my lips.

"I have feelings for you, my darling Heath," he murmured and pulled me into a deep, passionate kiss.

CHAPTER ELEVEN

It was still raining when my eyes popped open.

One of Costa's arms was sprawled across my chest. He was lightly snoring, sleeping next to me on his stomach. The light from the street lamp outside splintered and fractured through the falling raindrops and the water spattered all over the outside of the window. I could see he was naked, lying on top of the covers. The eerie yellowish light bathed his skin, and his bare backside glowed white in the semidarkness. I gently pushed his arm off my chest. He muttered a bit, shifted, and rolled over onto his left side, facing away from me. I took that as my cue to slip out of the bed.

The digital clock glowed 1:12 in red numerals on the nightstand as I pulled on my sweatpants and walked to the bathroom. I gently closed the door before turning on the light and staring at myself in the mirror. My hair looked like it had exploded, and my eyes were red. I sighed and turned on the water in the sink. I relieved myself as quietly as possible, then splashed cold water into my face.

What in the name of God were you thinking? I asked my reflection. The bruise on my forehead looked hideous in the bright lights of the bathroom, purplish with yellow edges, and the lump was pretty hard to miss. I turned off the water.

You were horny. It's not the end of the world, and it's not that big a deal. It's not like Costa is madly in love with you, or you him, either, for that matter.

"It was just sex," I whispered at my reflection before turning the lights off.

But it's never just sex for you, is it, Heath? You've never been able to differentiate between the two, have you? Isn't that what your problem has always been?

And no matter what he says—he's married to your cousin.

"Shut up," I whispered again as I opened the door to the bedroom.

Costa had rolled over onto his back but had pulled the covers up to his waist. I walked over to the window and glanced out. Everything outside was wet and glistening in the creepy yellow glow from the streetlights, and I shivered. *This wasn't the smartest thing in the world to do,* I thought, creeping out of the bedroom as silently as possible and heading down the stairs.

Sex isn't love, sex isn't love, sex isn't love, Aubrey's voice kept repeating inside my head. *That's what our problem was, wasn't it, Heath? You think sex means a relationship, means something more than just being horny and wanting to get off. That's not how it works. That's why your heart is going to be broken over and over again.*

So many times I'd met someone, at a party or in a club, seemed to hit it off with them and left with them, flattered and pleased with the attention, the idea that some good-looking guy with a good sense of humor and a great body was attracted to me. Back to my apartment, groping and rolling around on the bed, kissing and sucking and squeezing and pressing our bodies together, the sheets getting damp with our sweat, only to wake up alone in the morning, my date having slipped out in the night while I slept, not even leaving a note, not meeting my eyes the next time I saw him in a club, pretending like we'd never met, let alone gone home together.

Or the ones who took my phone number and never called, or gave me their number but didn't take my calls, didn't call back, or worse still, gave me a wrong number to call.

It never hurt any less when it happened, even if it wasn't the first time.

Every time I fooled myself, every time I believed this was the real thing, that this was the guy. It was why Aubrey had managed to get into my head. I wanted a boyfriend, I wanted a lover, I wanted someone to share my life with.

Costa was handsome, sexy, had a great body, and he was smart, talented. He said he cared about me, had feelings for me, thought I was good-looking...

But last night wasn't love.

He's just using you, Aubrey's voice whispered inside my head, *why else would he want someone like you? You're nothing, a nobody. Look at him! Go back upstairs and look at him! He could have anyone he wanted. Why would he settle for someone like you? Because he wants something from you, you're convenient to him, just like you're convenient to Jerry. Just like Jerry wants access to your grandmother's diaries, access to your family, access to Chambord, and access to your memories. If you're at Chambord and involved with Costa, he doesn't have to risk being seen in the gay bars anymore—and you're so willing to just let him have whatever he wants from you. He's married to your cousin. He has a* wife. *What kind of loser are you, anyway?*

I closed my eyes when I reached the bottom of the stairs and leaned against the wall, using all of my willpower to push Aubrey's sneering voice out of my mind for what I hoped was the last time. I gritted my teeth and walked into the kitchen. So what if it was nothing more than just casual sex?

I'd live. I'd lived through the other ones, hadn't I? Hadn't I survived Aubrey and his selfishness?

"Like falling in love with your cousin's husband isn't just sick," I muttered as I walked into the kitchen and flipped on the lights.

Our wineglasses were still in the sink, and the garbage from the Chinese food we'd ordered in hours ago was still sitting on the island where we'd eaten. I got the garbage can out from the cabinet where it was hidden and swept all the garbage into it. I rinsed out the glasses and put them in the dishwasher. I wet a sponge and wiped the island down. I sighed and got down another glass from the rack over the sink. I grabbed the open bottle of Chardonnay from the refrigerator and poured the last of it into my glass. *What's done is done,* I told myself as I walked over to the side door to the gallery, *and there's no changing it now. Whatever Costa's motives were is immaterial. All that matters is how I handle it now.*

My parents had raised me to believe that sex was special, and that I needed to respect women. When I came out to them when I was a sophomore in high school, they'd handled it far better than I had thought they would. They'd joined the local PFLAG chapter and started researching everything they possibly could think of. I got quite an extensive education in STDs, HIV transmission, and the importance of always using condoms. I'd slipped up a few times but always went and got tested, trying to keep my fears about being infected in the back of my mind, or I would have been a bundle of nerves. But my parents had emphasized that my attitude toward sex didn't have to change because I wasn't a straight boy, that I needed to respect myself and should only have sex with someone I cared about.

Needless to say, once I became sexually active I didn't tell them *anything.*

It wasn't that I didn't want to be in love, that I didn't want a partner to spend the rest of my life with.

But no one ever explained to me how to go about that when everyone you met was just looking for a hookup.

Or, if I was going to be completely honest with myself, sometimes that was all I wanted myself.

I slid the door open and went out onto the gallery with my glass of wine. The edges of the gallery were puddled with water, and in places there were spots and drops of water that had been shaken from branches and fern leaves onto the wooden surface. I sat down in a bamboo chair and curled my legs underneath me. It was very dark out there on this side of the house. The house next door, on the other side of the tall fence, was dark and silent. The wind was cool and wet but mostly blowing from the other side of the house, so it wasn't getting me wet from the rain. I sighed deeply and sipped the wine.

Yes, sleeping with Costa was a big mistake, but the mistake was worse for him than for me. Or was it? Who was more in the wrong here—me, or my cousin-in-law?

I laughed at my own naïveté. I could kick myself for being such a fool. But I couldn't change it now, couldn't turn the clock back and talk myself out of that impulsive decision, made after a couple of glasses of wine and probably because I was feeling a little vulnerable, because it felt nice after everything else that had been going on since I arrived in Louisiana to find out that Costa, whom I'd fallen in love with after a glorious Halloween weekend together, just might possibly have feelings for me, too.

You know you can't ever be with him. Imagine how your grandfather would react to that—Ginny's husband.

And saying I was vulnerable was an understatement. The truth was I was emotionally raw, physically battered, and had been dealing with blow after blow ever since my plane landed—what now seemed like months ago had actually only been a few days.

It was a lot to process under the best of circumstances.

That wasn't even taking into consideration the memory flashes I was having about that fateful day at the boathouse, either.

I closed my eyes and could see the red mask falling again, hitting the dark water's surface, the rings spreading out from it as it rested on the surface of the water for a moment before it started to submerge—

Submerge.

If my memory was correct, the mask had sunk into the pond.

So someone had to have gotten it out of the water, which meant someone else had to know it was there.

Someone else *had* been there that day.

Goose bumps rose over my body that had nothing to do with the rain and the chilly wind.

"You're the only person who knows what really happened that day," I said aloud. "If someone else *was* there, your life is in danger."

Someone had pushed me down the stairs.

I hadn't imagined that.

"You ought to just pack your shit and head for the airport," I said aloud as another gust of wind blasted around the corners of the house, shaking the ferns and live oak branches, rustling leaves so the trees seemed to be whispering to me *go home go home go home.*

It wasn't a bad idea. It wasn't cowardice. No one would believe me, except maybe Jerry, and he wasn't exactly a disinterested party. If I was right about someone else being there, talking to Jerry would put my life in even more danger.

Right now, the killer didn't know I remembered anything.

Maybe that was why your father took you and ran—because he suspected.

That didn't make any sense, I chided myself. And I had nothing really to go back to in Bay City other than my mother—my *stepmother*.

No, that was unfair. She'd raised me. She *was* my mother, not Genevieve. Genevieve was nothing more than a ghost, a connection to a family I didn't know, a connection to a long-ago crime I witnessed as a little boy.

All there was in Bay City for me were a lonely apartment, a dead-end job I hated more often than I enjoyed, a constant worry about money, and another semester at a second-rate university with no guarantee of employment once I finished my overpriced degree. I didn't really have many friends back in Bay City, and there was no boyfriend or loved one to go back to. Here, not only did I have blood relatives but a house, where I could live as long as I could pay the expenses and the taxes and whatever else being a homeowner could cost in New Orleans. There were any number of colleges here—University of New Orleans, Tulane, Loyola, even LSU up the highway in Baton Rouge—and the possibility that the Legendres might help me with the costs.

And there was Costa—whatever this thing was I had going on with him.

Maybe I should forget about him. Maybe this was just like the other time—a hookup born of convenience. Maybe he just wanted to see if I'd planned on outing him to the rest of the family. Maybe he thought if I slept with him again, I couldn't say anything without making myself look bad.

Maybe I should go pack my things and head back, pretend like I'd never come to Louisiana in the first place.

And you'll never be able to forget Costa. His thick, strong arms, his handsome smile, the big broad back, those gorgeous green eyes, that beautiful olive skin—and the fact that no matter what his marriage is about, he is still married. To my first cousin.

No, this wasn't the time to make decisions about my future. I didn't have to make up my mind about anything right now.

I put him out of my mind. That would never amount to anything.

Jerry, on the other hand...

What were the pros and cons?

I didn't know anything about him, really, other than he had a house a few blocks from mine and had written an enormously successful book he was still making money from, that was sold in every bookstore and gift shop in New Orleans. I didn't know about his family, I didn't know his romantic history, I didn't know anything about him other than I thought he was incredibly sexy and he was writing a book about my mother's death.

Which of course gave him every reason in the world to seduce me, to pretend like he was interested in me.

I was the only witness to my mother's death. I was the only person who really knew what happened that day in the boathouse.

And there was always a chance I could someday remember everything that happened there.

And I was also his entry into the Legendre family. Geoffrey might not let him have access to Chambord or anywhere near Nina's diaries or any other family papers, but I could access them. Hadn't Geoffrey placed one of her last diaries in my hands just yesterday afternoon? And at this very moment it was sitting on one of the tables in the living room. I hadn't told Jerry about it, and I wasn't sure if I should, to be honest.

I wasn't sure where my loyalties lay yet. A few kisses that might not be anything in the long run weren't something I was going to damage my chances with my family over.

That would be stupid. That would be the kind of thing I would have done a couple of years ago. I liked to think I was smarter than that now.

I got up and went inside, listening for any noise from upstairs. Nothing. I got the diary and went back out to the porch.

I couldn't trust Jerry. At least, not yet. He'd have to prove himself before I confided in him about anything.

I opened my grandmother's diary again.

February 1

This Carnival season seems even gloomier than past ones. Geoffrey thinks I am becoming melodramatic, acting melancholy, but as each year passes, I can't help but think how different things would be now if we hadn't been so headstrong, so adamantly determined that we were making the right choices and we knew what was best for everyone. Of course, no one could have ever guessed that separating Genevieve and Dylan by sending him to the military would end the way it did, with two dead bodies and my grandson lost to me, probably forever.

We were so sure we were doing the right thing, all of us. But as I sit here, with the temperature dropping and this enormous old white elephant of a house getting so cold that my fingers feel so numb that I can barely hold this pen, I cannot help but wonder at how stupid we all were, how arrogant in our certainty we were. It's as though God himself looked down upon us from his heavenly throne and laughed at our arrogance, laughed at our stupidity in thinking we could control the future, that we could change fate. Had we just decided to let them be together, to let them be happy despite her youth, would they both be dead now? I cannot stop thinking about it. I cannot stop thinking about that day, about walking down to the boathouse looking for my daughter and finding the bodies, and my poor grandson, staring at me with his wide-open eyes, unable to talk, unable to cry or do or say anything, his mother's blood drenching his little shirt...had I known that would be one of the last times I would ever see Heath, what would I have done differently?

The past is the past, Geoffrey always says, and brooding about it won't change the present, nor will it change the future. I don't want to argue with him—not that he would ever change his mind, that hasn't changed since he was a young man, he is always right—but I wonder if there are times when he wonders if we should have done things differently. I know when Genevieve married David she seemed happy in a way she hadn't been since we sent Dylan away, to separate them. Even her paintings changed after she married David. Instead of the gloomy depressing scenes of horror and death and misery she painted for years, she started using bright colors and painting happier scenes. I don't ever want to see those paintings myself again...I wonder if they are still in the attic of the New Orleans house.

I put the book down.

The attic of the New Orleans house?

Of course, there *had* to be an attic. I'd noticed from

outside that the house continued higher than the ceilings of the rooms with the balconies. And that attic would be the perfect place to store all of my parents' personal things after Dad had run away with me.

Given Geoffrey's dedication to the family history, I found it hard to believe he would have just tossed my mother's things. She was his daughter, she'd been a painter with a growing reputation—one that continued to grow after her death—so of course he wouldn't have gotten rid of her things, no matter how scandalized he was about the way she died.

I heard my cousin's voice again. *She was such a great mother, always laughing, always playing with you, that I was jealous and wished she was mine.*

A lump rose in my throat that I forced back down.

That was the answer, wasn't it, to the unasked question that had been haunting me ever since I'd found out the truth. Had my mother loved me?

Now I knew.

I slipped back inside the house, slipping the diary into the pocket of my sweatpants. I went back up the stairs and crept down the hallway. I looked in the bedroom to make sure Costa was still sleeping and picked up my phone off the nightstand. I closed the bedroom door behind me and switched on the flashlight app on my phone. I opened every door on the second floor, went into every room, looking up at the ceiling, checking inside every closet, and didn't find anything.

It didn't make any sense. How did one get up to the attic?

Then it hit me and I felt like an absolute idiot.

I turned the flashlight to the hallway ceiling.

About halfway down the hallway, I saw it, a rectangle in the ceiling. I climbed up on a chair and felt around, finally finding a place to slip my fingertips into the crack, and tried to pull down. At first nothing happened, and I could feel myself starting to sweat as I tried to pull the door down. I was just about ready to give up when there was a slight creaking noise, and the end I was pulling on began to come down from the ceiling…and a pull string dropped down from the blackness above.

I stepped down from the chair and grasped the string, pulling the trapdoor down. There was only a slight protest from springs that hadn't been uncoiled in years, and I shone my flashlight up into the darkness. A wooden stepladder uncurled as I pulled the trapdoor farther down, and I stepped up onto it, scooting up the stairs and into the darkness above. I pulled the door up behind me in case Costa woke up and came looking for me, and once it was closed I started shining the bright beam of light from my phone around.

It wasn't completely dark; there were dormer windows placed at strategic intervals throughout the attic, and despite the darkness outside, some of the yellow light from the street lamps managed to get in. I was aware of the smell of must and dust and cobwebs, and I turned my flashlight beam up to the ceiling, looking for an overhead light. I finally spotted a bare bulb hanging on a cable from the ceiling and yanked the pull chain, flooding the attic with harsh yellow glare. I shut my phone off and slipped it into the pocket of my sweatpants, the same pocket that held the diary.

There were dusty boxes everywhere, furniture—everything from rusty metal chairs to tables to bookcases. Lamps without shades or lightbulbs, box fans coated with dust and accumulated grime, tables and wardrobe boxes and artifacts from the mid twentieth century. I covered my mouth and sneezed twice. I approached some of the boxes, read the writing in black marker: *Clothes. Books. Magazines. Shoes.*

And then, out of the corner of my eye, I saw them:

canvases, stacked against a wall, with the images turned to face the wall. There had to be over fifty of them, I thought as I walked slowly and carefully across the wooden floor toward the rows of paintings, still kicking up dust and dirt in a cloud that tickled my throat and made me cough again. I turned the first painting around and stared at it, tears welling up in my eyes.

It was a painting of a baby in a crib, and the detail, the brushstrokes, the use of color, was absolutely incredible. It was a masterpiece that should be hanging in a gallery somewhere.

My mother's talent, even as obvious as it had been in the self-portrait, took my breath away.

I stared at it, unable to do anything, unable to move or speak.

The baby was lying on its stomach, holding up its head with a joyous smile on its face. There was a cloth diaper with enormous pins around the infant's lower torso, and it was lying on a purple knit blanket. In one upraised plump, pink hand, the baby was holding a silver rattle. Written across the bottom left corner in black ink were the words *My baby.*

My mother had painted me as a baby.

I felt my eyes fill with tears as an overwhelming sense of sadness filled me. *My mother.* I'd never known her, would never know her, didn't remember her. She'd always been kind of an abstract to me, not a real person who'd lived and breathed: Genevieve Melissa Legendre Brandon, a woman who'd married my father and given birth to me, nothing more than a name. But this painting brought her to life in my mind. She'd loved my father and married him. She carried me, nursed me, and took care of me the first three years of my life. There was no way of knowing what kind of mother she would have been, or what kind of relationship we would have had, whether she would have had a problem with a gay son or would have been supportive, the way Dad and the woman I'd always believed and thought of as my mother were.

How different would my life have been had she not gone down to the boathouse that afternoon?

I would have grown up in this very house, would have gone to school in New Orleans, would have started college here. We would have spent holidays at Chambord, and my grandfather and my cousin wouldn't be strangers to me. I would have known my grandmother, I would have been petted and spoiled and a part of this family.

If only she hadn't gone down to the boathouse that day.

I reached out with my trembling right hand and touched the painting, traced my fingers along the strong brushstrokes in the oil paint. I could almost feel the love radiating out of the canvas, the love my mother had expressed with every stroke of her paintbrush. The tears started spilling over, but I dashed them away quickly as sentimental nonsense.

She was dead. I would never get a chance to know her.

And, like it or not, someone in her family had tried to kill me.

But she *had* loved my father. I opened up Nina's diary again and looked at the words in her beautiful, curlicued handwriting, about how all the darkness in Genevieve's painting had gone away once she met my father, and how her paintings began to be cheery and colorful and happy again, as though Genevieve had somehow found the joy she'd lost when Dylan was sent away.

How on earth had they made Dylan go away?

And why?

It didn't make sense.

It wasn't that long ago—and the days when someone could be banished from a home and forced to do something they didn't want to do were long gone. It almost sounded like something from a Victorian novel. But Dylan had been over eighteen, so while he could have been evicted from Chambord, Geoffrey couldn't have forced him to join the military against his will.

Unless, of course, Geoffrey had some kind of hold over him, if it was either the military or something else, something much worse than joining the army.

My mother had only been sixteen when he'd been sent away.

Statutory rape?

What was it Nina had said in her diary? I turned back to the page I'd read out on the gallery.

We were so sure we were doing the right thing, all of us. But as I sit here, with the temperature dropping and this enormous old white elephant of a house getting so cold that my fingers feel so numb that I can barely hold this pen, I cannot help but wonder at how stupid we all were, how arrogant in our certainty we were. It's as though God himself looked down upon us from his heavenly throne and laughed at our arrogance, laughed at our stupidity in thinking we could control the future, that we could change fate. Had we just decided to let them be together, to let them be happy despite her youth, would they both be dead now? I cannot stop thinking about it.

I put the baby painting aside and started looking through the other ones.

They were, to a one, stunningly beautiful.

They needed to be cleaned, but the use of color and the brushstrokes were amazing. The details, even to the smallest one, were exquisitely and perfectly rendered. I didn't know much about art—my father had always discouraged me from any interest in art. I'd never really given it any thought, but sitting cross-legged on the floor in the attic of the house where my parents had lived, examining my mother's original paintings, it started to make a lot more sense to me.

My father had tried, my entire life, to make sure I was nothing like my mother.

I stood up and walked over to one of the dormer windows. It was still raining, and the cobblestones of Felicity Street glistened in the light from the street lamps. A car went by, driving slowly and throwing up a spray of water onto the sidewalk on the other side of the street. The paintings—the paintings had made me sad, sadder than I'd ever felt about the loss of my mother. I walked back over to the trapdoor and pushed it open, so the ladder unfolded and dropped down. I pulled the string to turn off the light and, wineglass in hand and phone tucked into my pocket, I slowly climbed down to the hallway below. I grabbed the pull string and left it out as the trapdoor closed, so that I'd be able to get it open again in the morning.

I yawned as I walked back to the bedroom. Costa was still sleeping but had rolled over onto his stomach. I stood there in the doorway, staring at the muscles in his back in the dim light. I took my sweatpants off and slipped under the covers. I finished the wine and lay back down, closing my eyes. Costa mumbled in his sleep, shifted a bit, and I cuddled up to the warmth of his back.

And managed to fall asleep.

CHAPTER TWELVE

I was alone in the bed when I woke up again. I rolled over and looked at the nightstand clock. 8:57.

I sat up with a yawn and a stretch, wondering where Costa was, and almost wishing he'd woken up and slipped out of the house. After all, it wouldn't be the first time that had happened. I shoved the covers off and swung my legs around to get up. I stood up and stretched. My head didn't hurt, and most of the aches and pains from my fall down the stairs seemed to be okay—no need for any more pain pills, thank God. I walked over to one of the windows and pulled the curtains open, letting sunshine flood the room. Looking out the window, you'd never know it had rained so hard and for so long during the night. The ground looked a little damp, but all the ferns and plants looked dry. I rubbed my eyes and walked into the bathroom. I turned on the water spigots and stared at myself in the mirror. The knot on my forehead was barely even noticeable, and the purple was starting to fade to an uglier greenish yellow. I grabbed the nail scissors out of the little caddy on the counter and cut the bandage on my shin off, peeling the layer of gauze gently away from the skin. The raw skin where the outer layer had been scraped away during the fall looked red and angry, but the doctor had said it needed air to heal.

I wondered how it would feel being washed in the shower.

I brushed my teeth and washed my face. I heard the buzzer from the gate over the running water and wandered out to the front room. I could see Jerry standing at the gate, holding a paper sack. There was no sign of Costa anywhere, so I buzzed Jerry in.

I opened the front door. "What are you doing here?"

"I saw the lights on here last night, and I called Ginny to see if you were here or at Chambord." He smiled as he pushed past me. "Go get cleaned up. I'll make breakfast."

When I finished showering and getting dressed, I came downstairs to see him setting up breakfast on one of the side tables, the one right in front of the window looking out over Coliseum Street. He turned and smiled at me. "I hope you don't mind me inviting myself over to make breakfast."

"It smells good, and I'm starving," I replied. "So, no, I don't mind at all. Thank you."

"I've actually been thinking a lot about you the last few days." He turned his back to me so I couldn't see his face. He was wearing his usual tight tank top and shorts, and I marveled at the play of the muscles in his tanned shoulders. He'd also done a great job of setting the table.

He'd certainly made himself at home.

I wasn't sure how I felt about that.

I wasn't sure if I could trust him, and what did he mean he'd been thinking about me the last few days? *He had to go through the cabinets and drawers to find the table settings and things,* I thought, again not sure how comfortable I was with him making himself so at home in my house. *My house.* I couldn't help but grin at the thought. I was already thinking of it as mine.

"You don't mind that I showed up here, do you?" He sat

down across from me, an odd look on his face. "I hope you don't mind—I thought it would be nice to…"

I laughed in spite of myself. "It's okay, it just kind of threw me," I admitted, buttering a piece of toast as he poured us each a cup of coffee from a black carafe. I helped myself to pancakes and buttered them as well before pouring the warm syrup over them. I picked up a piece of crunchy bacon and popped it into my mouth. "I'm not used to people treating me so nice—certainly not since coming to Louisiana."

"I find that a little hard to believe." He smiled back at me as he sipped at his coffee. "You're a good-looking guy, Heath. I should think men would be lining up at your door." His voice was silky smooth.

"Most guys tend to leave in the middle of the night while I'm sleeping," I retorted. *Like Costa just did last night. But on the other hand, I'm glad he wasn't here for Jerry to catch.*

"Aren't you a little young to be so cynical?"

I shrugged as I picked up another piece of bacon. "It's the voice of sad experience, I'm afraid." I popped the bacon in my mouth. It was crispy, just the way I liked it. After I swallowed, I smiled at him. "Have you never had someone slip out in the middle of the night?"

He laughed. "I'm usually the one slipping out."

I didn't laugh with him. I finished my coffee, holding the cup out for a refill. After he obliged, I added sugar and a touch of milk. "This coffee is really good, thank you for all of this." I took another sip and used my fork to cut off a piece of the pancakes. "So what made you decide to make me breakfast? This kind of seems a little romantic—have you changed your mind about us? Or do you want my help to write your book?"

He raised one of his eyebrows. "You really *are* cynical."

"Well, Jerry, you were the one who originally said you couldn't get involved with me because it would compromise the integrity of your book, weren't you?" I put the pancake bite in my mouth. They were delicious, and I tried to stifle an involuntary moan. I washed the bite down with some more of the coffee. "So what changed?"

"I don't suppose you would believe I couldn't resist your youthful masculine charms." He turned the full wattage of his smile on me, and I looked down at my plate. He was entirely too handsome for his own good—or rather, *my* own good. "No? All right." He leaned back in his chair and folded his arms across his chest. The biceps bulged, and bluish veins popped out like a road map. "I was actually thinking it would be a lot more interesting to tell the story from your point of view."

"What?" I stared at him across the table. I couldn't have heard that right. Then again, Ginny had, in her own way, tried to warn me that I couldn't trust him. "I don't understand. How can you do that?"

He reached across the table and grabbed my hands with his own. "I can see by the look on your face you don't like the idea. But please, hear me out."

I looked down at his hands, and he let go of me. "Okay. I suppose I can listen to what you have to say."

"You're the key to the whole story, Heath." He leaned forward, so close I could smell his cologne. "You were there when it happened. You didn't know anything about it. You grew up somewhere else, and your father didn't tell you anything. So you came here to meet your family for the first time, and even then, I had to tell you how your mother died. Not anyone in your family, me. You're the hook, the one the readers are going to identify with, feel sorry for, root for. The way I see it, I'll start the book with a prologue that tells the story of your mother's and Dylan's deaths, and how they wound up being reported."

"My grandfather will never go for it," I said when he paused. "You want to publish a book talking about how he not only interfered with a police investigation, but subverted justice. He could be prosecuted."

"No, I think he'll actually come across as sympathetic. He was just trying to protect you."

"He was trying to protect the *family*," I said bitterly. "Protecting me had nothing to do with it. He thought there would be a scandal, so he paid off the cops and bought what's his name a newspaper to cover it all up." I finished my coffee and pushed the plate away from me. I'd lost my appetite. "Just out of curiosity, how on earth did they explain away Dylan's death? There were two bodies."

He licked his lips nervously. "When the funeral home came to take away the bodies, they gave out the story that Dylan had been killed overseas in a car accident. A lot of people believed that was why Genevieve killed herself. That was the story whispered for years, you know. The official story was it was an accident. People whispered she killed herself in despair over Dylan's death."

"Even though she was married to my father by then."

He nodded.

"I don't know, Jerry, I need to think about this. Cooperating with you on this—well, in all honesty, it sounds like it might be a problem with my family. I don't want to...you know, I don't want to do anything that could damage my relationship with them." And then the truth dawned on me.

He figures if you get involved with him—if you date him— you won't be able to say no to helping him.

To give myself some cover, I reached for the carafe of coffee. I didn't need more coffee—the three cups I had already had me so wired I felt like I could easily climb the walls and dance across the ceiling, but I didn't want him to be able to read my facial expression. I poured the coffee and got up, then walked over to the other window, the one overlooking the side yard. It was the only thing that made sense. I didn't want to believe it, but I didn't have a choice. "It seems to me that your idea...well, if I agreed to this, wouldn't our involvement be an even bigger problem than if you wrote it the way you wrote the last one?"

He came up behind me, putting his big strong hands on my shoulders and pressing his lips to the back of my neck. His breath, his touch set my skin tingling. I closed my eyes and leaned my head back against his chest, and he stepped even closer so that our bodies were touching. He pressed his lips against my neck again, his breath coming even faster than before as his hands slid down my arms to my elbows. "Can we stop talking about the book for now?" His voice was husky, and even though I didn't trust him, my body was responding to him.

I put my coffee cup down on the windowsill and turned around. He was so close I could feel his breath on my face, and my face was practically in the center of his chest. I looked up at him. "You really want to do this?"

He gave me a rueful smile. "Maybe we should go slower, if that's what you want," he replied. "Is that what you want?"

"I don't know if I can trust you, Jerry." I pushed past him and stood in the middle of the room, my arms folded. He turned around and started to walk toward me, but I held up my hand to stop him. "Just stay over there, okay?" I didn't want him to, of course, but I also knew if he started kissing me again I was going to give in.

And I wasn't about to do that again.

"All right." He sat down on the windowsill, crossing his

muscular legs at the ankle. It took all of my willpower to keep my eyes focused on his. "I don't blame you for not trusting me." He cleared his throat. "Trust has to be earned."

I nodded.

"I like you a lot, Heath. I've never really been the relationship kind before." He lifted his shoulders in a slight shrug, the veins in his shoulder caps popping out. "I want you to know everything there is to know about me, okay? No secrets."

Seriously, he looks like he's never eaten a carb in his life.

"My parents threw me out when I was a teenager. My mother"—his face twisted into a sneer—"caught me in the barn with the preacher's son. That didn't exactly go over well." He laughed bitterly. "I grew up in upper northeast Mississippi, land of moonshine, meth labs, and snake-handling Christians who speak in tongues. It was hell, absolute hell. I was sixteen when she caught us. I wonder what ever happened to Joab sometimes…"

"Joab?"

He gave me a sad look. "Old Testament. All his brothers and sisters had Old Testament names." He sighed. "I ran away and came to New Orleans. I lived on the streets for a couple of years." He shuddered slightly. "I did whatever I needed to for money, okay? I'm not proud of it, but it's true. It's a wonder I never caught anything, but I didn't. When I was eighteen I was able to start dancing at a bar called the Brass Rail. You know it?"

I shook my head.

"It doesn't matter. I eventually was able to get a place to live, then my GED, and started saving money to go to college. And I did." He spread his arms wide. "And here I am. I worked as a personal trainer while I was in school. One of my clients was Delilah Metoyer's mother. And you know the rest of the story from there." He made a face. "I can't change my past, Heath. It is what it is. But I was also very sexually active for a long time after that, you know. I'm so used to being on my own, I guess it never really occurred to me to try to have a relationship with someone. I met Costa before he married Ginny."

"Wait—what?" I gaped at him. Him—*and Costa?*

He nodded. "I introduced them, in fact. And every once in a while, even after they were married, he would call me and have me meet him here. It didn't mean anything. I don't know if he and Ginny are intimate, but given what we saw here yesterday, I tend to doubt it." He shook his head. "I don't judge. You shouldn't, either."

I didn't say anything, just stood there feeling like a fool.

"I think I'm going to go." He took a step toward me, but I stepped back. "You have my number. Call me, okay?" He gave me one last look and walked out of the kitchen. I heard him walking through the house, and then the front door closed.

I collapsed onto one of the bar stools. "I didn't think he would ever leave," I said out loud. I took a deep breath and went upstairs, into the hallway. I looked up. The pull string for the trapdoor to the attic was exactly where I'd left it—not dangling, but tucked into the crease around the square. If you looked up it was pretty obvious, but you had to look up. I pulled the chair over, grabbed hold of the string, and pulled it down. Once the stepladder had unfolded, I climbed up into the dusty attic. The sun was streaming through the dirty windows, and it was much hotter up there than it was downstairs. I walked over to the stack of paintings.

I wanted to take the painting of me as a baby out to Chambord.

I was going to keep it. It was the only thing of my mother's I wanted. She'd painted me, her child.

But as I started flipping through the canvases, I glanced over at another stack of them and froze.

The painting in the front of that stack was of the red mask on a white background.

I stopped what I was doing and walked over to that stack. I swallowed.

"I don't love you anymore," a woman's voice was saying. I was afraid of this man, I didn't know who he was, but my mother was also afraid of him, and I could sense it. I wanted to run away, I wanted to scream, I wanted to protect her from him.

But she wanted me to hide, so I was hiding behind some dirty old shutters. She had told me to hide back there when we got here and told me we wouldn't be long, but I was there to help keep her safe. "He'll never hurt me if you're here," she'd said grimly, kneeling down in front of me. "Just hide back here and be ready to come out when I tell you to, okay?"

I just nodded and hid back there, I always did what Mommy and Daddy told me to, but I wished I knew why she was so nervous. I watched through the slats as she paced around, lighting a cigarette. She only did that when she was nervous or upset, Daddy hated it when she smoked, he always lectured her whenever she did it, they smelled nasty and made her smell nasty, too, so I didn't want her to do it, either, Daddy was right. She always just laughed when Daddy said anything to her and promised she wouldn't do it again but then something would happen to make her upset or angry and she would go to that drawer in the kitchen where she kept them, and she would go out onto the gallery and smoke one while she paced. She always paced when she was upset, that was how Daddy said he could always tell she was wound up in knots, that was what he always said whenever she started

*pacing, walking, going back and forth in a circle, worrying
and mumbling to herself the way she always did.*

*And I heard someone coming—footsteps on the wooden
deck. "Genny!" a male voice said, sounding happy and sad
at the same time, the voice quivering when he spoke. "I've
dreamed of seeing you again for so long…"*

I snapped out of it and was back in the attic of the house
in New Orleans, staring at a canvas, at a painting of the Orion
mask.

Why is it my trigger?

I took a deep breath and picked up the canvas, flipping
it over so I could look at the back. In the lower right-hand
corner, in plain block letters written with a Magic Marker,
were the words *The Orion Mask,* and my mother's signature
beneath the title. I carried it down the ladder, placing it against
the wall before climbing back up.

*Well, I remember now that she got there first, and she
didn't want to meet him, she was nervous and scared…but was
that because she planned to kill him? And why did she tell me
to hide, because I'd keep her safe?*

That didn't sound like a woman who was planning on
committing murder, did it?

I crossed the attic to the original stack of paintings I'd
looked at and flipped through the canvases quickly till I
found the one of the baby. I picked it up and looked at it in
the daylight. I frowned. Last night I'd been so thrilled to find
it I hadn't noticed some things about the painting. I just had
thought it was beautiful. But now, in the bright light of day,
some things were clearly wrong with it. The perspective was
skewed, for one—the baby should be larger on its left, given
how it—I—was situated, and the way she'd painted it. Instead,
the baby—me—I—was larger on the right side, the side farthest

away from the viewer. It was an amateur's mistake, one that someone who'd had formal training as a painter would never have made.

But…but that didn't make sense.

She'd already had one show at a gallery in the Quarter by the time I was born, and she'd signed with a gallery in New York as well.

She wouldn't have made this mistake at that point in her career.

I flipped it over again. There were the words again, in black Magic Marker. *My Baby*, and her signature beneath it.

Genevieve Legendre.

Genevieve Legendre.

I started trembling as reality hit me.

My grandmother's words.

We were so sure we were doing the right thing, all of us. But as I sit here, with the temperature dropping and this enormous old white elephant of a house getting so cold that my fingers feel so numb that I can barely hold this pen, I cannot help but wonder at how stupid we all were, how arrogant in our certainty we were. It's as though God himself looked down upon us from his heavenly throne and laughed at our arrogance, laughed at our stupidity in thinking we could control the future, that we could change fate. Had we just decided to let them be together, to let them be happy despite her youth, would they both be dead now? I cannot stop thinking about it. I cannot stop thinking about that day, of walking down to the boathouse looking for my daughter and finding the bodies, and my poor grandson, staring at me with his wide-open eyes, unable to talk, unable to cry or do or say anything, his mother's blood drenching his little shirt…had I known that would be one of the last times I would ever see Heath, what would I have done differently?

The past is the past, Geoffrey always says, and brooding about it won't change the present, nor will it change the future.

Why Dylan had so gladly gone into the military.

The big secret no one at Chambord wanted anyone to know.

And even as I saw the date scrawled in small numbers beneath her signature, so small that it was easy to understand why I'd missed it last night, I already knew.

My Baby wasn't a painting of *me.*

It was Ginny.

Ginny isn't my cousin. She's my sister.

Chapter Thirteen

My hands were shaking on the steering wheel as I pulled out onto I-10.

My bag and the two paintings were in the backseat.

At first I wasn't sure if I was okay to drive, but now that I knew the truth about Ginny, why had I not seen it before? We even *looked* alike, and the names—Ginny, Genevieve—were so similar.

But, I reminded myself as I pulled into the center lane to get out from behind a very slow-moving airport shuttle van, why would that be such a scandal? It wasn't like my mother had gotten pregnant as a teenager in the 1950s.

Geoffrey was big about the family name not being sullied, that much was true. Of course it seemed silly to me, so I had to put myself in his place. He'd seemed accepting of my sexuality. It was also entirely possible in the nineteen years since Genevieve—my mother—had died, his point of view had come into the modern world. Especially if his archaic notions about a woman's sexuality had indirectly resulted in what happened at the boathouse that day.

I gripped the steering wheel tightly and switched lanes again just before I-10 merged with another highway. The traffic was getting heavier and slower as I crossed the parish line into Metairie. It took all of my patience not to floor the gas pedal and start weaving around the slower-moving vehicles. "Come on, come on," I heard myself muttering as I got past the exit for the causeway and traffic started thinning out again. I sped up and before I knew it was on the bridge over the lake marshes outside of town, about twenty minutes or so before the Avignon exit. I glanced back over my shoulder at the painting of the baby. I felt a lump in my throat. I'd been on such an emotional roller coaster the last few days…it kind of broke my heart a little that it wasn't of me.

Just because that painting isn't of you doesn't mean there's not one of you somewhere else in the attic.

I wasn't exactly sure what my plan was going to be once I arrived at Chambord. It was possible I didn't even need one; all I had to do was show the painting to Geoffrey and demand to know the truth.

So many thoughts were swirling around in my head that I was at the Avignon exit before I realized it—I'd been driving and operating on autopilot, which scared me. I was lucky I hadn't been in an accident. I signaled and took the exit going far too fast, having to slam on the brakes when I reached the stop sign at the foot of the exit. I sat there for a moment or two, taking deep breaths to try to calm down, to get my heartbeat under control. Finally, I made the left turn and headed for Chambord.

The gates were open when I arrived, and I waved to the security guard as I sped past.

The big house loomed large in the bright sunlight, yet I shivered in spite of that. Chambord wasn't my home, would never be my home. I wasn't even sure I wanted to spend another night under its wide roof.

Someone had tried to kill me, and I was certain the three of us had not been the only ones in the boathouse that day. I sped up the driveway and screeched the car to a sudden halt at the foot of the steps up to the gallery. I turned off the car, grabbed the painting from the backseat, and carried it up the stairs. I unlocked the front door and slammed it shut behind me.

Olivia was standing by the sideboard in the front hall, sorting mail. She jumped when the door slammed, and she turned a startled face toward me. The shock wore off and her face settled into the usual disapproving lines the way it always did when she saw me.

"Don't slam the door—" she started to say, but her voice died away as soon as she saw what I was holding. The color drained from her face. Her right hand went up to the base of her throat. "Where—where did you get that?" Her voice was a hoarse, horrified whisper.

"It was in the attic of my house," I replied, hefting it up so she could get a good look at it. "I rather stupidly thought it was of *me* at first. But I know better now."

I walked past her as she tried to form words but couldn't. I walked down the hallway and burst into Geoffrey's sitting room. He wasn't alone; Costa was sitting opposite him on the other side of the desk. Both looked up when I charged into the room.

"Heath, I'm sorry but I'm rather busy right now—" my grandfather began, but his voice died away as I turned the painting so he could get a good look at it. Just as Olivia had before him, his face turned white, and he looked terribly old all of a sudden.

"All this time, you've kept this secret," I said, putting the painting down and leaning it against the wall. "Is that why—" But my own words died away—

—and another memory flash went through my mind.

"The only thing that has kept me going for the last few years is coming home to you," the strange man was saying. *"Six long years I was away, dodging bullets and fighting a war."* He held up the red mask. *"Do you remember the promise you made to me when you gave me this? Before I went away? Do you?"*

"I was a girl," my mother replied, her voice sounding sadder than I'd ever heard her sound. *"I was sixteen. I'm married to another man now. We have a child. I told you."*

"I wanted to believe—"

The sound of footsteps approaching on the wooden dock stopped him in midsentence.

Another voice. One I recognized, one I knew.

"I told you when you left never to come back here again."

"No!" my mother screamed as the loud bangs started. The mask fell out of the man's hands, falling in what seemed like slow motion as my mother's screams echoed in my ears, as there were more bangs, and I just stared in horror as my grandfather turned and saw me in my hiding place behind the shutter...

"You killed them," I said in a hoarse voice. "You killed them both."

Geoffrey pushed himself out of the wheelchair. "You don't...you don't..." He wheezed and his face went gray. He fell forward, knocking things off his desk.

I stood, watching, unable to move, unable to feel anything. Once again time seemed to slow to a crawl. Everything seemed to be a blur—Costa shouting and dashing around the desk to where my grandfather lay on the floor, Olivia pushing past me on her way to get to him, Costa trying CPR while Olivia called for an ambulance—all while I stood there, still holding the painting.

My grandfather murdered my mother.

Ginny was my sister.

Those were the secrets of Chambord my grandfather had never wanted to come to light.

But there was no saving him.

We found out later that he'd had a massive coronary and was dead before he hit the desk.

Later, that evening, we all sat around in the dining room.

"I always suspected," Olivia said, her voice a deadened monotone. "I think Mom did, too. I know afterward they weren't as close as they had been. Outsiders couldn't tell, but I could." She turned to me. "Yes, you were right, of course. Ginny is Genevieve and Dylan's daughter."

"I always wondered," Charlotte said softly. "But I never could be sure."

"But it doesn't make sense to me," I objected. "So Genevieve was sixteen and pregnant. Who cared? What difference did it make? Why run Dylan off?"

"I always felt like Geoffrey hated us," Charlotte said, taking a healthy slug from the whiskey and water in her glass. "From the moment we first came here, it was obvious to both of us we were only allowed to stay here because of Nina. If Geoffrey had his way, he would have gotten rid of us." She looked at me. "The very idea of Dylan despoiling his precious daughter—no, that couldn't be borne, of course. That was too much for the great Geoffrey Legendre." Her voice was angry and bitter. "But the child was a Legendre, and even if her blood was tainted, she was still an heir."

"I thought it was a terrible idea, and so did Genevieve," Olivia said. "But she wasn't given a choice. None of us were. She went away with my brother and his wife, and we gave out the story Denise was pregnant." She shook her head. "When it was time for Genevieve to give birth, she signed into the hospital as Denise. So the birth certificate would list Denise and Henri as Ginny's parents. The plan was perfect." She reached across the table and grabbed Ginny's hands.

"But before he left for the military, Genevieve stole the Orion mask and gave it to Dylan to keep as a symbol of their love, and she promised to wait for him," Charlotte went on. "Dylan never stopped loving her, you know. Even when she married, he still held out hope that once he was able to come home, she would—" Her voice broke.

"I don't think he meant to kill Genevieve," Olivia's monotone cracked with emotion. "I will never believe he went to the boathouse planning to kill her. He always suspected that Dylan was the one to take the mask, and she jumped in front of him to take the bullet for him...I will never believe he meant to kill his own daughter."

"Believe it," I said, but my voice sounded hollow and distant, like I was speaking in another room. "I was there, and now I remember everything." I started shaking again, and to my surprise, Costa put his arms around me and hugged me tightly. "He also pushed me down the stairs, didn't he, Olivia? And the real reason my father took me away wasn't because he was angry about my mother—he took me away because I was the only living witness, the only person who might remember and send Geoffrey to jail."

"No!" Olivia said, but she also didn't meet my eyes.

I stood up. "I need some air." I walked out the French doors to the gallery and sat down on the steps, putting my face in my hands.

I heard the doors open and close again but didn't look up until a warm, strong hand rested on my shoulder.

"I'm truly sorry," Costa said softly as he sat down beside me. He put an arm around my shoulders and pulled me in close.

The tears I'd been withholding since Geoffrey had collapsed finally came, and I started sobbing.

I cried for my mother, who died for no reason. For my father, who'd always believed his wife had loved another man and became bitter with that knowledge. For the grandmother I'd never had the chance to know. For the grandfather who'd killed my mother, kept my sister from me, and tried to kill me. He just held me as I cried.

And finally, I was finished. I picked up my head and wiped at my face.

"You can stay here now," Costa said softly, his arm still resting on my shoulders. "There's no more danger. There's no reason for you to go back to Florida anymore. You can stay and get to know your sister. And your aunt. You have a house in New Orleans"—he gestured with his other hand—"and all of this. I know Ginny will probably inherit everything, but she's your sister. I know she'll want to help you. I want to help you." He leaned over and kissed my forehead. "Ginny and I—our marriage was only until Geoffrey died."

"And now?"

"I would like to get to know you better." He smiled at me and used his big fingers to wipe tears from my face. "And maybe someday—who knows?"

I smiled back at him. "Who knows?"

He made a face. "And just think of the book Jerry can write now!"

I started laughing.

About the Author

Greg Herren is a New Orleans–based author and editor. He is a co-founder of the Saints and Sinners Literary Festival, which takes place in New Orleans every May. He is the author of over twenty novels, including the Lambda Literary Award–winning *Murder in the Rue Chartres*, called by the *New Orleans Times-Picayune* "the most honest depiction of life in post-Katrina New Orleans published thus far." He co-edited *Love, Bourbon Street: Reflections on New Orleans*, which also won the Lambda Literary Award. His young adult novel *Sleeping Angel* won the Moonbeam Gold Medal for Excellence in Young Adult Mystery/Horror. He has published over fifty short stories in markets as varied as *Ellery Queen's Mystery Magazine* to the critically acclaimed anthology *New Orleans Noir* to various websites, literary magazines, and anthologies. His erotica anthology *FRATSEX* is the all-time best-selling title for Insightoutbooks. He has worked as an editor for Bella Books, Harrington Park Press, and now Bold Strokes Books.

A longtime resident of New Orleans, Greg was a fitness columnist and book reviewer for Window Media for over four years, publishing in the LGBT newspapers *IMPACT News*, *Southern Voice*, and *Houston Voice*. He served a term on the Board of Directors for the National Stonewall Democrats and served on the founding committee of the Louisiana Stonewall Democrats. He is currently employed as a public health researcher for the NO/AIDS Task Force and is serving a term on the board of the Mystery Writers of America.

Books Available From Bold Strokes Books

The Heart's Eternal Desire by David Holly. Sinister conspiracies threaten Seaton French and his lover, Dusty Marley, and only by tracking the source of the conspiracy can Seaton and Dusty hold true to the heart's eternal desire. (978-1-62639-412-4)

The Orion Mask by Greg Herren. After his father's death, Heath comes to Louisiana to meet his mother's family and learn the truth about her death—but some secrets can prove deadly. (978-1-62639-355-4)

The Strange Case of the Big Sur Benefactor byJess Faraday. Billiwack, CA, 1884. All Rosetta Stein wanted to do was test her new invention. Now she has a mystery, a stalker, and worst of all, a partner. (978-1-62639-516-9)

One Hot Summer Month by Donald Webb. Damien, an avid cockhound, flits from one sexual encounter to the next until he finally meets someone who assuages his sexual libido. (978-1-62639-409-4)

Fool's Gold by Jess Faraday. 1895. Overworked secretary Ira Adler thinks a trip to America will be relaxing. But rattlesnakes, train robbers, and the U.S. Marshals Service have other ideas. (978-1-62639-340-0)

The Indivisible Heart by Patrick Roscoe. An investigation into a gruesome psycho-sexual murder and an account of the victim's final days are interwoven in this dark detective story of the human heart. (978-1-62639-341-7)

Big Hair and a Little Honey by Russ Gregory. Boyfriend troubles abound as Willa and Grandmother land new ones and Greg tries to hold on to Matt while chasing down a shipment of stolen hair extensions. (978-1-62639-331-8)

Death by Sin by Lyle Blake Smythers. Two supernatural private detectives in Washington, D.C., battle a psychotic supervillain spreading a new sex drug that only works on gay men, increasing the male orgasm and killing them. (978-1-62639-332-5)

Buddha's Bad Boys by Alan Chin. Six stories, six gay men trudging down the road to enlightenment. What they each find is the last thing in the world they expected. (978-1-62639-244-1)

Play It Forward by Frederick Smith. When the worlds of a community activist and a pro basketball player collide, little do they know that their dirty little secrets can lead to a public scandal...and an unexpected love affair. (978-1-62639-235-9)

GingerDead Man by Logan Zachary. Paavo Wolfe sells horror but isn't prepared for what he finds in the oven or the bathhouse; he's in hot water again, and the killer is turning up the heat. (978-1-62639-236-6)

Myth and Magic: Queer Fairy Tales, edited by Radclyffe and Stacia Seaman. Myth, magic, and monsters—the stuff of childhood dreams (or nightmares) and adult fantasies. (978-1-62639-225-0)

Balls & Chain by Eric Andrews-Katz. In protest of the marriage equality bill, the son of Florida's governor has been kidnapped. Agent Buck 98 is back, and the alligators aren't the only things biting. (978-1-62639-218-2)

Blackthorn by Simon Hawk. Rian Blackthorn, Master of the Hall of Swords, vowed he would not give in to the advances of Prince Corin, but he finds himself dueling with more than swords as Corin pursues him with determined passion. (978-1-62639-226-7)

Murder in the Arts District by Greg Herren. An investigation into a new and possibly shady art gallery in New Orleans' fabled Arts District soon leads Chanse into a dangerous world of forgery, theft... and murder. A Chanse MacLeod mystery. (978-1-62639-206-9)

CPSIA information can be obtained at www.ICGtesting.com
Printed in the USA
BVOW08s0601120815

412953BV00001B/65/P

Made in the USA
Columbia, SC
30 September 2019